Things We Knew Were True

Nicci Gerrard is a feature writer on the *Observer*, and the co-author, with Sean French, of the best-selling Nicci French thrillers. She lives in Suffolk with her husband and four children. This is her first solo novel.

Things We Knew Were True

NICCI GERRARD

MICHAEL JOSEPH
an imprint of
PENGUIN BOOKS

MICHAEL JOSEPH

Published by the Penguin Group
Penguin Books Ltd, 80 Strand, London WC2R ORL, England
Penguin Putnam Inc., 375 Hudson Street, New York, New York 10014, USA
Penguin Books Australia Ltd, 250 Camberwell Road, Camberwell, Victoria 3124, Australia
Penguin Books Canada Ltd, 10 Alcorn Avenue, Toronto, Ontario, Canada M4V 3B2
Penguin Books India (P) Ltd, 11 Community Centre,
Panchsheel Park, New Delhi – 110 017, India
Penguin Books (NZ) Ltd, Cnr Rosedale and Airborne Roads,
Albany, Auckland, New Zealand
Penguin Books (South Africa) (Pty) Ltd, 24 Sturdee Avenue,
Rosebank 2196, South Africa

Penguin Books Ltd, Registered Offices: 80 Strand, London WC2R ORL, England

www.penguin.com

First published 2003
1

Set in 13.5/16 pt Monotype Garamond
Typeset by Rowland Phototypesetting Ltd, Bury St Edmunds, Suffolk
Printed in Great Britain by Clays Ltd, St Ives plc

A CIP catalogue record for this book is available from the British Library

ISBN 0-718-14631-X

To Sean

PART ONE

In the middle of the night, she thought she heard him calling her name. 'Edie,' he said, 'Edie.' A drawn-out cry, as if he was falling from a great height, and calling to her at the same time. His voice echoed in her head, greeting her or saying goodbye or asking for help or simply shouting, shouting for her to come to him. She hadn't heard it for such a long time. Only in her dreams. She knew it wasn't him, of course, how could it be, and yet the feeling that he was near was so strong that she swung her legs out of bed and stood by the window, listening. Inside, the house slept, each person wrapped in their own warmth. Outside, it was a clear and silent dark. There were white-pricked stars in the sky and a low moon tangled in the trees. She pressed her forehead against the glass and waited, but the voice didn't come again. It would never come again.

I

The letter arrived on the same morning that Vic crashed into the milk float and scattered forty-three bottles of full-cream milk and eight cartons of standard-sized eggs over their driveway. He said goodbye to his daughters, bent to kiss Louise on the top of her head, his fraying striped tie hanging down over her face, picked up his empty briefcase and left. They heard the door slam shut, his feet scrunch across gravel, and the engine of the car stall, stall again, then splutter into life. Jude was leaning over the homework that she had forgotten about the night before, hiding the smudged scrawl from Louise with the crook of her arm, and Edie was eating her porridge slowly and dreamily. Louise piled last night's dishes into the sink and scrubbed ineffectually at the table. She knocked into a teacup that had been set down behind the door and stepped on a tomato that had mysteriously fallen out of the fridge when she opened the door. Little red pips shot out over the tiles and a mushy skin attached itself to the toe of her slipper.

'Oops!' said Jude cheerfully, and as she said it there was a deafening crash, an ugly tearing and screeching, and the sound of breaking glass which died away in a series of melodious clinks, as if hundreds of wind chimes had caught a sudden gust of wind.

'What the hell?'

'It sounded like a crash,' said Edie cautiously. 'Didn't it?'

The three of them rushed from the kitchen and stood at the front door. The nose of Vic's car was pushing against the side of the float. The car's dented bonnet and roof were daubed with milk and an egg yolk was sliding slowly down the cracked windscreen. Chunks and shards of glass lay in white puddles all around the car, along with several up-ended crates. Squashed egg cartons were oozing viscous yellow. Vic's face stared out of the window.

Louise opened her mouth but no sound came out.

'Blimey,' said Jude. She sucked the nib of her pen. 'Blimey,' she repeated in a louder voice. She sounded awed.

'What in flaming heck . . . ?' shouted the milkman, coming round the side of the float. His face was a mottled red, and his neck too. He kicked aside the bottom half of a bottle and knocked ferociously on Vic's window. 'Oy!' he shouted. 'You!'

Vic opened the door of the car. He swung his legs out and stood up, hunching his shoulders and moving his head around slowly, like a tortoise. Some of the bottles were unbroken, and a few stood upright on the drive. He picked one up, but then didn't know what to do with it. 'Sorry,' he said. 'I'm so sorry. Oh dear. I don't know quite how . . .' He righted a crate and slid the bottle into it. His shoes snapped on the glass.

And then the postman swung into the drive on his bike, steering one-handed and feeling in his bag for the Jennings' letters. He swerved violently to avoid the glass,

4

and a few of the letters scattered to the ground where they fanned out amidst the wreckage. The bike wobbled and ended up by the fence, in the long grass that was wet from the night's rain.

Louise gave a small sigh, then she tightened her dressing-gown and went over to Vic.

'What on earth happened?' She sounded genuinely curious.

'I must have been thinking of something else.' Vic stared around him. 'I'm really sorry.'

'The car . . .' said Louise faintly. 'The mess . . .'

'I know.'

'Well, I've got to finish my homework,' said Jude. 'Twenty minutes before the school bus goes.'

Louise was now talking placatingly to the milkman, laying a slim hand on his arm. Her dressing-gown opened slightly and his eyes flitted from her face to the swell of her creamy breasts. Edie stepped on to the drive, avoiding the glass, and walked across to the postman. She took the letters from his hand.

'Thanks,' she said.

'Bit of clearing up to do, eh?' he said. 'I'd call the council out if I were you. And that milk'll start smelling all rancid when it dries. Especially in this heat.'

But Edie didn't answer. She was looking down at a white envelope. It had her name on it. She wiped away the single smear of egg with her sleeve and smiled beatifically at the postman. 'Yes,' she said. 'Terrible, isn't it?'

She had been waiting for the letter for over a week now. The postman usually arrived as they were eating

5

breakfast and she would hear the clatter of letters out in the hall and rise from her chair, but slowly, as if it didn't matter to her, and put her napkin by her plate. And her heart would rise up in her throat. And morning after morning there had been no letter – just the usual pile of bills and perhaps a postcard, that her mother would read out to her father while he methodically crunched his toast and raspberry jam, crumbs scattering down his tie, and smiled and nodded and didn't hear a word she said. Edie got used to the dullness that settled over her every time, but she never let it show. She would simply sit down again at her place and finish her breakfast and then go upstairs to get ready for school.

But this morning the letter had come at last. For a moment she felt hollow and light-headed, as though she hadn't eaten for days. She held it for a moment, as if she could tell something about it just from the way it felt between her fingers. Then she carried it back to the house with the other letters, leaving the milkman shaking his forefinger in her mother's face and Vic staring at the glass that glinted in the sun. One bill for Vic; two letters for her older sister, Stella, who was still in bed in spite of the cacophony outside, and would be for hours; one handwritten letter for her mother, and nothing for Jude.

Edie slid her finger under the gummed flap and lifted out the piece of paper. Through the open front door, she heard the milkman saying, 'You shouldn't be allowed out on the road.' She glanced across at Jude, who had acquired a black ink-stain on her lips, like the skin of a berry, then read the letter. It was very short. '*Dear Edie,*' it said. '*I promised to give you my address, so you could send me*

6

an invitation to your party. It's 19 Beckett Road, Kelsey. I look forward to seeing you then. Love, Ricky.' That was all.

She closed the letter and sat down. She dipped her spoon into her hardly touched porridge. But she couldn't eat. '*I look forward to seeing you then.*' That meant that he would definitely come. On Saturday week she'd see him again. She closed her eyes for a moment. '*Love, Ricky.*' *Love.* What did that mean? She knew it meant nothing, just a word that everyone used at the end of a letter, but she couldn't stop smiling. She put her spoon down and wiped her twitching lips. A small giggle of happiness lodged at the back of her throat.

'Jude, time to get ready. Edie? *Edie?*' Louise was back in the room. She looked weary.

'Is everything all right outside?'

'Well, you saw it, didn't you?'

'Can I help?'

'No. You're going to be late for the bus and I'm going to be late for work. Vic'll have to deal with it.'

'Is he all right?'

'Apart from being on another planet, you mean? Yes, fine.'

'He can't help it.'

'Oh, go and get ready for school, Edie. And remember your swimming stuff.'

'OK.'

Upstairs in her bedroom, she put the letter into her satchel. The cat, Tangle, was asleep on her pillow, stretched out in a rectangle of sunlight. Edie leant over him and pushed her face into his warm fur, felt the way his stomach rose and fell with his breathing. Then she stood in front of the long mirror and stared at herself. Stella looked like Louise, with hair like apricots, or golden syrup by the end of winter, regular white teeth with a gap between the two front ones, and full lips: effortlessly beautiful. Jude looked like Vic, broad-boned and tall, with the same coarse dark hair and high brow and white Welsh skin. Edie was the smallest, least visible, of the three sisters. Her face was rather pale and too round, she had always thought. She had brown hair, a few freckles over her nose, and a chipped tooth from where she had dived into the shallow end of the swimming-pool last summer. But Ricky had sent her a letter. Her. She smiled at her reflection. She laid two fingers against the pulse in her throat. From the outside, she looked calm and still, but inside she could feel the drumming of her heart, the fizz of her blood, the electric thrill of gladness.

'Who was the letter from then?' Jude was in the room. She picked up Edie's hairbrush and started to drag it through the tangles in her hair.

'Just someone I met.' But she had to say the name out loud. 'Ricky.' She watched herself as she said it, and then started twisting her hair into a single plait at the back of her neck, the way Stella usually did.

'Ricky? Who's Ricky?'

'He's coming to the party.'

'You're sweet on him. I can tell.'

'He's just a boy I met at Fran's. We talked.' She couldn't stop the little smile that kept twitching at her lips. 'I said I'd ask him to the party. Rose won't mind one extra person.'

'You fancy him,' Jude repeated.

'Don't be stupid.'

'You do.'

'Girls!' Louise called from downstairs. 'You've got seven minutes till the bus goes.'

2

On the school bus, Edie sat on her own near the back, and read the letter again, though she already knew the few plain words off by heart. She had met Ricky eight days ago, at a friend's party that she hadn't really wanted to go to. She wasn't much good at parties; she didn't have the knack. She envied the ease of someone like Rose, who would giggle and flirt and put her hand, with its long painted nails, on a shoulder or arm, or talk in a light-hearted, fluent babble, her earrings swinging, her bangles clattering on her arm. But Edie was self-conscious; she talked too little and blushed too much. She felt awkward and heavy-footed when she danced, although at home, when she was on her own, she would often put a record on and leap around the living-room. She would look at herself in the mirror as she danced and wish that she could be like this when other people were around. This was the girl she wanted them to see, flicking her soft brown hair, throwing a radiant smile back over her bared shoulder, full of grace. Sometimes she would go up close to the glass and stare into her own face until it misted over. Then lean in and kiss her fogged lips.

Of course, Edie had kissed boys before, as well. At the end of parties, when the music slowed down and the light dimmed, whoever you happened to be with would put his arms round you and draw you close. That's just the way it was – unless you were one of the girls standing on the edge of the room, eating salted nuts and sipping at empty glasses, watching and pretending that they didn't care that they hadn't been chosen. Edie remembered the shock of the first kiss; her arms gingerly around the broad, damp back of a boy whose name she'd forgotten now, swaying in the gloom, and his lips had suddenly pressed against hers; their teeth had clashed and she'd felt his warm, beery breath in her mouth and then his cool tongue, and she'd nearly screamed out loud in horror. Afterwards, Rose had giggled and told her she'd get used to it. Sometimes she would escape to the lavatory and wait there until the music stopped and the lights came on and her father, who'd been waiting outside with the other parents, came in to take her home. He would put an arm round her shoulder and ask her if she'd had a good time and she would say, 'Fine, Daddy.' That was all. She still called him Daddy, although Jude called him Dad, and Stella, newly, Vic.

It had been quite different with Ricky, who had walked up to her half-way through the evening. He hadn't asked her what groups she liked, in order of preference, or what school she went to, or how she knew Fran. He'd backed her into a corner and told her that his favourite writers were Samuel Beckett and J. D. Salinger; that he wanted to be a film director; that his brother had died when he was two. He was thin and bony, with brown eyes, thick eyebrows, and ragged, slightly greasy hair. He looked undernourished and pallid, as if he spent too much time in dark rooms. He stared at her as he talked, with the intensity of someone who was very stoned. He danced wildly, but without any embarrassment. Edie looked at his denim shirt, open at the neck, his old jeans, his thin wrists with a leather bracelet round the left one, his knuckly fingers. She saw his nails were bitten to the quick and for some reason that gave her hope. She wanted the music to slow down so that he would put his hand on the small of her back, hold her against him. She would be able to feel his breath on her cheek.

But instead he went to get more drinks. A girl stopped him and said something and he smiled and turned towards her. Edie watched and the girl put a finger against his cheek. He took a tin of tobacco out of his pocket and deftly rolled a cigarette for her and then for himself. Their heads leant together over the flaring match, almost touching, and she placed her hand over his as he lifted the flame to her cigarette. Edie went to the bathroom and stared at herself in the mirror. Her shallow breasts and brown hair. Her cheeks were flushed and all her lipstick was gone. She looked about twelve.

When she returned, Ricky wasn't there. She sat down on a chair at the side of the room and watched the couples wrapped together, bodies straining against each other. She saw Rose taking the face of a boy she had fancied on and off for a whole year in her two hands and kissing him full on the mouth. Then she threw back her head and Matt blindly kissed her on the neck, stumbling her back against a wall. Rose's eyes were shut and her yellow hair rippled down her back.

'Sorry. Here you are.' Ricky was back, holding a drink

for her. She tried to smile. The evening was about to end. There were cars outside; parents gathering to collect their children. The girl who'd touched Ricky's face with her finger was back in the room, walking towards them, keeping an unwavering, purposeful smile in place. 'I need somewhere to hide,' said Ricky. 'Can I hide against you?' And he kissed her. His lips were soft and he smelt of tobacco and beer. Edie closed her eyes.

Then it was over. The lights went on and couples on the floor separated abruptly, blinking in the harsh light. Girls adjusted dresses; boys glanced across at each other, smirking. Vic was in the doorway; Edie could feel his anxious glance before she even looked up. She stood, smoothing her skirt and pushing her hair behind her ears.

'I've got to go,' she said. She hesitated. 'Goodbye then.'

'Goodbye, Edie. See you.' He stayed sitting in the chair.

'Yes.' She waited, but he didn't say anything else. ''Bye.'

She left, walking over to Vic who held out an arm. 'Hello, Daddy,' she said. There was a lump of misery in her throat and she fought the urge to turn around.

'How was it?' He helped her into her coat.

'Fine.'

But when they got to the car, she said there was something she'd forgotten and ran back to the house. Ricky was still in the main room, a cigarette hanging off his lower lip. There was no one with him; he was just staring into the distance.

'Would you like to come to my party?' she said. 'Mine and Rose's, that is – a joint birthday party for us; except my birthday isn't for a couple of months. It's in a pub in Baylham. The Three Kings.'

He took the cigarette out of his mouth. 'I was just thinking about you,' he said. Then, 'Sure. When?'

'Two weeks on Saturday. I'll send you an invitation if you want. Where do you live?'

'Have you got anything to write with?'

'I'll remember it.'

'How about if I get your address from Fran, and send it to you. OK?'

It was an unnecessarily convoluted arrangement, probably just a way of letting her down gently. 'OK,' she said. Before she could lose her boldness, she leant down and kissed him again on his thin, soft lips and he put a hand up to the back of her head and held her against him for a moment. Then he let her go and put his cigarette back in his mouth.

She thought about it all the time. The two kisses; his hand on her hair. In the bath, lying in bed, in the middle of a conversation with friends, in lessons, she would let herself remember the feel of his lips. Edie was nearly seventeen, but it was the first time that she had felt sick and loose with desire. Now she sat in the school bus and stared down at the letter; the way he signed his name, the way he wrote hers. She touched the words with her finger.

She put her address very neatly at the top of the paper, in her best italic writing, with her phone number underneath. *'Dear Ricky, thanks for writing. I thought you'd forgotten . . .'* No. *'Dear Ricky, I was glad to hear from you and look forward to . . .'* No. *'Dear Ricky, here's the invitation that I promised to send. I hope you can make it. Love, Edie.'* That sounded so curt; he might think she didn't care and not come. But if she was too warm, he might not come either. She stared at what she had written, then pushed it inside the envelope with the invitation and sealed it. She went out straight away to post it. Louise was still at the shop, stock-taking, and Stella was out with a group of friends who were all waiting to go to their separate universities in October, and in the meantime were drifting round at their respective homes, sleeping late in the mornings, taking long, steamy baths, going through their clothes, putting books into boxes, meeting friends to discuss the lives that were waiting for them.

Outside, the car stood in the driveway with its crumpled bonnet and cracked, sticky windscreen. The glass had been cleared away though, and someone must have hosed down the tarmac and gravel. Edie ran up the road to the post-box, taking a deep breath before sliding the envelope in and even then holding on to it by a corner for a few seconds. Then she let it go and heard it clatter to the bottom of the empty box.

You go on, she thought, as if nothing new was happening. You look neat and placid, demure, and that's what people think you are, the same inside as you are on the surface. They never guess the teeming emotions, the way your heart bangs and your blood rushes and fear and longing cascade through your body. Everything that's important is hidden, secret. She sat in her bedroom and did her science homework. She wrote very neatly, underlining her answers with a ruler, mapping her graph carefully with a sharpened pencil, blotting her work. Her room was small and orderly: the counterpane pulled over her bed with a sharp crease at the pillow, her clothes folded and put into drawers, her glass ornaments arranged on the table, her books slotted back into the bookcase when she'd finished them.

Edie had always loved order. In Rose's house, everything was quiet and clean and neat. You came in through the front door and took your shoes off by the mat, and hung your coat up on the row of hooks, and the waxed floorboards led you into a living-room with a beige carpet that showed the recent tracks of the vacuum cleaner, and there were plumped-up cushions on the sofa, and windows without smears, and walls fresh with magnolia paint and six photographs of the family in silver frames along the mantelpiece. And in Rose's kitchen, the surfaces were clean, the toaster and food mixer set back against the wall, and the polished table had nothing on it except, occasionally, a small vase of flowers, a bowl of four green apples. Each object was in its proper place. The books were arranged alphabetically. Whereas their house was old, rambling and shabby. The floorboards creaked, the kitchen tiles were coming loose, there was a crack running up the stairwell. The windows needed washing, the curtains had been bleached by years of sunlight, the carpets were worn through and covered in bits of lint and fluff, and objects swept in like an incoming tide, and piled up in drifts around the rooms.

Even Louise's frantic cleaning binges, like the one that seemed to be going on downstairs at the moment, failed to achieve the immaculate order of other people's houses.

Today, Louise had started clearing up before she had even taken off her jacket. She had marched into the kitchen, dropped her bag and keys on to the chair, picked up a broom and shoved it round the kitchen floor, gathering dust and crumbs and dropped coins and hair clips into a pile. She rammed the broom head against Jude's feet, but Jude didn't look up from her book, just shifted her feet a few inches sideways. Louise put away pots and pans with furious bangs and a lid hit the floor with a cymbal's clash. She tipped faded roses and wilted peonies into the compost bin and picked the rotten pears out of the fruit bowl. She collected school folders, empty envelopes, incomplete decks of playing cards, old magazines, books with cracked spines that had been left face downward on the arms of sofas, bangles and lidless lipsticks and hair clips and brushes and sanitary towels; the leaking pens, snapped rulers, cracked protractors, that had slipped down the backs of chairs. In Jude's bedroom, where the curtains were closed, Louise stared in dismay at the tangle of sheets on the bed, the clothes lying in drifts on the floor. She opened the windows in Stella's room to let out the smell of sleep, sweat, perfume, camomile shampoo. In the living-room, she paused for a moment in front of herself and Vic on their wedding day. There she was, looking at the camera with a radiantly optimistic smile; Vic – much slimmer then, with his hair falling in a glossy black wing over his brow – was gazing at her, very grave. His left arm was round her and his hand almost hidden in the silky folds of her skirts. She had been twenty years old, in love, and in love with the idea of being so adored. That was 1960, twenty years ago, and she felt she had wings on her feet and was flying towards the future. A year after she and Vic married, she was a mother. Two years later, they were living in this house, where the wind rattled the panes at night, and in the winter flowers of frost bloomed on the inside of the windows.

Vic came in from the garden. A rusty leaf fluttered from his hair on to the table; his boots made marks over the tiles. In his cupped hands he held four plums.

'Look,' he said. His fingers were stained with juice. 'Taste one.'

'Vic, did you phone the insurance about the car?'

'The first of the season.'

Louise sighed. 'Go on then.'

She opened her mouth and bit into the plum he held out. She felt the juicy sweetness trickle down her throat.

'I'll do it tomorrow,' he said.

3

Louise and Edie went from shop to shop. The smell of perfume clogged their nostrils. They trudged up and down escalators, drifted along racks of dresses that looked promising from a distance but up close were too frilly, too bright, too sober, too low, too staid. Louise kept holding up garments, urging Edie at least to try them on, but Edie would shake her head stubbornly. Rose was going to wear a long black skirt with a slit all the way up the side and a black halter-neck top; she said she would be irresistible. Edie wanted a miracle dress that would transform her. She had a churning stomach every time she thought of the party. Excitement and fear trickled through her.

'Try this,' said Louise in the seventh shop.

'Oh, but it's too much. Look at the price.'

'Who cares?' said Louise recklessly.

Edie took the dress into the changing-rooms, wriggled out of her jeans and tee-shirt and pulled it over her head. It was long and russet-coloured, and had a deep neck and a wide skirt that flared out if she twirled around. Her skin looked milky and her neck long. She held her hair on top of her head and stared at herself. What would he think if he saw her like this? She stood on tiptoe. She smiled.

'Edie? Show me. Oh, that's the one! You look

gorgeous.' And she did, thought Louise. She looked slim and fresh, like a sapling. A wand. She held her by her narrow shoulders and kissed her. 'Really lovely,' she repeated and saw the flush of pleasure on her daughter's cheek. 'He'll be bowled over.'

'Mummy!' Edie blushed to the roots of her hair.

'I'm not blind, you know.'

'Mum . . .'

'Yes?'

'Thanks.'

Edie stared at herself once more, smiling at her reflection. One week.

The days were hot and dry; the summer's last gasp. The grass turned yellow, the leaves hung limply on the trees. Every morning, Edie woke early and lay in bed watching the cloudless sky through her curtains, hearing the birdsong from the garden. She would get up at half past six and lay the table for breakfast, feed Tangle, wait to hear the alarm go off in her parents' bedroom and the sounds of the day begin: floorboards creaking above her, taps running, Vic humming tunelessly in the shower, a voice calling out, a radio turned on. Sometimes she went out into the garden, where the grass was still wet with dew and mist plumed from the shrubs, where nettles were growing tall in the ditch and leaves were gathering in soft golden heaps along the wall. She'd pick a plum from the tree and eat it sitting on the swing that Vic had put up when they moved here, with its slimy green seat and fraying rope, watching the grey sky brighten to turquoise and the sun break through the thin layer of clouds.

She and Jude would leave the house at a quarter past eight and walk down the dusty lane, through the avenue of limply hanging beech trees, to catch the school bus. At a quarter to five they were home again, except on the days when Edie went swimming. She would make a pot of tea, then do her homework in the silent house. Her pen nib scratched across the paper. Bees clicked against her window pane. The shadows lengthened across the garden, wrapping the roses and the lilac trees in early darkness. She felt strange – slow and listless, yet agitated. She was waiting. Waiting for life to start in earnest.

On the day of the party, Rose came round in the late afternoon. She sat in Edie's room, plucking her eyebrows, while Edie lay in the bath. Vic was outside, mowing the lawn. The window was open and Edie could smell the fresh-cut grass. Downstairs, Jude was playing the piano, the same few bars over and over again, tinny and insistent. Edie looked down at her body, her flat white stomach and her ladder of ribs; her bony knees and her long feet. She noticed for the first time that her toes had hairs on them. She washed her hair twice, and soaped herself carefully all over. Out of the bath, she brushed her teeth and gargled water round her mouth. She was intensely aware of herself, every move she made.

The two girls sat in their bathrobes and painted each other's nails. Rose blow-dried Edie's hair and piled it on top of her head, fastening it with a tortoiseshell claw and teasing loose a few wisps to curl around her face.

They sprayed body perfume over each other until the room reeked. They put talcum powder on their feet, leaving white footprints on the carpet. Then they put on their make-up, both kneeling in front of the mirror together and applying foundation, eye-shadow, eye-liner, mascara, lipstick. Rose put blusher on her own cheeks, then some on Edie's. They were very serious about the task, quite silent. Then they gazed at their heightened reflections: two vivid faces with glowing red lips.

'We look fabulous,' said Rose. She kissed Edie on the cheek, leaving a scarlet oval.

New underwear, feet slipped into shoes, clothes pulled carefully over their heads, more lipstick, a dab of perfume behind the ears and on the wrists, then another because after all there was still nearly an hour till the party started and the perfume would disappear, the make-up would rub off, their faces would gradually fade and become ordinary again. They stood back from the glass and examined themselves.

'Half of me wishes I was staying in,' said Edie. She looked like a stranger, she thought; someone she didn't know if she would like, bright and hard.

'Don't be daft. It's going to be brilliant. Think positive.'

They went down the stairs, tottering on their heels and suddenly self-conscious. Vic and Louise were there, waiting. Together with Rose's parents, Simon and Alison, they would be downstairs in the pub all evening, occasionally coming up to make sure no one was mis-behaving. Louise widened her eyes dramatically.

'You look wonderful, both of you,' she said. 'Knock-outs.'

'Thanks,' said Edie. She glanced at Vic who smiled at her, but it looked more like a grimace of surprise. She saw that he had cut himself shaving and a shred of tissue was stuck on to his neck.

'Lovely,' he said. 'I would hardly have recognized you.'

For two and a half hours, Edie danced. They had hired a disco run by a friend of Rose's cousin. Afterwards, she couldn't remember the music, just the frenetic wretchedness. She danced with Jonathan from school, then his elder brother Tom, then with a boy she'd never met who tried to kiss her when the music stopped, but she backed away; then Bob, back home from university for the weekend, who arrived late with Stella, then with Jonathan again. She jumped up and down to the punk rhythms, a dull ache bumping around in her skull. She swayed and gyrated. She could feel blisters forming on her feet in their high heels. Ricky sat at the side of the room and smoked roll-ups. She had seen him arrive with a couple of other boys, and she'd pretended not to notice. She'd gone on dancing with increasing flamboyance, though she couldn't find the beat and jolted around clumsily. She tried to flirt, smiling too much at whoever she was with. Her cheeks burned and her head ached and her mouth was dry. She waited to feel the touch of his hand on her shoulder. But he didn't come to her. He sat there with a glass of beer and looked at all the people jostling in the middle of the room. He was wearing the same clothes as last time, but his hair was shorter and cleaner. She saw him all the time, out of the corner of her eye. She felt him behind her when her back was turned.

Eventually, she went to the toilets and sat on the closed seat and put her hot head in her hands. Everything was wrong; all her stupid, childish dreams. He didn't care. It never occurred to her that he might be shy among strangers. She just knew that the party was nearly over and they hadn't even said hello to each other; hadn't even met each other's eyes. After all the waiting, this was how it had ended; crying in a smelly cubicle.

When she came out, she went to the bar and asked for a glass of wine. The music was slowing now. She drank the wine in rapid sips. Someone came up and asked her to dance but she shook her head and stumbled down the stairs. Louise and Vic, and Simon and Alison were sitting at a small table with glasses of wine and a plate of sandwiches. Louise was talking animatedly, laughing, gesturing with her hands. The silver bracelet on her arm slid up to her elbow. She leant towards Simon and put a hand over his, then took his cigarette out of his mouth for a single puff, though she didn't usually smoke. They didn't see Edie, who went outside into the chilly dark. She walked through the car park and over to the river bank. She tipped her head up. The moon was a vague, diffuse light behind the gauzy clouds. She let the breeze blow over her burning face. Upstairs, the disco was playing 'Without You'. One day, she thought to herself, not really believing it but knowing it was probably true, one day she would be married with children and she would look back to this evening and smile to think how unhappy she had been because a boy she hardly knew hadn't asked her to dance to 'Without You'. Perhaps she wouldn't even be able to remember his name. Ricky.

She heard a crunching of footsteps over the gravel but she didn't move. She felt a hand on her shoulder, very tentative. She turned then. She could feel the tears drying on her cheeks. He put up one hand and tucked a wisp of hair behind her ears and she gave him a watery smile.

'I thought you were having a good time,' he said.

'Not really.'

He placed his arms round her waist, hardly touching her, and she moved a step forward so that her cheek was lightly against his chest. She put her hands on his back, just the fingers really, pressing them into the denim shirt.

'I've been thinking about you all the time,' Ricky said into her hair.

'Me you too,' she said. Happiness bloomed inside her.

'You ignored me though. When I came in.'

'I was scared.'

'Scared?'

'That you didn't care.'

They kissed each other very lightly on the lips, just once, not wanting to break the spell. She shifted her fingers, moving them along his back. He pulled her closer. The last sentimental strains of 'Without You' died away and 'Hi, Ho, Silver Lining' started up.

'Shall we go and dance then?' he said.

'I'd like that.'

Holding hands, they walked back inside. Just the press of his fingers sent little pulses up her arm. Her whole body felt soft and loose; each breath had a tremor to it. Vic, still sitting at the table with his chin in his hand, looked at her as they walked in, then his eyes slid towards Ricky. She saw a crease appear in his forehead, but she didn't care. She smiled at him and tugged Ricky by the hand and they went upstairs together. She was dimly aware of Louise standing at the bar with Simon, looking after her.

They danced and smiled at each other. In the corner, Jude was sitting alone with a bag of crisps in her hand, but Edie looked away; this was her night. Ricky put his hands in her hair and kissed her mouth and her neck. He said he'd like to see her again and she said she would like to see him, too. Very much, she said, and put her hand against his cheek. Suddenly she knew all the right moves. When the lights came on they blinked at each other.

'I've got your phone number,' he said. 'On your letter, right?'

She nodded. Vic and Louise were in the room now. People were leaving, trooping down the stairs towards their coats and lifts. They were coming towards her to say goodbye, thank you, lovely party, see you on Monday ... She lifted Ricky's hand, with its fingers stained yellow, nails bitten to the quick, and turned it over. She kissed the palm.

'I'll be waiting.'

4

'Edie? It's Ricky.'

'Hello, Ricky.' Her voice sounded rusty. She cleared her throat. There was a short silence. There was nothing she could think of to say. Not a single word.

'I thought I could maybe meet you after school tomorrow. If you'd like to, that is.'

'I'd like to,' she said.

'Four o'clock then.'

'OK. I wear school uniform, you know.' She blushed at her gaucheness.

'Yeah, well, I think I'll recognize you anyway. See you tomorrow then.' The phone went dead.

'Have you heard, Edie's got herself a boyfriend.'

Edie prodded the omelette with her fork. It was too runny in the middle, and speckled with chopped chives.

'A boyfriend?'

'He rang her up just now. Dick.'

'Ricky,' said Edie. She smiled as she said the name; she couldn't stop herself. 'Ricky Penrose.'

'Is he that boy last night?'

'Yes,' said Edie. 'I'm seeing him tomorrow. After school. I'll be back later than usual.'

'He's a weirdo,' said Jude suddenly.

'Don't be stupid. You don't know anything about him, anyway.'

'I know he's weird. Sarah Caldecott's brother knows him. He was at the party.'

'Weird how?' asked Louise.

'Just, you know, *odd*,' said Jude. 'He hangs around with all these people who've dropped out of school and stuff. Or that's what Greg said.'

'Why don't you invite him back here?' said Louise. 'So we can meet him. I don't like the idea of you just wandering off with him after school.'

'No.'

'Why not?'

'Honestly, Mummy. I'm not going to ask him to be vetted by my parents, the first time I meet him!'

'Edie, just for . . .'

'No!'

'I don't want you just going off with some strange boy we know nothing about.'

'He's not strange. Anyway, I'm sixteen, for good-ness' sake. Soon seventeen. People can leave home at sixteen.'

'But you're still living at home, aren't you?'

'We're not in the Victorian age. Anyway, you didn't behave like this with Stella.'

'That was different.'

'Why? Why was it different?'

'I knew Bob already,' said Stella calmly. 'Louise and Vic even knew his parents a bit.'

'Well, thanks for your support, Stella. I'm not bring-ing him here and that's that. And I *am* meeting him tomorrow after school. There's nothing you can do about it.'

'We're not trying to stop you meeting him, we're just saying . . .'

'I'm sixteen. I'm meeting a boy after school. I'm not going to go and take drugs or run off or anything. I'll meet him and then I'll come back here and do my homework and behave like a dutiful daughter. Like I always do.' She was shocked by the fury in her own voice.

'Sarah Caldecott's brother said . . .'

'Shut *up* about Sarah Caldecott's stupid brother. I don't care what he says or anyone says.'

'You're really in love with him,' said Jude with glee. 'I've never seen you like this before.'

'Oh, shut up. I'm not in love, I'm just going to meet him after school. No big deal. Let's talk about something else, OK?'

'OK,' said Louise, and silence fell.

He was leaning against the wall with his roll-up dangling from his lower lip. She walked up to him, aware of how she must look in daylight, in her uniform, the navy woollen skirt with its itchy waist, the dull-blue shirt. She wasn't wearing any make-up and her hair was pulled back into the severe pony-tail that she always wore for Chemistry. She smelt of the laboratory.

Ricky just nodded at her and took her bag and they walked, not touching or speaking, down to the river where they sat on a bench set back from the bank. There was writing along its back: 'In memory of beloved

Gareth, 1949–1970, who fears no more the heat of the sun.' For one panicky moment, she wanted to sob. She tightened her lips and took a few breaths, then tried to think of something to say – something arresting; anything would do. There was nothing in her head at all. She stared beyond the river bank, out at the slow, brown water with its submerged cargo of litter and dead wood. A man in a slender boat rowed past, bending to his oars. His body moved backwards and forwards on its coaster, and even from the shore, Edie could see the muscles in his arms rippling as he pulled.

Ricky fished in his top pocket and brought out a joint, seeming not to care about the woman with her red setter dog straining at its leash, the man jogging past with sweat staining great circles under his arms.

'Here's one I made earlier,' he said, and Edie smiled, though her mouth was dry with nerves. She'd smoked dope once before, with a group of school-friends, and it had had no effect except to make her feel dizzy and sick. She watched Ricky as he leant forward, striking a match and cupping the flame in his hand, lighting the joint, drawing in deeply and holding the smoke in his chest before exhaling. She didn't want to say to him that she didn't really know how to do it. She was miserably conscious that she called her father Daddy, was in awe of her mother, was polite to her teachers, won school prizes for effort and cooperation; that she didn't smoke, didn't take drugs, rarely swore and had never gone beyond kissing and the odd inadequate and undesired fumble. She felt encumbered by all the things that hadn't happened to her yet and by the lightness of her life.

He passed the joint to her and she took it. She tried to copy him, making a funnel of her fist to pull the smoke through. It made her cough and a slight nausea swept through her as she held the smoke in her lungs. Then she let it out, slowly like he'd done. She repeated the action once more, and passed it back in relief.

They finished the joint and he stood up, grinding it under his heel.

'Shall we walk for a bit?'

'Sure.' She took a step and the world swam in front of her eyes. She put out a hand to steady herself and giggled.

'Look at you!' said Ricky. 'You're stoned already.'

'I'm not. Not really. I'm just – glad.' As soon as she said the reckless words, she heard Rose's voice in her head, telling her to play it cool.

But Rick took hold of her hand and lifted it up to his lips, which were dry against her palm. She turned to look at him. His pupils were dilated, just like when she'd first met him, and she could see her face mirrored there.

'Hello,' she said. She stepped closer so she was no longer reflected in his eyes, and lifted her other hand to place it against his cheek.

His arms went round her then, under her blazer and over her school shirt. She put her hands in his soft hair and pulled his face towards her. Their lips touched and he made a small sound, like a groan of pain. Joy rose like a bird in her chest. A woman tutted disapprovingly as she marched past them.

'Do you know something?' he said when they moved

apart. 'I wrote about twenty notes to you before the one I sent.'

'Did you? Really? What did they say?'

'I'll write them again. If you'd like.'

'I'd like that.'

They joined hands and walked on slowly. Every so often they stopped and moved nearer each other. Their hips touched, their shoulders. His hair grazed her cheek. A few yellow leaves fluttered down and one landed in his hair. She picked it out and put it surreptitiously into her blazer pocket.

'I was worried about you seeing me in my school uniform,' she said.

'That's just mad,' he said. 'You're beautiful.'

'No,' she said, flushing with delight. 'Rose's beautiful, other girls at school. Not me. You know, last week some of the boys voted on who was in the top ten and I wasn't on the list; I never thought I would be.'

As soon as she said this she regretted it. She didn't want Ricky to start looking at her through their eyes and suddenly to see her ordinariness. But he just shrugged. 'They're ignorant. They're so ignorant they make lists and give people points. They just want blonde hair and big tits and short skirts. A pout and a fuck-me look, like the women in the Miss World competition. That's not beautiful; that's all on the surface.'

'Well, that's good,' she said, giggling.

'I'm serious. Things should be kept secret. Cherished. Like a gift.'

'OK, I give you my beauty, such as it is,' she said lightly. 'All right?'

'Do you?' He stopped and held her by her shoulders. She was taken aback by his intensity; the wild look in his eyes, the press of his fingers against her skin.

'Yes,' she said. And at that moment she would have given him anything in the world.

Edie woke and it was dark and silent in the house, except for the creak of pipes and the sigh of the wind outside her window. She got out of bed and put on her tatty dressing-gown. All the lights had been turned off, and the bedroom doors were shut. She padded in her slippers to the kitchen and put on the kettle.

It occurred to her that she was hungry. She hadn't eaten properly for days, weeks even. She put a slice of slightly stale bread in the toaster and, when it popped up, spread it with butter and then raspberry jam. She and Victor had made the jam together, just a couple of months ago. They'd gathered the raspberries in the pick-your-own fruit farm a couple of miles away. She remembered the day clearly: cloudlessly hot and still, the earth baked in dusty ridges underfoot and the canes limp in the dusty heat. Edie had crouched down to look under the leaves where the fruit hides, pulling gently so that the berries slid over their white hulls. She remembered the smell of her suntan lotion and the sweet, rotting fruit. Above her Victor, in his wide-brimmed sun-hat with his white arms turning a stinging pink where his tee-shirt ended, had picked steadily, refusing to eat a single raspberry. They'd collected two full baskets of soft, purpling berries that were melting under their own weight, then that evening cooked them with sugar, bringing the scarlet liquid to a rolling boil, cooling spoonfuls on a saucer to test its thickness. The jar had Victor's spidery writing on the label and when Edie bit into her toast she remembered the way he'd looked that day, with his paunch swelling the blue tee-shirt he'd owned as long as she could remember, and his legs, pale and thin, in their baggy white shorts, his pink elbows, his stupid hat above his white forehead. She bit into the toast and looked out at the massed shapes of trees in the garden.

The cat was curled up on one of the chairs, eyes closed and half-purring. Edie stroked his spine and felt the vibrations running along his body. She opened the back door and stood looking out for a moment. The wind sighed in the trees. A few fallen leaves rustled on the ground. There was a half moon above the tree-line and next to it, a single white star. There was a song her father used to sing when he was saying goodnight to her. He would pull her sheet under her chin, smooth back her hair and stroke her cheek.

> *I see the moon,*
> *The moon sees me,*
> *The moon sees the one*
> *That I want to see . . .*

She sang it now to herself, softly. Her mouth was full of joy. Behind her, the kettle boiled furiously. She pulled the door shut, scooped two spoonfuls of tea leaves into the pot and poured in the water. The kitchen clock said it was two in the morning.

'Edie? What on earth are you doing? I thought you were a burglar or something.' Even when her face was puffy with sleep, Stella was golden and beautiful.

'I couldn't sleep. D'you want a cup of tea?'

'All right. I've got a dreadful period pain. Something warm might help.' She sat at the table and cupped the mug in her two hands.

'Did I wake you?'

'Not really. Are you all right?'

'Yes. I feel a bit restless, that's all.'

'Why's that, then?'

Suddenly, Edie wanted to tell Stella everything. She half-opened her mouth to begin. But after all, what was there to say? Ricky kissed me. I kissed Ricky. I wanted to swoon with happiness. I've got this feeling of dread and excitement in the pit of my stomach. I can't sleep, I can't eat, all I can do is think of him. All those emotions boiled down into a few paltry words that made her sound young and ridiculous. So she shrugged instead and took another gulp of tea, while Stella looked at her with a tender expression on her face.

'It's two weeks tomorrow,' said Stella after a pause.

'What?'

'That I leave home, of course.'

'Is it that soon?'

'Yup. Make the most of me.'

'How do I do that?'

'Oh, you know – bring me breakfast in bed. Help me clear out my room. Things like that.'

'Are you excited?'

'Kind of. I already feel a bit homesick. Weird, eh?

I've been looking forward to leaving home and being at university ever since I was about thirteen, and suddenly I want more time. To lie in bed and smell coffee being brewed downstairs; wander around in my dressing-gown, mooch about doing nothing in particular, just being here. Everything's changing, isn't it? You wait and wait for change, then when it comes you wish things could go back to being how they always were.'

'Mummy minds you going terribly, you know.'

Stella blew on her tea and wrinkled her forehead. 'Yeah – but it's a bit like I'm having the life she never had herself. It makes me feel a bit guilty I'm going away.'

Edie and Stella had almost never talked like this together. Although she was only two years older, Stella had always been emphatically the eldest daughter: responsible, self-reliant, generous towards her younger sisters in a way that made it clear they were no threat to her. She'd led the way towards adulthood with self-assurance, painting her nails in her bedroom with her friends, calling her parents by their names, leafing through glossy magazines, dealing discreetly with her periods, buying lacy white bras which she washed herself and hung above the bath, dating nice enough boys, passing exams with good enough grades, coming home before midnight or phoning to say she would be late, losing her virginity after a visit to the family planning clinic.

'That's true,' Edie said now to Stella, nodding her head, sipping at her cooling tea. 'But the house will feel very empty without you.'

'You'll soon get used to it.'

'I don't think so. I think you not being here will make us feel incomplete. We'll always be waiting for you to come home again. Mummy especially.'

She suddenly felt wise and old, sitting in the kitchen with Stella, her lips still sore from kissing. It's possible, she thought to herself, to be happy and sad all at the same time.

'What?' She suddenly became aware Stella was talking to her again.

'I was saying, you don't know anything about him.'

'No,' said Edie. Then she smiled. 'But I will know, won't I? Bit by bit, I'll know.'

He was the only child of a single mother. His father was often drunk and sometimes violent; he had left when Ricky was three, just after his baby brother had died, and now didn't even remember to send Ricky a birthday card. They lived on a council estate and about once a week one of their windows was broken or paint thrown against the walls. His mother did lots of odd jobs — she cleaned, made curtains, did bits of child-minding, sometimes helped out in the fish and chip shop. In her spare time she read glossy magazines and biographies of actresses. She wanted Ricky to be an accountant or a teacher; something middle-class and safe. He wanted to travel and make films that would hold a mirror up to the world. His greatest friend, Cal, had left school after O-levels and spent most days in bed and most nights out of his head. His first girlfriend was a year and a half older than him; now, she was anorexic and weighed about five and a half stone.

Ricky smoked dope, took acid and sometimes, for a change, drank opiated cough medicine that made him feel drowsy and peaceful and far away from himself. He played the saxophone and the guitar, neither very well. He didn't eat meat. He was left-handed. He smoked about twenty-five cigarettes a day, roll-ups that he could make with one hand. He got migraines that made him ill and sick, but which left him feeling oddly renewed afterwards, like a landscape after a storm.

He shoplifted, but only from big stores. He thought school was crap and the system was corrupt. He bit his nails. He masturbated in bed at night, but not every night. He had insomnia. He sometimes thought about killing himself. He loved cats, but didn't own one. He loved birds of prey. He loved Baudelaire (in translation), and Neil Young. Loved walking in the early hours of morning, when the streets were deserted. He didn't believe in God but if he'd been religious he would have been a Buddhist. He hated suits and ties. He hated football and heavy metal and beards. He hated his father.

He had a scar on his stomach from an appendectomy two years ago. He lifted up his shirt to show it to Edie and she stared at his thin, milky stomach and the tightly puckered line that ran down below the belt of his trousers. Shivered with apprehension. She'd never before let herself imagine a man's body, not really.

And he had a scar on his thumb from where he had tried to open a beer bottle with a stone. She lifted the thumb and held the scar against her lips, feeling its ridge with her tongue.

In the café near the school, their legs tangled under the table and their hands touched lightly. Outside, rain was falling steadily; the street was full of umbrellas. They leant towards each other. They gazed at each other's faces, each other's mouths.

*

He came and watched her swimming. She wore a plain black suit and tucked her hair into a black cap that snapped over her temples and gave her a headache. She wore blue goggles over her cap that bit into her flesh, leaving rings round her eyes afterwards. He watched her from the gallery, one of the dozen or so swimming steadily up and down the stretch of turquoise water below him: crawl, breast-stroke, back-stroke. She was a good swimmer, with a flat stomach and strong shoulders, large hands and feet. When she swam, she made it look effortless. Afterwards, wrapped in a yellow towel, she stood near him and pulled off her black cap, shook free her damp tendrils of hair. He put one hand on her sharp collar-bone, fiddled with the strap of her costume.

'You smell of chlorine,' he said.

'Mmm. I'll have a shower.'

'I like it.'

She swallowed and leant a bit closer to him. Her flesh ached.

Her days in the sun. Sun inside and out, and she could hardly tell where one stopped and the other began. She lay in the garden, wearing a pair of denim shorts and a bikini top and soaking up the lingering heat of the evening. She put her hand on her stomach. She touched her ribs and her pelvis. She touched her neck and her face, very gently, the way Ricky did. She ran her fingers along her slightly swollen lips. Her limbs felt heavy and there was a sheen of sweat along her arms and in the hollow of her stomach. There were house-martins dipping in and out of the eaves on the garden shed, and she watched them for a while, then closed her eyes drowsily. The sun burnt on inside her head, a fuzzy golden disc.

Louise and Vic were sitting at the garden table with Rose's parents, Simon and Alison. She could hear their voices rising and falling, the chink of glasses, Louise's laughter; smell the honeysuckle, the night-scented stock and the smoke from the barbecue. There was a sudden sharp exclamation, raised voices – something had burnt; someone was angry. But it didn't matter. Nothing mattered. Just this.

Rose asked her if she and Ricky wanted to go out with her and Matt, in a foursome.

'Maybe,' said Edie, evasively.

'Go on, it'd be fun.'

'Later perhaps.'

'You can't just spend your time gazing into each other's eyes. You'll get bored of each other. Come skating in Birmingham with us at the weekend. How about next Saturday?'

'I'll see.'

'If you don't want to come, just say so. I'll ask Laura instead.'

'OK.'

'You've changed, you know.'

'What d'you mean, changed?'

'You can't just forget about your friends, as if we'll sit here waiting for you to come back again.'

'It's not like that.'

'Isn't it?'

'No.'

'You're going to get hurt. You've got to learn how to hold back a bit, play the game.'

'It's not a game.'

'That's what I mean.'

Rose turned away and walked towards a group of girls who were giggling in the yard.

She told him about herself, too, though sometimes it seemed there wasn't much to tell. She told him about her sisters, and how she had always thought of herself as the one in the middle – Stella was the beautiful, amiable and popular one, Jude the clumsy, difficult and clever one. She was always in between – smart enough, cheerful enough, well liked enough not to worry about. She told him she was going to be a doctor – either a GP or a paediatrician. She wanted to make people better, and give a name to their chaotic ailments. As a doctor, you could diagnose the causes of suffering and take away pain. She said all this, but her future suddenly seemed unimportant – what mattered was here, now. She had stepped out of the shadows, into the dazzle of the present.

She described holidays she'd been on. Walking in Scotland – purple heather and mist and swimming in the icy waters of lochs. Camping in Brittany; the way all the houses had shutters, and there were avenues of pollarded trees in the towns, and how they'd eaten croissants for breakfast, and crêpes in the evening. He'd never been abroad; he'd never been on a ferry or a plane.

He hardly ever went on holiday – except for the time when he and Cal had hitched to Devon and slept on the beach and eaten nothing but bread and cheese for six days.

As she talked, she became more and more aware of herself as part of a network of people – parents, sisters, grandparents, concerned adults – while he was un-attached. She lived in a house of noise and friction, where everybody was aware of everybody else and there was a queue outside the bathroom each morning; she was bound by responsibilities and expectations. But he lived in a tiny council house and was often alone. He could do what he wanted, go where he chose. Nobody told him what to believe. Nobody told him what the rules were; he made them up for himself, a weird mixture of Romanticism, existentialism, youthful pessimism and raw need.

She told him about her parents – that Louise had married young, and now worked in an interior design shop, selling fabric and brass door handles. When she said that Vic was an estate agent, he raised his eyebrows at her.

'He's not like that,' she said defensively.

'Like what?'

'Like an estate agent is supposed to be. You know. It's just something he does.'

'So what is he like?'

'He's . . .' She tried to think of the right word. Estate agents were meant to be smooth, enthusiastic, with fake sun tans and big gold watches. Vic was a shy and silent man. He thought before he spoke, frowning and putting one finger against his nose. Often people were too impatient to wait for his reply and would talk over his considered pauses.

'Sweet,' she said at last. 'Hopeless,' she added, feeling a pang of disloyalty.

And sitting on the river bank, she told Ricky about the boys who had kissed her, trying to make them sound more significant than they were.

And she told him she was a virgin. She said it looking at the ground as they were walking up the road together, hands loosely linked. She didn't look up. She didn't want to see his face. Her words seemed to float in the air between them. The pressure of his fingers didn't alter, nor the pace of his stride.

'So I'll be your first.'

They went on walking up the street in silence. She could hear her heart, banging like a drum.

'Yes.'

Her grandmother was arriving for the weekend and Louise insisted on a family meal together.

'And it's Stella's last weekend. You should try and be here. After she's gone – well . . .' She was pressing cloves into a ham. Their pungent aroma filled the kitchen. Then she said, 'Why don't you invite this boy . . . ?'

'Ricky.'

'Why don't you invite Ricky round for supper on Saturday? We'd like to meet him.'

'Supper?'

'Yes. What's wrong – doesn't he eat supper?'

*

44

'OK.'

'Really? I mean, you don't need to, if you don't want to. It's just, my mother, she wants to, well, you know.'

'See what I'm like.'

'Yes.'

'What time then?'

'I don't know. Sevenish?'

'All right.'

She resisted the urge to tell him to wear clean jeans and wash his hair and shake hands firmly with Louise and look her in the eye. After all, why did it matter if they liked him or if he liked them?

'Thanks,' she said.

6

Ellen was a compact, restless woman. Her clothes were crisp, her brown-grey hair cut short and brushed decisively behind her ears. Her mouth was set in an expression that was hoping to be a smile. She always stood very straight, shoulders back, and walked fast. She hated to be idle, or perhaps she feared it. During a week planned in advance and organized into grids of time, she kept her house and garden immaculate, learnt Italian at evening classes, read books about history, politics and the glory of country houses, took long, vigorous walks, met friends. She cooked proper meals for herself each evening, setting the kitchen table with the correct cutlery. She allowed herself a finger of whisky and one third of a bottle of wine every day, half on a Friday and Saturday. When she ate, her knife and fork chinked on the china, she could hear herself chew and swallow, hear the fly trapped against the window pane. Only after she had cleared away her meal would she let herself settle in the chair in front of the television and relax. She disapproved of too much television, and she had never in her life watched it in the daytime, except for tennis during Wimbledon. She was sixty-four and scared of becoming an old lady nodding in front of a flickering screen. She didn't like to look back at the crowded past, and she was fearful of seeing too far into a future of regularly spaced activities and long, empty nights.

Louise made a gesture of apology as they went into the house together, Ellen carrying her small bag.

'I've let it all get into a bit of a mess, I'm afraid. I should have cleared up before you arrived. It's just – well, I've been busy, what with work and Stella leaving on Monday and, well, everything. You know how it is.'

'Yes. Of course,' said Ellen, who didn't. 'But I can get it straight in no time.'

'Oh no, Mum! I didn't ask you here to do our housework. You really don't need to do that. I'd feel awful.'

'I'd like to,' said Ellen firmly. 'After all, what are mothers for?'

She rolled up her sleeves and put her hands on her hips while she surveyed the mess. The laundry piled up by the ancient washing-machine that didn't spin things properly any more, unmade beds, a sense that clutter was taking over. The kitchen had obviously been cleaned recently, but in the cupboards, rice spilt out of its bag, and there was a thick dusting of porridge oats and biscuit crumbs over the surfaces. And the boiler was on borrowed time, Louise said apologetically; it kept going out. Paint faded or flaked, wood rotted, iron rusted.

Louise carried Ellen's bag up to Edie's room, where she would be staying. It was the only neat room in the house. There were no posters on the wall, just a line drawing of two deer that had faded so that now it looked more like a framed blank canvas. Clothes were folded in their drawers or hung in the cupboard; shoes were in pairs under the radiator that was making a gurgling, banging sound now. Edie's glass ornaments, which she had collected since she was a child, were arranged on the window sill. Even the elephant with the broken trunk was there, and the pink cat the size of a fingernail. Her school work was stacked on the table under the window, with sharpened pencils and a ruler in a mug.

There was a postcard propped up on the table too, with a black-and-white photograph of a man standing in a dark doorway. Ellen turned it over. *'Edie,'* she read, *'here is one of the messages I didn't send you before: I can't stop thinking about you. I see you in my dreams. R.'*

Ellen put the card carefully back in its place and pursed her lips. Clearly, things had changed around here. Something was going on in this bare little room. She sat on the bed and pulled off her shoes, slipping her aching feet into the slippers she had made sure to bring with her. Plain, demure Edie had a boyfriend, 'R', who saw her in his dreams. Ellen wondered who had ever dreamed about her. Bill? If he had, he'd never told her so; that wasn't the way their marriage had worked. Had she ever dreamed of him, though? She didn't think so. She dreamed of ships and planes and trains, of long journeys.

She stood up and smoothed her skirt. She'd start with the living-room.

'Edie's got a boyfriend.'

Jude speared a chunk of ham on her fork, then shovelled broad beans in parsley sauce and a whole new potato on top. She opened her mouth very wide, inserted the mouthful, and chewed violently.

Vic poured wine into everyone's glasses, even Jude's. He was wearing an ancient brown sweater with zigzag green stripes and blue cotton trousers and Ellen didn't think they went very well together.

'Have you, dear?' said Ellen. 'What's his name?'

Edie blushed. 'Ricky,' she mumbled.

'He's coming tomorrow for supper,' continued Jude, mouthful finished. 'Mum wants to inspect him.'

'Poor boy,' said Stella. She winked at Edie and leant back. Her black polo-neck sweater stretched over her breasts; her hair was piled on top of her head.

'I just want to meet him,' Louise protested. 'That's all right, isn't it, Edie? I'm not going to interrogate him.'

'It's fine,' said Edie neutrally.

She looked different, Ellen thought, watching her. There was a light about her, a glow. She drank the rest of her wine and Vic poured her some more. Why was he so silent? She wondered if he'd said anything at all this evening; she couldn't remember a single word. She turned her glance on him. His hair needed washing and he was wearing such terrible clothes. He had just taken off his heavy-rimmed reading glasses, and there was a small indentation across the bridge of his nose. She decided she should make an effort.

'How's work then, Vic?'

'Fine,' he said. 'Thank you.' He smiled at her, then cut himself a square of pink ham and an oval of potato and pushed them on to the back of his fork. He rolled a single broad bean on top and lifted the fork very carefully to his mouth.

'But it's a worrying time to be in the housing business.'

He chewed several times before replying, 'It's always a bad time.'

'Oh.' Ellen was stumped.

'It's the time of year when the swallows start to leave,' he said, as if he was continuing the conversation.

'Is it, Vic?' She picked up her glass and took a sip of wine. 'I didn't know,' she added.

Across the table, Louise was talking arrangements with Stella: how she needed to get up earlier than usual the next morning so she didn't miss her haircut, how she needed to go to the chemist's for last-minute things. And was she sure that two suitcases were enough? And did she really need to take an electric heater with her?

'What does your young man do, Edie?' said Ellen. She was beginning to feel rather light-headed. She never usually drank this much wine. She took another cautious sip.

'A-levels,' said Edie. 'He's in the year above me.'

'At your school?'

'No. The boys' comprehensive across town.'

'Oh,' said Ellen. She didn't know what else to say. She wanted to have a conversation about politics or foreign affairs – something impersonal and robust. She wanted to have her opinions stirred up and to hear everyone getting passionate about things that didn't really touch them. Vic filled her glass once more; she hadn't noticed she'd emptied it. She heard herself saying, 'It all happens so much younger than when I was a girl. Bill was the first man who kissed me.'

'How old were you?' asked Jude.

'Eighteen, I must have been.'

'No one's ever wanted to kiss me,' said Jude. Her voice was triumphant. 'But then, why would they? Look at me.'

'You're a very handsome girl,' said Ellen.

Jude grinned at her. 'I'm fat, Granny.'

'Oh, I wouldn't say that, it's just something that will . . .'

'And getting fatter.'

'How are things with you, Mum?' Louise intervened. 'That's what we want to know. Have you planned your holidays this year?'

'I thought I'd go to the Isle of . . .'

'You're not fat, Jude,' said Vic, breaking in. 'You mustn't say things like that.'

'Why not? Everyone else says them about me.'

'Who says them?'

'It doesn't matter, Dad. I *am* fat. Edie's thin, I'm fat and Stella's just right.'

'No one's just right,' said Stella complacently. 'Everyone's got their weak points.'

'You sound like one of those agony aunts in your stupid magazines. What are yours then?'

Stella pursed her lips. 'Lots of things,' she said vaguely. 'Too many things.'

'Hah!'

'Looks aren't everything,' said Ellen, meaning well.

'Thanks, Gran,' said Jude. 'Speaking of being fat, what's for pudding?'

'Stewed plums,' said Edie. 'Daddy picked the plums and I cooked them.'

'Blimey. That's a change from fruit salad.'

'I'm going to branch out,' said Edie. 'I made a real egg custard too. Six egg yolks, a bit of sugar and a pint of milk. You have to cook it really gently over a low heat or it'll curdle. It's ready when it coats the back of the spoon.'

'If you ate a bit less . . .' began Louise.

'There you are, I am fat. See? Mum thinks so anyway.'

'I never said that. People have different shapes and you . . .'

'. . . are fat.'

'Girls worry too much about their weight nowadays,' said Ellen valiantly. 'You know the history of art course that I did last year? One of the things we talked about was the changing shapes of women's bodies. Our tutor was a women's libber, or whatever you want to call it . . .'

'Feminist,' said Jude.

'Yes. Well, she taught Women's Studies as well as History of Art. Anyway, take Rubens' women for example, they were very large you know. And yet that was thought of as beautiful at the time: large thighs and breasts.' Ellen blushed and took a hasty swallow of wine.

'The trouble is,' said Jude, 'we don't live then, we live now. Who wants to kiss a Rubens' woman?'

'I've always liked Rubens,' said Vic.

'Who else did you study in your course?' asked Louise, and Ellen sat back gratefully and started to talk about the History of Ideas, though her words slipped a bit, tumbling into each other. She thought some of her dates might be a bit wrong. Never mind. The evening was drawing in, cold and sharp, and soon she would be lying in Edie's narrow bed.

7

Ricky had made an effort. He was wearing baggy brown trousers, a white shirt buttoned over a tee-shirt, a woollen jacket that was a bit too small, so his wrists poked out. He'd shaved. His hair, still damp, was brushed flat over his scalp, making his face look thinner. For a moment, Edie saw him through the eyes of others: gaunt, ungainly and pale, with chewed nails and cheap clothes. He looked poor, she realized. Poor and strange.

And nervous. His hand was cold when she touched it and his smile forced. She was washed through by love for him. She lifted his hand and kissed it, held it against her flushed cheek.

'Hi.'

She was nervous too. All day she'd been thinking about the evening, as if it were a wall to climb over. She had gone for a brisk walk with Ellen in the morning, the wind whipping the dead leaves around their feet and stinging their cheeks; she'd helped Vic in the garden, piling stones into a pile to make a rockery, until her back ached and sweat trickled down between her breasts. She had imagined Rose and the rest of them skating in Birmingham, blades cutting through the ice; falling over and shrieking with laughter, holding on to each other for support, collapsing on the side with mashed feet. For a moment, she had allowed herself to wish she was there, with her friends, not here, waiting with butterflies in her stomach for Ricky to arrive. But she'd pushed the thought away and done her homework at Jude's table, among the crumbs and scraps of paper, staring out at the windy, blue day. All the while, Jude lay on her unmade bed, reading *Lord of the Rings* for the third time and crunching boiled sweets.

It took Edie a long time to decide what to wear, standing in her bedroom that had been transformed into Ellen's bedroom, with Ellen's possessions arranged on all the surfaces and Ellen's smell of lavender soap and cold cream in the air, staring at the few clothes that were folded in her drawer. Her favourite jeans, she thought, but which top? She pulled on her blue cheese-cloth shirt with its dozens of tiny buttons and looped buttonholes. It had hardly been worn, because she kept saving it for the right occasion, but now she was finally wearing it, she didn't look the way she'd imagined she would. She pulled it over her head and one of its buttons flew off. She tried on her skinny-rib pullover, but immediately felt claustrophobically hot. Then her plain white shirt, but that had a black smudge on the shoulder and made her look whey-faced anyway. In the end, she'd put on a black flannel shirt, which was old and loose-fitting but which she knew suited her. She pulled her hair back and tied it in one thick plait. She applied mascara, then lipstick. Rose-water that she bought for fifty pence a bottle from Boots behind her ears. Silver studs in her ears. A bangle round her wrist. She looked in the mirror, rubbed colour into her cheeks, grimaced at her reflection.

Downstairs, she could hear the sound of Ellen and Louise cooking together, their voices murmuring among the clatter of pans and chink of plates – Louise's low and quiet, Ellen's brighter and more emphatic. And she suddenly remembered, as the doorbell rang and she ran downstairs to get it, that she hadn't told Louise that Ricky was a vegetarian. The smell of garlic and rosemary filled the air. Lamb, she thought, as she pulled the door open.

'Hi.'

'Hi.' She saw his pupils were dilated; he was a bit stoned.

'How did you get here?'

'Walked. It's only a couple of miles.'

'Oh.' There seemed to be nothing to say. Her head ached with the effort. 'Come in, anyway.'

He stepped into the hall and wiped his feet on the doormat for an unnecessarily long time. The voices in the kitchen rose and fell.

'I'd better introduce you then.'

They walked into the kitchen, which was filled with the smell of lamb cooking. The two women looked round. Louise was wearing a silvery-green dress that made her eyes look green too, and an apron tied round her waist. Her hair was tied in a coil on the top of her head and her mouth was pink and smiling. She held a long knife in her hand.

'This is Ricky,' said Edie. 'Ricky, my mother and grandmother. Um, Louise and Ellen, I guess.' She gave a surprised little giggle and then steadied herself.

Louise held out her hand. Edie could smell her perfume.

'Hello, Ricky,' she said, still smiling. 'I'm pleased to meet you. I've heard so much about you.'

Edie winced and looked down at the table. Lilies in a vase, filling the kitchen with their heavy scent, candles waiting to be lit, two bottles of wine. She tried to block out the kitchen, Louise's polite smile and her words, Ricky's muttered response.

'Hello, Ricky,' said Ellen. 'Pleased to meet you.'

They shook hands over the table.

'We've hardly seen Edie since she met you,' said Louise.

'Well . . .' said Ricky. He glanced at Edie. 'I, um . . .' He stopped dead and looked across at Edie.

'I forgot to say, but Ricky's a vegetarian,' Edie blurted.

'Oh,' said Louise. She looked at the carving knife in her hand. 'Well . . .'

'It doesn't matter,' said Ricky. 'I'm not hungry. A few potatoes . . .'

'Why are you a vegetarian, Ricky?' asked Ellen brightly. 'I know a lot of youngsters are nowadays, but I must say I would miss my meat. A meal doesn't seem to have a centre unless you have meat or fish.'

'Would you kill the lamb that you're going to eat?' asked Ricky. His voice came out in a loud rush.

'Oh no, I don't think so. Unless I was on a desert island and starving and there was no one to do it for me. I suppose if I was desperate enough – but I would have to be desperate.'

'Everyone should be able to kill what they eat. I wouldn't kill an animal, so I shouldn't eat it. Most people only like buying meat that doesn't look like flesh – all shrink-wrapped on supermarket shelves.'

'I must say, that's extremely thought-provoking,' said Ellen.

They all gazed at each other hopelessly. Ellen cleared her throat.

'I was going to make a green salad as well,' said Louise. 'Do you and Ricky want to go and pick some herbs for me, Edie?'

'Sure.'

Edie gave her a grateful smile and Louise smiled back.

'I think Vic's still out there building his rockery. Tell him we'll eat in half an hour or so.'

They went through the kitchen doors into the garden. The wind had died down and the evening sky was clear, with a few rippled clouds. Later it would be chilly, but now there was still a warmth in the air, and the smell of flowers, mown grass, fallen leaves. Vic was at the end of the garden; they could see his shape through the tangle of shrubs. But they lingered by the swing and the rose bushes. Ricky took out his tin of tobacco and papers and rolled himself a cigarette. Edie shielded the flame of his lighter while he inhaled deeply. She wished he wasn't here; she wished he wasn't going to sit at dinner, eating boiled potatoes and answering questions about his school, his plans (impossible), his father (absent), his mother (a cleaner), his opinions (confused). He had been her secret, belonging to no one but herself.

She didn't want him reduced to the ordinary and quantifiable, nor did she want anyone to have opinions about him, or them. She had a sudden feeling of their vulnerability. They needed to shield their relationship from the bright glare of the world.

'Ricky.'

'Yes.'

'Are you all right?'

'Fine.'

They kissed each other briefly on the lips. Not a kiss of desire, or affection even; just a kiss that was keeping things going, until they were together again away from everyone else.

Edie loved Jude. She loved the way she talked, even with her mouth jammed with roast potatoes, lamb and mint sauce, her voice riding over the conversation between Stella and Louise. She was wearing a strange orange shirt-dress with the belt undone, her hair was unbrushed and pushed back behind her ears, her cheeks were red with the heat of the room. She was talking about *Lord of the Rings* to Ricky, who'd read it three times as well. They were having a conversation – a real conversation, not the stilted question-and-answer session which had preceded it, where everyone had been on their best behaviour, and each attempt to ignite a discussion had been like turning the key in a car whose battery had gone flat.

'It's a journey,' she was saying. 'Everything's so complicated, but all the time there's a journey that leads us through. A quest. And it's about power, isn't it? Power and saying no to power. That's why it's not just a children's book. In fact, I don't think it's a children's book at all; hardly any of the people in my class could read it; they'd just give up. People who think it's about hobbits and elves and wizards just don't get it.'

'It's about giving things up,' said Ricky. His face loomed across the table in the guttering candlelight. 'You have to say no to things you love and you want. Frodo gives up everything.'

'That's very sad,' said Ellen, gamely trying to join in and spread the animation round the table. 'Very sad indeed.' Really, she thought, he wasn't so bad, this boyfriend of Edie's. A bit odd and awkward, but she warmed to him. And, she realized with surprise, she felt sorry for him. She wanted to comfort him, though really, she knew nothing about him except what he'd told them earlier – that he lived with his mother, was studying English, History and French for A-levels and wanted to make films and travel. But any fool, she thought, could sense his need, rising like steam off damp clothes. Perhaps that's what Edie had fallen for: drawn by Ricky's loneliness; in love with his burning brown eyes.

She drank some more of her wine. When she went home, she would have several abstemious days. No alcohol, and early nights – get back into a routine. She swallowed back a dreariness at the thought of her neat little house where everything was just so; her structured days where nothing was unplanned.

Ricky was saying something about purity and Ellen saw Louise glance across at him, her fork suspended half-way to her mouth. She looked a bit low, and Ellen thought she knew why that should be: because she was getting older, because her daughters were growing up and taking her place, because she had grey in her hair and pouches gathering under her eyes and lines running down the side of her mouth, because her husband was silent, because she was worried about money, because Edie was in love with a beetle-browed boy, because her eldest daughter was leaving home and nothing would ever be the same again, because she was filled with an impossible yearning for worlds she'd never know, and had dreams in her head which weren't coming true and never would now.

There comes a point, Ellen thought, when you suddenly know it's too late. This is your life and you can no longer tell yourself that soon it will be different. She sat up straighter in her chair and refused a second helping from Louise. Her head was buzzing.

Louise bounced her knife against her glass.

'I want to make a toast,' she said. 'I want to toast Stella, who's off to university on Monday.' Stella smiled. She seemed to glow mysteriously in the flickering light, her eyes shining. 'To the future,' said Louise. She raised her glass. Everyone could hear the tears in her voice.

'To the future,' they all chorused, picking up their glasses.

Stella reached across and took her mother's hand. 'I'll be back soon. I'm not really leaving, you know.'

Ricky and Edie's eyes met, for the first time since they'd sat down at the table. They gave each other a small smile. It would be all right.

*

Louise sat beside her on the bed.

'Is this a bad time?'

'No,' said Edie, putting down her book and sitting up.

'I thought we should have a talk.'

'All right.' Edie waited, then said, 'Is something wrong?'

'No. I've just been thinking about you and Ricky.'

'Why?'

'I just want to make sure you're not getting out of your depth.'

'What does that mean, out of your depth?'

'Edie . . .'

'No, really, I don't know what you mean.'

'I don't want you to do anything stupid, that's all.'

Edie knew what Louise was talking about, of course. She pressed one hand against the other.

'Have you two, have you . . . ?'

'What?'

'Had sex?'

'Oh, please, Mummy. Don't.'

'Edie, I'm just concerned for you.'

'You don't need to be. Look, I'm seventeen in a few weeks' time. I'm not a child any more. I know about condoms, if that's what you're on about.'

'I see. You have.'

'As a matter of fact, no. Satisfied now?'

Louise gave a sigh. 'It's not like that, Edie. I like Ricky, but – well, there's something odd about him, isn't there?'

Edie pictured Ricky's face, the way his brown eyes

looked at her and the odd half-smile he gave when he was happy. 'You shouldn't say things like that to me. I love him.'

'Love's a big word, Edie, and you're too young . . .'

'*I love him.*'

They never said the word to each other. They said miss, need, want, gazing into each other's eyes while the rest of the world fell away.

'I miss you,' Ricky said, holding her against him as they stood by the river where it left the town and meandered over fields. There were hardly any people on the path; they could almost fool themselves they were alone.

'How can you miss me when I'm still here?'

'I don't know, but I can.'

They had kissed for hours. Kissed and touched each other and occasionally said things like that. Her skin felt raw and her lips stung. He put a hand under her shirt and her bra. His lips were against her ear.

'The other day, when you said not yet, how long did you mean?'

'I don't know,' she said.

'Are you scared?'

'No. Yes. Yes I am. I don't know why.'

'Don't be scared.'

8

Ricky was thin. His body looked crooked, and his skin was milky-pale. He had freckles on his shoulders and a narrow trail of dark hair running down from his stomach to his groin. She made herself look at him. She had never seen a naked man before, except Vic, and even that was several years ago, before he started wearing pyjamas. She had certainly never seen a penis that wasn't small and soft before. She stared, then looked away, her cheeks flaming. It all seemed so impossible. She sat in his bed with a sheet pulled up to her shoulders. The room was narrow and bare, just a chest of drawers in the corner, under a small window that had no curtains. Books were stacked in piles against the wall, and a broken guitar lay in the corner. The wallpaper was hanging off in shreds. The air smelt stale; the sheets unwashed. She drew her knees up and shivered. She wished it was tomorrow; or yesterday.

Ricky came across and touched her shoulder. His hand was cold. He was probably nervous too, she realized. She tried to smile. They should just have done it when they were standing under the tree, trembling with desire. They should have lain down out of sight on the wet grass there. Now all desire had gone and she was chilly and tense. She watched as Ricky tore open the packet of the condom with his teeth. He climbed under the sheet. She lay down beside him. Their cold feet touched. He put a hand on the small of her back and she shuddered. Her body felt dry and narrow and impassable.

'You've got swimmer's arms,' he said.

'Have I?'

'Edie?' he said.

'Yes.'

'You don't have to, you know. If you don't want to.'

'I do want to.'

'Are you sure?'

'I'm here, aren't I?'

She lifted her hand to his face and stroked her fingers down his cheek, then closed her eyes. She wished there were curtains; the room was too light when she didn't want to see. He kissed her neck and then her shoulders, and she closed her eyes. He kissed one breast and then the other, and she heard him sigh softly. She touched his hair, his bony shoulders, ran her fingers along the bumpy ridge of his spine. His mouth was on her stomach now. She opened her eyes and stared up at the grimy ceiling. Then he was lying beside her again, and his hand was between her legs. His face was looking into hers as he rolled on top of her, his mouth slightly open and his eyes narrow.

'Does it hurt?'

'Yes. No. It doesn't matter.'

At school, some of the girls talked about sex a great deal, in a knowing, sophisticated kind of way. They said they could tell, sometimes at a single glance, if someone was a virgin or not. They knew that Edie was. Everything about her gave away the fact that she *hadn't done it yet*. Would they know, she wondered. Tomorrow, when she walked into school, would there be something about her that would show them she'd joined them? And what about Louise and Vic? Would they know too, when she came back that evening, carrying her swimming bag with her, making non-committal noises about her day at school, sitting down to supper but picking at her food – would Louise glance sharply across at her, her eyes shrewd, her mouth pursed?

'Edie?'

The word came out in a ragged gasp. He was pushing into her, thrusting. His face was screwed up, his mouth still slightly open. There was sweat on his forehead. His hands were on her breasts, then on her hips, pulling her closer.

'Edie?' he said again. 'Oh my lovely, lovely Edie.'

She thought he might be crying, but perhaps it was the sweat.

She was glad when it was over and he pulled away from her with a little sigh, as if he'd been winded. She was still chilly. She lay back and stared at the ceiling again, overcome with a feeling of unreality. There he was, walking naked out of the room, and she was lying naked under the sheets where he'd left her, and she wasn't a virgin any more. She looked and saw that she'd bled a bit, just like you're supposed to. So that was it, she thought. In this dreary little room, she'd crossed some sort of a line.

*

When Ricky came back in he had showered and was wearing different clothes. He'd rolled a large joint and after a few drags, he passed it to her. She sat up and pulled the acrid smoke into her lungs and held it there. He watched her until she dropped her eyes.

'Are you sore?'

'A bit.'

'But you're all right?'

'Yes.'

He pushed her hair behind her ears. 'You're beautiful,' he said.

'I should go. They think I'm at swimming.'

'Don't go. Not just yet. Let me get you something to drink.'

'All right. Coffee, and then I really will go.'

'I'll bring it to you.'

'No, I'll get dressed now.'

When he'd gone, she got up and went into the bathroom. She washed herself between the legs and she splashed water over her face. Then she put on her school clothes, which felt gritty against her skin, and joined Ricky in the kitchen-sitting-room. She sat on the sofa and he put a mug of coffee on the table in front of her and tried to find biscuits in the cupboard, but there weren't any. She looked around her: the walls were beige, there was a bare bulb above the cooker, the sofa was hard, the linoleum was tatty, the window, that looked out on to a small yard and a stairwell, was cracked. She thought of her own house, whose shabbiness was homely and welcoming, and shivered. Ricky sat on the floor at her feet and picked up her hand, twined his fingers through hers. She kissed the top of his head and he leant back against her knees and closed his eyes.

'I don't want you to go,' he said.

'I must.'

'I keep thinking you won't come back.'

'That's just mad. You know that's mad.'

'Mmm,' he said. 'Maybe. I could go to sleep like this, with you stroking my hair. That'd be nice. I haven't been sleeping too much recently, but now I could.'

'You can't, because I'm about to get up.'

'It'll be better next time.'

'Ricky.'

'Mmm.'

'Everything's fine.'

'Is it?'

'Yes. I promise.'

'Go on then. Go.'

She slid her arms around him from behind and leant forward, his hair tickling her face. ''Bye.'

He tipped his head right back and she kissed him, upside down, on his lips.

'You're my lover,' she said.

9

A few days later, they made love again, at a party thrown by a friend of Ricky's while his parents were away. Louise fretted about Edie going. She insisted that she drink a glass of milk beforehand to line her stomach but Edie poured it down the sink when her mother turned her back. Louise drove her to the party at nine and said that Vic would collect her at eleven-thirty sharp.

When Edie went into the main room, she saw that Ricky was talking to the girl that she'd seen him with before, at the party where they'd first met. She was tall, with eyes heavily rimmed in kohl and a mass of bright curly hair. She looked robust and omnivorous, and she was holding Ricky by his forearm and laughing too loudly at something he was saying. Ricky laughed back. He put a tip of one finger on her nose. Edie went into the kitchen and took a can of beer from the table. She pulled back the tab and took a gulp. She wished she'd put on more make-up, worn high heels and a top that plunged like that girl's. She took another swallow. It was like seeing him for the first time, across a room and smiling down at someone else.

When Ricky found her, she put her arms round his neck and kissed him, put a hand beneath his shirt on his bare warm back. She was pliant with beer and jealousy. They didn't speak. He took her by the hand and led her upstairs to a room full of coats. He shut the door and pushed a chair against it. His hands were on her soft breasts, his mouth at her neck. She felt for his belt. He pushed her against the wall and pressed himself against her. Then they stumbled back on to the bed and he was on top of her, pulling at her clothes and saying her name.

Afterwards, they lay among the coats and smiled into each other's faces and touched each other with the tips of their fingers. Music pounded in the room beneath them; once or twice someone tried to push the door open. A voice shouted raucously, 'Hey! We know what you're doing in there!' But Edie didn't care what they thought or how it looked. They didn't have a clue. What they were doing was lying together and loving each other. She wanted to stay here for ever in the blissful dark.

When Vic arrived, ten minutes early, they were down-stairs among the dancers, hardly moving, holding each other. Someone called to her, and she collected her coat from the bed where they'd lain and left, ignoring the knowing smile of the boy by the door. Vic stood hunched on the threshold, his hands in his pockets. A girl was throwing up in the front garden and her friend stood beside her watching helplessly.

'Hello, Daddy,' Edie said.

'Hello. Did you have a good time?'

'It was fine,' she said. Her skin tingled. She put her arm through his. 'Let's go home.'

The next day she lay in bed till eleven, half-stupefied by desire and love. Outside, the sky was low and grey. She could hear Louise, downstairs in the kitchen, banging pans. There was the smell of food: toast, bacon, coffee beans, something sweet, as if bread was baking in the oven. And she could hear Vic, too, in the garden; the sound of a hammer in sudden rhythmic bursts.

Eventually, she got out of bed. She was going to see Ricky at midday, down by the old chestnut tree in the lane. In one hour, his mouth would be on hers again, his hands tugging at her clothes. She cleaned her teeth vigorously, washed and put on jeans and her black flannel shirt. No bra. No make-up. She stood in front of her mirror and brushed her hair until it crackled. She rubbed cream into her sore skin, put lip balm on her mouth, and smiled at herself. Sick with anticipation and longing.

'Edie.'

It was Jude, standing at her bedroom door still in her pyjamas, with jam on her chin.

'Hi.'

'Are you going out?'

'In a minute.'

'Can I come with you?'

'I'm going to see Ricky.'

'Oh. I just thought it would be nice to have a walk. Talk. We haven't for ages and there's something I want to ask you. Tell you. Something I've done.'

Edie heard the appeal in her voice. 'I would have loved it,' she said. She gave a rapid glance at her watch. 'We'll do it soon. But I've got to rush now, OK?'

'Will you be back soon?'

'Probably.'

'Edie?'

'Mmm?'

'Oh – nothing. I'll tell you later.'

'See you then.' On an impulse, she gave Jude a kiss. 'Have a nice day.'

'Back soon,' she called to Louise, grabbing her jacket and running out of the house.

'Where are you going?'

'Just to meet Ricky. I won't be late,' she said over her shoulder.

'You haven't even had breakfast and you never said . . .' But Edie was gone, running down the road.

They didn't greet each other. They left the road by the chestnut tree, climbed over the fence and pushed their way through the dense autumnal wood. Branches snapped back against Edie; brambles clutched at her clothes. Wind shook small showers from the leaves. She could smell soil, rotting fruit, decay. The earth was damp and rich, and soft when they lay down on it, though twigs stuck in Edie's hair. Through the branches above her, clouds rushed past.

Ricky took off her jacket and undid the buttons of her shirt, giving a murmur when he saw she was naked underneath. He untied the laces of her trainers and tugged them off. Peeled off her socks and balled them up together, then put them into one shoe. She lay back flat while he pulled her jeans over her hips and off, and folded them carefully before putting them to one side with her other clothes. He took off her knickers and, very delicately, he unhooked her earrings and put them into his pocket. A scatter of soft rain dampened her

72

skin. She watched while he stood up and took off his own clothes, placing them in a neat pile beside hers. He was knobbly and crooked and pale, the most beautiful person in the world.

'Are you cold?' he asked, kneeling down beside her.

'It doesn't matter.'

It didn't. Nothing mattered any more. Only this, the way he looked at her as if he was in pain.

'I'll never get over you,' he said.

'You won't need to get over me. You've got me.'

They gazed at each other, very solemn, very young. A car passed on the hidden road, but they took no notice.

He reached across and took a condom out of his jeans. 'We didn't last time.'

'My period's due any minute. It'll be all right.'

They smiled at each other. Everything will be all right, she thought. Nothing can harm us now.

The following day, after school, Ricky came to the house. Jude and Edie had arrived home already, and Jude was busy baking a cake for them. They sat in the kitchen, which was warm because the boiler had been mended during the day. Jude brought down her chess-board and taught Ricky the moves. Edie noticed that she had brushed her hair and put on lip-gloss and blue eye-shadow, but that her face was puffy, as if she'd been crying.

Later, while the cake was still rising in the oven, they went up to Edie's room, ignoring Jude's disconsolate glance. They sat on the bed and kissed each other. They kept their eyes open and their mouths kept smiling under each other's lips. Ricky loosened Edie's pony-tail and ran his fingers through her hair. He sighed.

'What is it?'

'That was a happy sigh,' he said.

'Are you happy then?

'Yes. I can't remember being as happy.'

'Oh,' she said, profoundly touched. 'Is that true?'

'Yes.'

'Because of me?'

'It must be.'

They kissed again and he started to undo the buttons of her blue school shirt. She drew back.

'I don't think it's a good idea, not here. . . Jude's just in the kitchen, and –'

'I only want to look at you.'

He pulled her shirt open, undid her bra and then laid his head against her breasts. 'One day we'll spend the night together. Go away somewhere, to a hotel.'

'Yes,' she said. She ran her fingers through his hair and closed her eyes.

'I was thinking. Usually I hate winter, Christmas, all that crap. But this year, there'll be you. Everything will be different.'

'Oh, Ricky,' she said.

He turned his head and took the nipple of her left breast in his lips and she started unbuttoning his shirt.

The door clicked open.

'I've brought you . . .' a voice said, then stopped dead.

Edie's eyes snapped open, and Ricky lifted his head.

Vic was standing in the doorway with a plate in his hand. He stared down at them, at Edie with her breast bared, his mouth slightly open. He was wearing his grey suit but no tie and his shirt was grubby round the collar. The plate tipped and a slice of chocolate cake slid to the floor.

Ricky stood up. Edie started doing up her shirt. No one said anything for a long while, but Vic went on staring into the room. And suddenly, Edie felt a wave of revulsion towards him – because he looked so defeated, because he had stared at her naked breasts, because he made her ashamed when she had been feeling so joyful, because he looked sad and lumpy and hopeless and helpless . . .

She fixed him with her gaze, then said in a new voice, that was as hard and bright as a newly minted coin, 'Why are you looking so shocked? I'm not a virgin, you know.' She hesitated, gripped by terror, and then added, '*Vic.*'

Vic bent down and picked up the slice of cake at his feet. He placed it carefully back beside the other one. He put the plate on Edie's table. Then he left the room, closing the door with a click behind him.

'Oh dear,' said Ricky, rather blithely.

'Shut up. You don't understand a thing.'

'Edie . . .'

'Don't say anything.'

'All right.'

Ricky picked up the cake and bit into it. There was a chocolate smudge on his chin and Edie felt a flash of hostility so violent it left her breathless.

75

'I think you'd better go,' she said, making an effort to keep her voice calm.

'Edie, what is this? Just because you've upset your dad.'

'I don't want to talk about it. Just go, all right?'

'I'll meet you tomorrow then.'

She hesitated. 'Make it the next day, OK?'

'If that's what you'd prefer.'

'I think I should be here tomorrow, that's all.'

'OK.' He kissed her on the cheek and was gone.

Edie and Louise cooked supper together, waiting for Vic to return. Edie made cauliflower cheese and Louise did the chips in the deep fryer, filling the kitchen with the smell of oil. It started to rain: occasional big drops from the heavy twilight sky.

'It's going to pour. He'll get wet,' said Edie.

'Then he can dry himself when he gets in,' said Louise calmly. She shook the basket and the oil hissed and bubbled. 'Do you want to tell me what happened?'

'Nothing really. I mean, he kind of barged in on me and Ricky – we weren't doing anything, don't look at me like that. But he looked all wretched and – oh, I said something to him because I got irritated, and he left. But he looked as if I'd slapped him across the face. I feel terrible.'

'Mmm,' said Louise. She looked out of the window. The rain was falling steadily now.

'He thinks I'm just a little girl,' said Edie, trying belatedly to defend herself.

'Oh, darling, you are, aren't you? You're *his* little girl.'

'I'm nearly seventeen.'

'I know. Sometimes it's hard for us to realize that though.'

They both heard the front door open, then bang shut. Edie ran into the hall and Vic was standing there, wiping his shoes methodically on the mat. His wet hair was plastered to his forehead and his grey suit had splashes of water down it.

'Daddy,' said Edie. She went up to him and put her arms round him. 'Daddy, I'm really, really sorry.'

He patted her shoulder distractedly. 'You don't need to say that.'

'Yes, I do. There are probably lots of things I need to say, but the first one is that. Sorry. I was cruel.'

'I should have knocked.'

Louise came out of the kitchen. 'You're soaking, Vic. Go and get some dry clothes on and we'll eat, all right? Have a cosy family evening for a change.'

A cosy family evening. Chips and cauliflower cheese, and then mashed bananas and cream and golden sugar. Vic sat at the end of the table, looking dazed, like a man who has staggered out of a car crash with blood pouring from his head but thinking he hasn't been hurt. Jude washed the dishes and Edie dried them, while Louise sorted the clothes for ironing and put out a note for the milkman, and Vic sat at the table with the spikeful of bills, leafing through them, squinting at the figures as if the sun was in his eyes. Louise went across and stood behind him and he leant back against her, his coarse black hair spilling over her white shirt. She bent forward and kissed his forehead and he closed his eyes as if he wanted to sleep.

Edie woke in the morning with a dull pain low in her back. Her period was coming. And she felt as if a cold was brewing too. Her throat ached and her head throbbed; her eyes stung when she turned on the light. She wanted to stay in bed. She wanted to be ten and have Louise bring her lemon barley water and toast with honey, and put a cool hand on her brow, and lean over her, the waft of perfume and baking, a smell of motherhood, of being both beautiful and good. But she was having a Physics test this morning, and Louise was going to work anyway. She sat up in bed. The day, seen through a narrow strip in the curtains, looked grey and chilly after the night's rain. It wouldn't be so long now till all the leaves were stripped from the trees. At least Stella would be coming home for Christmas. Reluctantly, Edie swung her legs round on to the floor and stood up, her head pounding. She drew open the curtains a bit more and peered outside; the sun was pale behind the layer of clouds, and the ground looked drenched.

There was a figure in the garden, by the plum tree. It was Vic, but what was he doing at half past seven in the morning? She squinted. He was picking plums and piling them up in the basket beside him. She watched as he reached up and twisted off the plump fruits, then bent down to place them carefully among the others. He took a thick branch and shook it gently. She couldn't hear but she could imagine the soft, heavy patter of falling plums. Vic was searching in the tall grass, wiping the fruit against the leg of his grey suit.

She turned away and got herself dressed in front of the mirror, then brushed her hair for a long time before braiding it in two tight and girlish plaits. She was glad she wasn't seeing Ricky today. She felt empty of desire.

Louise and Jude were already in the kitchen when she came down, Louise in her dressing-gown. There was a pot of coffee on the table and toast cooling in the rack.

'Do you want anything special?' asked Louise. 'I could make porridge if you wanted.'

'Toast is fine.' Edie took a piece and spread butter thinly over it. Vic came through the kitchen door, carrying the basket piled high with damp and glistening plums. The ends of his trousers were wet and his hair too, where water had dripped from the tree. Grass blades stuck to his hands. He placed the basket on the middle of the table and stood back.

'There are almost no plums left. Just a few high up that didn't want to fall and that I couldn't reach.'

'Brilliant, Daddy,' said Edie, too vivaciously. He didn't look at her.

'Toast and coffee? And I think I just heard the mail.'

Edie rose and collected the letters: two bills and nothing else. Vic didn't even look at them. He poured himself a cup of coffee and drank it standing up.

'I need to leave early today,' he said.

'Busy at work?' asked Louise.

He didn't answer, just sipped his coffee and gazed out of the window.

'Right,' he said suddenly, putting his cup down on the table with a sharp little rap and picking up his briefcase. 'I'll be off now.'

He kissed each of them on the top of their heads; Jude, then Edie, and last of all Louise. 'Take care,' he said, and turned and left the room. They didn't watch him go.

Edie did her Physics test. And she told Rose about sleeping with Ricky. She hadn't thought she was going to, but then suddenly heard herself blurting it all out – even the bit about Vic walking in on them. And strangely, saying it all out loud – how it was sore, how she'd bled, how they'd had sex again among the coats at a party, how her father had stared at Ricky's head against her naked breasts – made it seem less momentous. Rose had gasped and hugged her. She asked her to repeat details. It was all right after all, Edie thought. It wasn't the end of the world after all. She wasn't a different person. Love didn't have to be dangerous. Sex didn't have to be tragic and swooningly intense; it could be funny and carefree as well, something that other people did too.

She went home straight after school, on the bus with Jude. Her period had started so she had a bath, though the hot water ran out half-way through, washed her hair, and changed into old leggings and the baggy yellow sweatshirt that used to belong to Stella. She'd said to Louise that she would cook supper, so she rooted round in the fridge and cupboards before deciding to make something new for a change. Vegetable lasagne, she thought; filling and comforting. Ellen had told her how to make it. It didn't sound too complicated.

She chopped an onion and put it into a heavy-bottomed pan with oil, and crushed garlic over it. Then she added diced courgettes and carrots and dried herbs. The kitchen was filled with the smell of frying vegetables and garlic. She poured in a tin of plum tomatoes and chopped them up in the pan. She made a white sauce, and for once it was smooth and creamy. She seasoned it and remembered to add nutmeg, then set it to one side. When the cheese was grated, she layered a dish with lasagne pasta, vegetable ragout, sauce, cheese. She put it into the oven, and washed all the utensils. Later, she would make a green salad, with herbs from the garden, and Vic would open wine. She washed her hands and dried them on a kitchen towel, filled with a lovely sense of her own competence.

Louise was home by six, and she sat in the kitchen drinking tea. She was wearing her cream suit and calf-length brown boots; her hair was in burnished coils at the back of her head. Edie remembered, when she was younger, how she had loved to watch her mother getting ready to go out. How she would sit at her winged mirror, brushing her hair until it prickled with electricity, then twist it into a loop and hold it in place with long pins. She would always take great pains over her make-up, as well; she called it 'putting on her face'. Foundation cream, blusher on her cheekbones, the delicate dabbing of eye-shadow on her lids, a pencil over her arched eyebrows, all the while frowning in concentration at her reflection. She would put on her lipstick and then close her lips over a tissue, leaving a serrated red oval on it that for Edie had seemed an emblem of adulthood. Perfume dabbed behind her ears and on her wrists – the same perfume she still wore. 'How do I look?' she'd say, turning in triumph to Edie, and Edie would always say, 'You look absolutely beautiful.' And she always did.

In the same way that Edie had watched Louise putting make-up on in the evening, she used to watch Vic shaving in the morning, sitting in the corner of the bathroom, against the radiator. He had a beautiful shaving kit that he kept in a leather case, and he'd lather the soap and spread it over his face with a small wooden-handled brush so that his mouth looked very pink. Then he'd scrape the lather away steadily, leaving smooth stripes of flesh. At the end, he'd splash cold water over his skin and pat on some lotion that smelt of pine woods and mountains.

That's what she remembered: Louise at her dressing-table and Vic at the bathroom sink, and herself watching them and feeling safe.

Vic hadn't come home by seven-thirty. Louise poured herself a gin and tonic; Edie put the lasagne into a low oven to keep it warm. She put lettuce and cucumber and celery into the salad bowl and made a salad dressing in a jam jar. Upstairs, Jude was practising her typing again; the keyboard thumped above their heads.

Louise called the estate agent, but the phone just rang and rang. The office was closed.

'Don't worry,' Edie said.

'This is ridiculous,' said Louise at eight-thirty. 'Honestly, he should have phoned and warned us. We'll just eat without him, OK?'

'But . . .'

'Come on! Put the plates out, Jude. Edie, it looks perfect.'

It was. Cheese blistered on the surface. Oily tomato sauce bubbled up round the edges. Edie served out three portions, and dressed the salad. Louise poured herself a large glass of red wine.

'Where on earth can he be?'

'Loads of places,' said Louise. 'He could easily have had a late-night viewing.'

'But he would have rung.'

'Maybe he couldn't get to a phone. Or he's stopped off for a drink with a colleague.'

'But he never . . .'

'Eat up. Delicious.' Louise put an extra-large forkful into her mouth and chewed vigorously.

Edie and Louise ate their meal. Jude toyed with hers, pushing the lasagne messily round the plate. Outside, the wind blew through the trees and in the grey darkness their branches dipped and swayed. It reminded Edie of the sea, waters drawing in.

At half past nine, Edie called one of Vic's colleagues.

'William, it's Louise Jennings . . . yes, that's right . . . I'm sorry to disturb you at this time of night but I'm a bit concerned because Vic hasn't got home from work yet and he never said he'd be late, and I just wondered if you knew. . . .sorry? . . . yes . . . no . . . no, I see. I see. Goodbye.'

She put the phone down very slowly and turned towards Edie and Jude. Her face was blank, as if someone had taken a cloth to it and wiped away all expression.

'Mum?' Jude walked towards her. 'Mum, what is it?'

'He said. . . .' She swung her head from side to side to clear it.

'What? Tell us!'

'He said Vic lost his job. They told him months ago, and he hasn't been at work for over two weeks now.'

'No!' Jude put her hands over her open mouth.

'But that's not true!' Edie clenched her fists and dug the nails into her palms. She realized that she was shouting but she couldn't stop herself. 'It can't be true. He's left for work every morning, just like usual. And he would have said. He would have, wouldn't he? Mummy?'

'What shall I do?' said Louise in a whisper, and put a hand against her throat. Edie felt panic rising up in her at the question – if Louise didn't know what to do, they were lost.

'Call the police,' she said. She picked up the phone and held it out. 'Now. We've got to find him.'

'I can't call the police just because he's two hours late home. They'd tell me not to be so stupid.'

'We can't just sit here.'

'And I probably am just being stupid.' She smiled at them, making a visible effort. 'You'll see, in a minute he'll come through that door.'

'But why didn't he tell us?' said Edie.

'Oh, darlings, I don't know. Because he was wretched, or felt he was letting us down maybe. It'll be all right.'

'Can you imagine what it must have been like for

him?' said Jude. She had bright pink spots on either cheek. 'Pretending to go off to work every morning. Can you imagine? Fucking hell.'

'That's enough, Jude.'

'He must have been desperate,' she continued.

'Jude!'

'And so lonely. Think of the loneliness of that. What have we gone and done?'

'That's enough.'

'What have we done?' repeated Jude.

'Stop it now!' Louise glared at her. 'Do you hear? We can talk about these things later, but stop it. The thing to do is to remain calm.'

'Calm! Oh right, yeah, we've got to stay calm. Our father's gone missing but we just ought to continue as if nothing has happened.'

'He's not gone missing. Don't be hysterical. He hasn't come home yet, that's all.'

'Ha!' Jude flounced from the room and ran up the stairs. They heard her door slam. Louise sank into a chair and put her head in her hands. Edie sat opposite her.

'Are you angry with him?'

'Angry?' Louise looked at Edie. 'No, I'm not angry.'

'You're sure it'll be all right?'

'Of course it will.'

'I'll make us some tea, shall I?'

'That would be nice.'

She put on the kettle. 'Jude's right,' she said softly.

'Mmm?'

'About how he must be feeling.'

Louise lifted her face. 'Am I such a terrible person?'

'No!'

'So how come he wouldn't dare tell me?'

'Don't think about it like that. It'll be all right now we know. Won't it? Mummy – now we know we can make everything all right again.'

'The kettle's boiling.'

Edie made tea and poured it into three mugs. She got some chocolate digestives from the cupboard and they sat at the table, dunking biscuits into tea.

'Go to bed now,' said Louise when they'd finished.

'I want to wait up till he comes.'

'No. Waiting is the worst thing you can do. And you've got a cold, I can hear it in your voice. Go to bed.'

'Will you tell me when he comes home?'

'Yes. Go on now.'

Edie lay in bed and listened. Her whole body felt taut with listening and with waiting. Cars drove past the house, and sometimes she thought that they were stopping, and her skin would tingle with expectation; she would let herself imagine the relief that would sweep through her cramped limbs. But they never did. She heard Louise moving about downstairs, and once she made a phone call though Edie couldn't make out to whom. Then she came up the stairs, her footsteps slow and heavy. Edie turned over and looked at the glowing green hands of her clock in the darkness. It was nearly midnight and Vic hadn't come home. The wind buffeted the garden and shook the window panes. It sighed in the trees. Edie was chilly. Her stomach ached and her throat prickled; her head was blocked up with cold. She lay, in her separate darkness, listening.

She must have fallen asleep, because when she jerked awake and focused her sore eyes on the clock it was nearly three. She listened and heard nothing but the wind. She got out of bed and tiptoed on to the landing. Every door was shut. She stood for a moment by Louise and Vic's bedroom, straining to hear a sound. Nothing. Cautiously, she opened the door a crack. It was too dark to see if there were two shapes in the bed or one. She crept forward and placed a hand very gently where Vic's feet should be, but touched flat covers. She moved them further up. Louise moaned something in her sleep and turned restlessly.

Vic wasn't there. Of course not. She would have heard the car, heard his key in the door. She would have surfaced from her fragile, shallow sleep if he had mounted the stairs. Anyway, Louise would have woken her when he came home.

She lay back in bed again. She wished that Stella was here, being calm and practical. She remembered how she used to put her hand in Vic's and see how his large brown fingers closed over her slender white ones. He would pick her up and put her on his shoulders and she'd hold on to his thick black hair and feel absolutely secure, high above everyone. She knew he would never let her fall.

'I'm not going to school today.'

'Oh yes you are!'

'But how can I when . . . ?'

'You're going to school and that's the end of it. Both of you.' The last bit of the sentence was directed at Jude, who was standing at the kitchen window, looking out at the sodden garden.

'I don't feel very well,' persisted Edie – and it was true, she didn't. Her legs ached and her head throbbed and her eyes felt raw in their sockets.

'There's a pot of tea all brewed, help yourselves. And I've made porridge for all of us. I thought it would do us good. Come and sit down, Jude.'

Louise spooned thick, steaming porridge into three bowls. She held a spoon of golden syrup over the top of hers and watched while it puddled over the surface. It was not even seven o'clock and she was still in her dressing-gown. Her hair was loose and pushed back behind her ears, and her face looked creased and puffy with tiredness.

'Are you going in to work today?'

'No.'

'So how come you make me go . . . ?'

'Because I'm the adult round here, God help me, and you're my children.'

'What are you going to do?'

Louise put her spoon down and looked across at Edie. She hesitated, deciding how much she should tell her, then her face softened. 'I don't know,' she said. 'But I think I should start by calling the police.'

And although this was what Edie had been insisting that she do, Louise's words made her feel clammy with fear.

'What's happened to him?' she said. 'He'll be all right, won't he?'

'Yes,' said Louise. 'Eat your breakfast.'

Edie sprinkled soft brown sugar over her porridge, where it darkened and melted in streaks. She lifted a spoonful to her mouth. She thought she would gag on it. She looked across at Jude, who was stirring her porridge round and round in the bowl; it had turned a queasy beige colour.

'Should we tell Stella?' said Jude.

'No! What for? So she'll worry herself sick, a few days into her first term away?'

'I suppose you're right.'

'Except,' said Edie, 'it just feels so wrong . . .'

'I know, poppet,' said Louise.

At the endearment, Edie's eyes filled with tears. Jude stood up suddenly, scraping her chair against the floor. She looked lumpy and wretched, her face and neck blotchy. Louise put out a hand and caught her by the arm.

'It's going to be all right,' she said. 'Jude? I promise you it will be all right.'

'You're just talking crap,' said Jude.

'Jude!'

'Crap. And it's all your fault.'

'Don't say that.'

'You know it's true.'

The day passed in a strange daze. Everything that happened seemed to be taking place at a great distance. Edie got through all her lessons, although later she couldn't have said what she had learnt. She copied formulae neatly into her exercise book, in her small, spiky writing, the nib of her pen scratching across the paper. She drew neat diagrams with her sharpened pencil and her old wooden ruler that had the dates of English kings and queens along its length. She stood in the Science lab among the Bunsen burners and the test-tubes, the smell of gas and chemicals, methodical in her white coat and goggles. She walked up the long corridors to the next classroom, gazing down at the polished tips of her shoes that clacked along the wooden floors. At lunch, she sat in the common room with the other sixth formers, and ate nothing and drank black coffee. Nobody noticed that she said nothing. She was always quiet anyway; a listener not a talker, someone who was in the background. Even Rose didn't notice, or if she did probably put it down to the cold that was turning Edie's nose red and making her eyes water. Every so often she would glimpse Jude, alone in the playground, or on her way to the next lesson, hanging back from the groups of girls ahead of her, but they didn't speak. Every so often she would look at her watch; at the hour hand which crept towards the end of the day. She tried not to tell herself that if Vic had come home, Louise would have found a way of letting her know.

At ten to four, the bell rang and she packed her bags and put on her raincoat. Only when she saw Ricky waiting for her outside the school gates did she remember they had arranged to meet. He was slouched against a wall, smoking as usual, but he stood up as soon as he saw her and raised a hand in greeting. His face opened up in gladness. Edie walked towards him.

'You look a bit rough,' he said, and put a hand towards her. He was bedraggled from the rain and his hair stuck to his scalp. He looked as if he'd shrunk, she thought. She stepped back from his hand.

'I can't see you today,' she said.

'Why? What's up?'

'Daddy's disappeared,' she said.

'What do you mean, he's disappeared?'

'He's just not come back home. And he hasn't been at work for days, though he's been pretending to go there. They gave him the push, but he didn't say and now he's not come home.'

'Shit.'

'Yes.'

'Shall I come back with you?'

'No.'

'What can I do?'

'Nothing.' She just wanted him to be gone.

'Ring me.'

'OK.'

'When he gets back.'

'Yes.'

'Promise?'

'Yes.'

'He'll be all right.'

'How do you know?'

He looked at her and half-smiled. 'You're quite right, I don't know.'

''Bye,' she said. It all seemed such a long time ago, loving Ricky.

When Edie and Jude arrived home they saw, through the window, that there were two figures in the sitting-room.

'He's back!' said Edie, but then realized as soon as she'd said it that the man wasn't Vic but a stranger – a man in a dark green jacket, with thinning brown hair, who looked nothing like her father.

Louise heard them open the door and she came to meet them. She was wearing an old red jumper that made her face look pasty, and she was holding a cigarette between her fingers, although she had given up smoking many years back. She shook her head before they could ask the question.

'Come out of the weather,' she said. Her voice was flat and gentle.

'Who's in the living-room?' asked Jude.

'He's a policeman,' said Louise. 'I'm going to make us some tea. Then we can talk.'

'Just tell us,' said Jude.

But Louise turned and walked into the kitchen, and they followed her, still in their raincoats, with their school bags slung over their shoulders.

'They found Vic's car,' said Louise. Her back was to them, and she was filling the kettle with water.

'But . . .'

'Where?'

She turned to face them. 'By Crossley Bridge.'

'I don't understand,' said Edie into the silence that followed.

'He left the key above the passenger mirror and his wallet was in the glove compartment.'

'I don't understand,' said Edie once more.

Jude banged her school bag down hard on the table, so all the mugs rattled. 'What don't you understand?' she shouted in a voice raw with anger and contempt. 'Are you so stupid and blind? Huh? Do you want me to say it out loud? Well, do you? Do you?'

'There's nothing to understand yet,' said Louise, in her new dull voice.

'Please,' said Edie, not knowing what she was asking for.

'Your father has been very depressed,' said Louise. 'He hasn't been himself lately.' Then, as if transfixed by the phrase, she repeated it slowly and softly: 'He hasn't been himself. Not himself.'

'The bridge,' said Edie. 'That doesn't have to mean anything in particular. Don't look at me like that, Jude!'

'Ellen's arriving here this evening,' said Louise. 'And I've told Graham and Rona what's going on. I thought I ought to.' They were Vic's parents, and had always treated Louise with a mixture of timidity and suspicion.

'What about Stella?' Jude asked.

'I've left her a message. She'll ring when she gets it.'

'But Daddy . . .' said Edie. 'Daddy . . .' She heard her voice, far off and tremulous, a little girl's voice. It was a dream, she told herself. They were living in a dream, a nightmare. It wasn't real. It couldn't be real. 'He wouldn't leave us,' she said, in the tinny accent of despair.

'I need to go back to Detective Shaw now,' said Louise. She stood up from the table, like an old woman with arthritis, and Edie saw that her hands were trembling badly. 'But I love you both very much.'

Edie and Jude sat at the table together and a ghastly silence held them. They did not even look at each other. Then Jude got up and rummaged in Louise's bag. She pulled out a packet of cigarettes. Six had gone. She pulled one out and looked at it, then struck a match and lit it. She inhaled and started coughing violently, her face turning puce. But she persevered, puffing hard. After a few minutes, Edie followed suit, sucking smoke into her lungs and knocking ash into her mug, where it sizzled briefly in the dregs of her tea. Smoking made her feel dizzy and sick; made her throat ache even more, her head throb, but that didn't matter. It was better than the icy trickle of dread round her body.

She tried not to think. She didn't want to remember his face as he'd gazed at her with Ricky leaning against her breasts, or his expression when she'd rounded on him, called him 'Vic' with all the cruelty she could muster. His pale, soft, heavy face; his brown, beseeching eyes; his bulky body and his spindly legs. She could hardly breathe. She tried not to think of him, and just concentrated on the red tip of the cigarette and the pain it made in her chest. She tried not to think of him parking the dented car, putting the ignition keys under the mirror flap, the wallet in the glove compartment, walking along the bridge ... They'd walked over it together, many times. It had a steep arch, and on a dark night, with the lights of cars shining on the black tarmac, it looked as if the road just headed up to the sky and stopped. The wind whipped across the bridge, and the brown river ran fast underneath it. If you peered through the high, spiked railings, you could see detritus dragged along in its current. Sometimes it flooded, and then the paths where Edie and Ricky had walked, the tangled shrublands where they had kissed, were under water.

Don't think of the bridge, of the river, of the tugging waters. Don't think about Vic, about his hurt eyes, his black flop of hair.

She knew why he'd parked by the bridge, of course she did.

'He'll come home soon,' she said out loud. 'You'll see.'

Jude stared at her. 'He's never coming home,' she said.

'Don't say that!'

'He's never coming home. He's never coming home. He's never coming home.' The hysteria swelled in Jude's voice.

'Stop it!'

He had picked all the plums from the plum tree, only yesterday, and carried the basket into the house like an offering. It stood on the surface near the fridge now, brimful of pulpy, rotting fruit. She closed her

eyes. She could feel the kiss he'd placed on her forehead.

'You're lucky,' said Jude in a bleary voice, as if she'd
tipped half a bottle of gin down her throat. Edie opened
her eyes. 'You've got Ricky to love you.'

But Edie didn't want Ricky, not any more. She would
trade Ricky for Vic. She would promise God that she
would never see Ricky again, never touch him, if only
Vic was safe. If Vic walked in through the door now,
she would be satisfied for the rest of her life with that.
Only that. Nothing else. She didn't mind if she was a
doctor, she didn't want to have sex again, she never
wanted to go dancing and drink warm beer and feel the
earth tilt and giggle with her friends and wear dresses
with plunging cleavages and put make-up on her pale
features and kiss boys and stay out late and let them
love her . . . Never again. None of that. Just home, and
Daddy walking in through the door with his funny smile
just for her, and the way he looked as if he was about
to cry when he was happy, and family meals round this
table where she and Jude now sat in horror. Cauliflower
cheese and chips and Daddy saying nothing because he
was a silent man but she had never thought, never, not
ever thought, that his silence would end like this, walking
out one morning and just planting a kiss on each forehead and going away and not knowing that it didn't
matter he had lost his job, it didn't matter that the boiler
broke down, that the bills stacked up on the gleaming
spike; it didn't matter, nothing like that mattered . . .

'He'll come home,' she said again. She looked at the
clock on the wall. It was only six o'clock; the depth of

waiting ahead gave her a sense of vertigo. 'Waiting is the worst thing.'

Still dark. Still quiet. Branches tapping at her window. Edie gazed out at the sky that was clearer now, and pin-pricked with stars. Leaves rose up in the air like bats. It would be cold outside, she thought. Cold blackness and a wind curling and sharp. He was out there somewhere, in the unkind weather. She held her pillow against her body, clutched it. She felt as if she was lying on a high ledge and all around her was danger. One move and she'd plunge through the moving air. 'I'll be good. I'll be good for ever,' she said in a whisper. 'Just let him be all right. Let him be all right. Let him be all right.' Then she added, 'Daddy, come home. Please come home.'

12

The body was carried by the current several miles down-stream. It was spotted by a young mother pushing a buggy along the river path: a grey shape among the reeds, a hand, palm upwards.

The police came to the house to tell the family. Louise opened the door and saw the two figures standing on the step, their faces already composed in expressions of sorrow. She shrank from them, pressing a fist against her heart. She backed into the kitchen, where Ellen was cleaning the windows with a soft cloth and the radio was on and steam was rising from the spout of the kettle. They followed her apologetically, their thick black shoes stepping on the scrubbed floor. Behind them, the door banged shut in the wind.

'No,' said Louise. She heard her voice, like the voice of a stranger. 'No.'

But Ellen came and stood behind her and wrapped her arms round her as if she was a small child again and if she hugged her hard enough everything would be all right.

Louise identified the body through a glass screen. She looked at the grey suit, which he'd worn every weekday morning for a year or more. A button was missing and the left arm had a rent in it. She looked at the striped tie that she had given him three Christmases ago. The watch with the frayed strap on his wrist. Its hands had stopped at nineteen minutes to ten. The white shirt. The old shoes with scuffed toes. She didn't want to see his swollen face or his staring eyes or his gaping mouth. She mustn't see that because if she did, then every time she remembered him, the drowned face would float into view and nothing would remain for her except that dead stare from the murky brown eyes.

What journey had led to this moment? One moment she had been a young woman hanging on the arm of her besotted husband and laughing, while people threw confetti in her face and cheered and the sun rose in the sky and flowers opened and happiness was a word they said easily. And now she was staring at her husband's corpse. He'd waited until he was sure no one was watching, then he'd walked along the bridge and climbed over the sharp railings and stepped off. And it was her fault. Bit by bit she'd let go of everything that held them together, until at last he'd fallen out of his life. Her fault: she felt the knowledge lodge in her like a stone, a great boulder.

She nodded. 'Yes,' she said and turned away from the body. 'That's my husband. Vic.'

Later, Edie could hardly recall the funeral. All its details were erased and instead she saw herself from the outside, as if she was an image in a formally posed photograph. There she was, in her dark, ill-fitting clothes, sitting beside Stella and staring at the cheap, shiny coffin. She couldn't remember feeling anything, except perhaps the pressure of Stella's hand on hers and tears sliding down her cheek and salty on her lips, nor could she remember any of the conversations that she must have had. Just sitting there surrounded by the unreal world.

The next day, they scattered Vic's ashes under the plum tree.

Louise put the house on the market. She had decided to move back to Shrimpley, the town where she was born, and where Ellen still lived. It was only a forty-minute drive away, thirty on a good day, and they would be able to stay in touch with friends, but she thought that they needed to make a fresh start; the sooner the better. They could stay with Ellen until they found a house to buy, and she would look for a new job. Edie and Jude would have to change schools.

It didn't seem to matter very much that the estate agent that was to sell the house was the one where Vic had worked for seven years, and the one which, a few weeks ago, had made him redundant. Two men came to the house. They had with them a camera, a tape-measure and a notebook and on their faces shifting expressions of gravity, embarrassment, eagerness and curiosity. They said how sorry they were about poor old Vic, everyone liked him, not a mean bone in his body, what a nice chap, what a terrible waste ... Louise, expressionless, poured tea and handed out biscuits, and they made their way round the house, in and out of bedrooms, looking round the toilet door, opening the cupboard where Vic's shirts still hung among Louise's dresses, and his shoes stood beside hers. One of them tapped his pen against his teeth and stared at the widening crack in the hallway, the damp patches on the walls, the dripping taps, the ill-fitting windows, the fading wallpaper, the threadbare carpets; he made busy marks in his notebook and murmured to himself. The other measured the rooms with the tape-measure, and then walked the length of the garden, counting his paces. They made everything seem poky, shabby and of little value.

The sum they mentioned made Louise wince, but then she shrugged and accepted it.

Stella went back to university. Ellen stayed on and helped Louise, Edie and Jude pack up all their belongings. Most of them were going into storage. The removal men brought dozens of boxes, folded flat, which Ellen and Jude assembled in the hall, securing the bottoms with masking tape. Louise said that they should throw away anything they didn't absolutely want. Be ruthless, she said. She had hired a skip, and was already steadily filling it with the contents of the kitchen cupboards: rusty pans, bent egg whisks, chipped mixing bowls, lidless tupperwares, a teapot that always gushed water out of its spout, a small pasta-making machine that had never been satisfactory, jam jars, a whole set of dinner plates that were discoloured and veined with hairline cracks, pastry cutters, jelly moulds that hadn't been used since Jude was small . . . Louise kept going for hours. She wore old jeans that were held up by a red tie of Vic's, her sleeves were rolled above her elbows and she had tied her hair back in an old flowery scarf. Her face looked pinched and angry.

She got rid of most of the food in the store cupboard. Anything past its sell-by date was tied up in big bags and plonked by the back door: flour, jam, yoghurts, tins of baked beans and sweetcorn and plum tomatoes, tea, pasta, rice, hot pickles that Vic used to like with the curries they once ate as a family on special occasions. Louise flung all the small packets of spices into the bin too: turmeric, coriander, cayenne pepper, cumin, hot chilli powder. Food colouring went, they weren't going to cart all of that to Ellen's, and half-boxes of cereal, pulses, stock cubes, ancient bottles of raspberry vinegar and sesame oil.

She made a bonfire in the garden and carried armfuls of rubbish out to it – old newspapers and magazines, cookery books with unhinged spines, the contents of the cork tile notice-board, half-filled notebooks, last year's diaries, postcards, unanswered letters, catalogues, accounts. She threw the bills on too, the ones in black and the ones in red. They curled up in the fierce flames and became petals of ash, floating over the wall at the back. She stood by the flames in her black Wellington boots and threw on clutches of soggy leaves to control the conflagration. Acrid smoke billowed round the garden. Edie, looking out of her window, saw Louise remorselessly feeding the fire with Vic's old gardening books. The one about roses and the one about wild flowers. She wanted to run down and rescue them; she would have kept them and one day used them to grow a garden herself. But even as she thought this, it was too late. The glossy illustrated pages curled and blackened, then crinkled into orange.

Edie turned back to her own room. She packed a bulky suitcase and a sports bag with the things she would need at Ellen's: two sweaters, three pairs of trousers, several tee-shirts, trainers, a waterproof, her denim jacket and her coat, old boots, pyjamas and her dressing-gown and slippers, underwear, swimming costume and goggles, shampoo and deodorant – functional clothes for autumn and the coming winter. She didn't need much. Her strappy tops, her tight trousers, the rusty-brown dress that she'd bought for her party and the black dress she'd pictured herself wearing at Christmas, her bangles and necklaces and earrings, her velvet choker, her high-heeled shoes – all these she put into a box for storing. She couldn't imagine ever wearing them again.

She was methodical and slow. She picked out four novels, all ones she'd read before, and her science books, to take to Ellen's, and put the rest of her books for storage. She wrapped her glass animals in tissue paper and made sure they were on the top of a box, between layers of newspaper. She took the picture off the wall and put it between towels and her sleeping-bag.

Some things were more difficult. In the large drawer at the bottom of her wardrobe were her memorabilia. Here, she stored old school reports; flimsy exercise books in which she'd written stories at the age of seven; swimming certificates and prizes; paintings in primary colours. She sat back on her heels and leafed through one school report, from when she was twelve and a year into secondary school. 'She tries hard,' it said on the first page; 'diligent', it said on the next. Diligent, steady, obedient: that was the verdict.

Maybe, she thought, she should throw all these things away – the poster, done at primary school, showing what she wanted to be when she grew up; she'd drawn a picture of a ballet dancer, with pointing legs that seemed to connect at the knees and a pink, semi-circular tutu. Or the magazine that she, Stella and Jude had produced one year. It was called *The Jennings Journal*, and Stella had written a story about a white horse while Edie'd copied out a recipe for almond and cherry flapjacks.

She glanced out of the window again to where Louise was still making trips to the fire. Someone was with her now: it was Rose's father, Simon, standing helplessly beside her, his shoes sinking into the mud, and watching books – and now clothes as well, Edie saw – consigned to the high, dancing flames. He stepped forward to put a restraining hand on Louise's arm, but she turned sharply away from him.

No, thought Edie, she wouldn't throw everything away. She would keep them and maybe one day she would open them all up again and let herself remember.

She came last to the letters that Ricky had written to her over the past weeks. He had written several a week, even when he knew he would see her the next day; some were on postcards, some on plain paper. She had put them all into a small wooden box, with a sachet of lavender on top, and the yellow leaf she'd picked out of his hair. She knew the letters all by heart, but nevertheless she took them out of the box and read through them once more. They were in chronological order, and began with the one in which he'd sent her his address. She half-smiled, recalling how she had pored over the letter, looked for special meaning in the word 'love'. It seemed such a very long time ago. Some were simply one line: '*I want you and I need you too*', or '*You left ten minutes ago and I miss you already.*'

The last one had arrived this morning. It was quite short.

> *I hate to think of you in pain. I wish I could help – I wish you would let me help you. Please don't push me away. We are meant to be together. You know we are. Please see me. I was so happy and I am very lonely without you. Please.*

He underlined the final *please*, and didn't sign his name.

Edie laid the last letter back in the box and shut the lid. She closed her eyes, but in her mind she did not see Ricky's face, but the face of her father, staring up at her through muddy waters.

Edie and Jude went back to school. They had six more days before they left – four more school days. Louise had found a school where Jude could do her O-levels, and a sixth form college for Edie. They were going to travel back with Ellen; she would wait for two or three more days, tying up loose ends, then she too would leave, lock the door, leave the keys with the estate agents and the negotiations in the hands of her solicitor.

Edie made sure she had the right number of knickers and socks left, and a spare school shirt. Stella rang each evening, at seven o'clock. They ate sandwiches and fish and chips from the mobile van that stopped at the top of the road on Wednesdays and Fridays. Louise drank wine at lunch and whisky in the evenings; her days lost their cutting edge and took on a blurred, autumnal quality. Wet leaves, grey rain, ragged trees, mist drifting off the grass in the mornings, the sense of things coming to their end.

They didn't talk much – not about the things that mattered. What they had to say was too massive, like a cliff to climb, and nobody had the energy. Not yet.

At school, Edie felt as if she had already left; that she was a stranger who had returned after a long absence, just to say goodbye formally. She went to lessons, did her homework punctiliously, sat in the common room at break and listened to other people's conversations, did tests, but all the time she was leaving in her mind. She would look at the face of a teacher and think: this is the last time I will sit in her classroom; the last time I will raise my hand at his question. She memorized the ugly stained-glass window in the school hall and the smell of linseed oil near the caretaker's shed. She joined in conversations with friends, but knew that their future was no longer the same as hers. Her road, which had seemed so straight and steady, had veered sharply away from theirs. Everybody was very kind, and that as much as anything else made Edie realize she had become some-one who was different. She was Edie-whose-father-had-killed-himself; she saw it in their eyes and heard it in their voices, in the pity they offered her. No one argued with her, or disagreed with her opinions. No one told her their problems any longer. They didn't complain about boyfriend trouble or the argument they'd had with their mother, or how this teacher picked on them or that friend was manipulative. How could they, when her problem was so large and incurable?

Even Rose, who came round to the house most days, or called on the phone, drifted away from Edie, She was on the lookout for her new close friend, the one who'd replace Edie when she had left to start her new life, the one who would tie her plaits for her, hear her secrets, tell her which colours suited her, walk with her down corridors and across roads, giggle at nothing in particular, wait for her outside school. They would stay friends, but would no longer know when the other had bought a new cartridge pen or seen *Top of the Pops* that night.

13

A man walked slowly up a bridge that curved up into the sky, like an unfinished road, climbing steeply nowhere, spectral and uncanny. Underneath, the deep and muddy water carried branches torn from trees, like arms that wave for help; sodden objects bobbed along the surface for a bit, then gradually were dragged down, to drift and disintegrate on the unseen bottom. At some point, Edie slept and she dreamed of him walking the bridge, and then she dreamed of him jumping, flying, falling. She woke and the images were still the same. She imagined him straight and keen in the air, with his arms raised in a V and his legs together, toes pointing. Aiming for death; entering the water with hardly a ripple. And then she imagined him flailing through the air, arms thrashing, hands grasping at nothing, his whole body tipping, spinning, crashing through the air.

But sometimes she dreamed he was still alive, and walking towards her with that old sweet smile, and she'd look up and say, 'Hello, Daddy,' as if he'd never left, and put her arm through his, and he'd ask her how she was, and she'd reply, 'Fine.'

Edie met Ricky on Saturday. It was a beautiful, cold day, blue and still after all the wind and rain. The world looked like a photograph. He was waiting at the end of the lane, and she filed away the image of him, standing motionless under the chestnut tree, shielding his eyes from the low sun. There were rooks in the trees above him, swaying in their nests of sticks, shouting hoarsely into the clear air. He was wearing his denim shirt and his old jeans and as she drew closer she saw he had washed his hair and shaved, and she was jolted by love and pity. It would have been so easy to step forward and take him by his hands and kiss his fingers with their bitten nails and fold herself into his familiar smell of sweat and tobacco and let herself be comforted. It was all she had left to want – the feeling of being held in his arms and the way he still looked at her, in spite of everything. He looked at her as if he was looking through her, to a person no one had ever seen before or would ever see again.

If he had put his arms round her, or if he had broken down and appealed to her – but he didn't. He just waited, looking at her with his brown eyes that reminded her, suddenly and horribly, of Vic's.

'You look pale,' he said.

'Oh, well . . .' She put a hand up and touched her cheek.

'Are you OK?'

'Kind of. Thanks.'

'I've missed you. You've no idea how much, Edie. Every minute of every day.'

'Ricky,' she said. 'Listen. I can't . . .'

'Like a hole in my heart.'

'I just can't any more.'

He looked away from her, down the hill to the town. Silence trembled between them.

'I'm so sorry,' she said at last. 'Nothing's right any more.'

'Including me.'

'Not you. Us.'

'Is it because of that time when he . . . ?'

'No!' she said too quickly. She didn't want to think of that now.

'Because you can't stop having a life, you know, because your father's dead.' His voice was stony in a way that was new to her.

'I know that.'

'You should have had more faith.'

'What do you mean?'

'Faith in us. I did.'

They stared at each other. Now that she was no longer tempted, she put out a hand and laid it on his arm.

'It's no good,' she said. 'Everything's changed, don't you see?'

'So that's it? Just like that.'

'I'm going away on Monday.'

'But I love you,' he said, laying down his final card.

'I love you too,' she said. 'I still can't.'

He put his hands in his pockets. His face became blank. 'Oh,' he said.

'I'll go now,' said Edie. 'I hope . . .' What did she hope? 'I hope things go all right for you.'

'You hope I have a good life, is that it?'

'I suppose so. It sounds stupid.'

'Very stupid.'

'Ricky . . .'

''Bye then,' he said.

'Goodbye.'

She turned away and started to walk down the lane, back to the house. At the corner she paused. If he was still there, watching her, she would go back to him, because her chest ached and her eyes hurt and she couldn't bear any more.

She took a deep breath to steady herself and looked back, but the road was empty.

On Monday, Edie and Jude left. They packed their last few things and ate breakfast in a kitchen echoey with its bareness. Even the blinds were gone and naked bulbs hung from the ceiling. Then they heaved their cases into the back of Ellen's car, and Louise came out to say goodbye. Jude sat in the front, crying. Her eyes were red; her face newly gaunt; her clothes hung off her now. Edie told Ellen she wanted to check she hadn't left anything, but really she needed one last look around, by herself.

She wandered through the house, her feet tapping against the boards. Every room was stripped and empty, dust stirring in the corners, but memories came rushing to fill the spaces. Slowly, she mounted the stairs. To stand for the last time in her bedroom, to gaze out of the window at the climbing rose and the broken swing. There were a few house-martins in the eaves still, though soon they too would have to leave. And there was the plum tree, leaning towards her in the wind. For one moment, she saw Vic beneath it, his pale, heavy face turned towards her; his shy smile. Then she blinked and he was gone. Of course he was gone. He would never come again.

She closed the door and went down the stairs again and out to the car, where they were waiting for her. Louise pressed a cold cheek against hers and murmured something in her ear. Edie climbed into the back.

'All right,' she said. 'Let's go then.'

PART TWO

14

Edie woke in the night. She lay quite still, hoping to slide back into sleep. It always happened at about the same time, in the scary hours before dawn. Beyond the dirty orange glow of street lamps the sky was dark, and the silence wasn't yet broken by birdsong or the postman, only the occasional far-off car, the sound of a door shutting somewhere, a cat's solitary yowl – sounds which made the quiet seem even heavier.

She turned her head to see the green digits on her alarm clock as they clicked over to 3.05. Beside her, Alex stirred and murmured something, in the lovely thick of sleep. They weren't touching, but Edie could feel the warmth of his solid body. She reached out and put a hand flat against his back, which was slightly damp, like a loaf of bread still warm from baking. His breath was steady; his mouth was slightly open, and every so often he made a faint sound, like an inquiry. Edie propped herself up on one elbow, so that the duvet fell away from them both, and looked at him in the dim orange light through the curtains. His waist was thickening, his chest was broad and hairless. His face was slack in sleep; the brown hair was turning grey. He looked very serious when he slept.

Edie pulled the duvet carefully back round him and lay down again. She closed her eyes. The whole house seemed to be filled with sleep and dreams, to rise and fall with it. Not just Alex beside her, but the children, each in their separate rooms. She imagined them: Jessica, her face laid on her folded hands, as if she was praying. Before long, she would perhaps climb in beside her and nuzzle her face into her neck. She'd smell of grass and clean sweat and her toes would be cold. Lewis, in a tight ball with only the top of his bristly head showing; the thin white scar along his scalp where he'd fallen off his bike last year. And Kit, on his back, with his arms stretched above his head as if he'd fallen from a great height and landed like that – the way he'd slept since a baby. But she didn't want to think of Kit in the middle of the night, because then she'd be filled to the brim with an insomniac's panic about her middle son, who had Vic's bewildered eyes.

She tried to breathe regularly. She tried not to think about things, just make her mind a blank; an empty space. At university, she'd had a friend who practised meditation, sitting in a lotus position with a beatific smile on his face. He'd told her that she had to repeat a syllable – a mantra – over and over again inside her head, until at last everything was swallowed up by the meaningless word. The world slipped away, with all its snags and thorns. In a moment of generosity he'd told her his secret mantra, but it had never worked for her and she couldn't remember it now. There was so much she couldn't remember. Facts and figures; people's birthdays; the capital cities of Europe, the speed of sound, the circumference of the earth, how to convert Centigrade to Fahrenheit, the periodic table she'd once known off by heart, her car's registration number, her old telephone numbers, how to video films, though Alex had told her often enough . . .

And so much she remembered; so much she carried around with her and couldn't get rid of. Her head was an attic full of treasure and junk. Today Kit had PE at school and Jessie had swimming. Leah and Gabriel, Alex's teenage children by his first marriage, were coming in the evening, for their midweek visit, and she had to remember to get the fish out of the freezer before she left for work and make up their beds. She hadn't phoned the dentist to make an appointment about Lewis's brace. Kit had to check he knew his spellings for the test today. She must remember to buy the surgery's receptionist a birthday present, from all the partners. Was there enough bread for their packed lunches, or maybe she should make a pasta salad? She had to remind Lewis to take in the periscope they had made together, for his science project. Had she reminded Alex about her training day on Thursday, when she needed to leave the house earlier than usual? Would she have time for her swim today? The car needed servicing. They were nearly out of guinea-pig food. Alex's jacket to the dry cleaner's. New shoes for Kit soon. Visit to Lewis's secondary school, where he'd start in September. Organize child-minder's times for the next few weeks. Chicken drumsticks and ice cream for Jessie's sleepover on Friday. That referral for her patient with cancer of the throat. A babysitter for Thursday. Parents' evenings coming up, for one child after the other – waiting in a line for half an hour to get five minutes. The assembly where Jess would play 'Three Blind Mice' on her recorder – could she get away from work to hear it? The broken fence at the end of the garden. Puncture on Lewis's bike. School jumble sale, she'd have to find things to donate. Phone Louise, suggesting a visit. Sort out the locum for the summer months. Ante-natal clinic tomorrow. Problem with their trainee: talk to Kevin about it. Return library books. Accounts to do. Visit Ellen in the old people's home soon – but when? When could she? Dates clicked through her restless mind. Recipes. Shopping lists. Unanswered letters. Odd socks.

And tangling with them were other concerns which she could sense rather than name. Vague, deep worries, which came when she was losing the glaring clarity of insomnia and sleep was sucking her under again. The way Kit came out of school alone every day, shuffling, eyes cast down and thin shoulders hunched – though Alex always told her to stop worrying about Kit and allow him to be the strange, dreamy boy that he was. The way life was going too fast, doors shutting behind her, and what were the secrets behind them, decades going like years used to? The way the past seemed very close and a long way off, and when she looked back at her life she seemed to herself like a diminutive figure silhouetted at the far end of a long tunnel; and she didn't understand the journey she'd made, how the girl she'd been then had become the woman she was now. A half-time GP with three children and a husband, a tall house and a long, narrow garden, two cars, two cats, a guinea-pig . . .

She was nearing her forties, with glasses for reading,

stretch marks on her stomach from her pregnancies, a scar from her Caesarean, wrinkles round her eyes and running from her nostrils to the side of her mouth, rough hands, grey hairs in her eyebrows, insomnia at night. A very long time ago, she had thought that growing older meant growing more serene about life. But increasingly, she cried when she read books out loud to Jessie, Kit and Lewis and found the ending was always about growing up and leaving childhood behind. And she cried when she saw the news, or watched corny films, or listened to the music she'd listened to when she was young. Sometimes she even cried without knowing she was doing so. Driving home, she would feel a sheet of tears streaming down her hot cheeks and stop the car for a while until the mysterious emotion passed. She was just about the age that Louise had been when Vic had died. She thought of her mother, alone in the neat and empty house. She thought of her grandmother, in her neat square bedroom in a home for the elderly that smelt of cabbage, polish and piss.

Edie turned over and found a cool spot on the pillow. She thought that perhaps she should buy Ellen a teddy bear – something to hold through the days she spent staring out of the window. When Edie went to visit her she would hold her hands that felt like a sheaf of twigs between her own, and talk to her, trying not to sound as if she was talking to an infant, trying not to croon and baby-talk to the woman she'd once considered indomitable. Ellen always smiled and blinked her milky eyes and then asked when she was going back home again. Edie never knew what to say. It was easier to do practical things, like dress the sores that kept opening up on Ellen's arms, or cut her thick yellowing nails, wash her thin hair.

She heard the first few notes from a blackbird outside the window. She should get up, rather than just lying here passively in the grip of thoughts. Or she could even wake Alex and they could make love, before the children got up. It had been ages – she'd been tired, he'd worked late, she'd been on duty, the children had come into the room with bad dreams, a stomach ache . . .

There were more noises outside now and it was definitely getting lighter. It was late May, and dawn came before the milk float and the newspaper boy. The sky was turning a grey-blue; the birds were singing. She would get up and go into the garden to listen to their chorus. But even as she made the decision she felt herself softening towards sleep. Images floated through her mind. Water. Waves breaking over the brown sea-weed and grey, shining pebbles. Rock pools. There were lights in the depths of the rock pools and people in long cloaks were walking towards her, ringing the bells they carried in their hands. She wanted to run away from the sound but couldn't move and the bells kept on ringing, and then Alex was leaning across her to turn off the alarm clock. He kissed her on the forehead.

'Good morning, my beautiful,' he said, which was what he said every morning.

'Oh fuck,' Edie groaned.

'Did you sleep all right?'

'Oh well, you know . . .'

'It's nearly twenty past seven.'

'Yes.'

'We should get up.'

'I know.'

'Two more minutes.'

He put his arms round her from behind and held her against him. His hair tickled her face and his warm hands enfolded her.

'Bliss,' she said. 'I could lie here all day.'

There was a pattering in the hall and the door was flung open.

'I've wet my bed, but it doesn't matter one little bit,' said Jess. 'And the cat's been sick on my carpet.'

Toast and jam for Lewis and a white roll with honey for Kit and porridge for Jess. Big pot of tea. Empty the dishwasher. Open the bills. Iron her shirt that had the cat's paw-prints down the back, but no one would see them. Fill out permission slip for Lewis to go with his class to the Globe Theatre. Write a cheque. PE bag. Swimming things. Packed lunches: three sandwiches with tuna and mayonnaise, three oat biscuits, three apples, three bottles of water.

'Tracey's mum always gives her crisps and choco-lates.'

'I'm not Tracey's mum, Jess.'

'I'm not feeling very well today . . .'

'Oh, Kit. Eat up your breakfast and then you may feel better.'

'I don't know if I should go to school.'

'Headache?'

'And I feel sick.'

Edie looked at him. He felt ill most mornings before school. Every so often she would let him have a day at home, especially if it was on one of her days off, bringing him squash, slices of cake, carrying the portable CD player into his room so that he could listen to tapes while Bilbo purred on his pillow.

'I've got to go to work myself this afternoon, Kit. See how it goes,' she said.

He nodded glumly and fiddled with his roll. 'I've got PE,' he said.

'I know. It'll be OK. Just do your best, and ignore anyone who's stupid, all right? Remember you've got those spellings. Finish your breakfast and then you can go over them. You've got golden syrup on your chin, Jess. By the way, Lewis, why on earth are you still in your pyjama bottoms?'

'Because I can't find my school trousers.'

'Your trousers? Aren't they in your room?'

'No. You must have put them somewhere.'

'*I* haven't put them anywhere at all.'

'The allotment's come through, Edie. At last!' Alex brandished a letter in her face.

'What?'

'The allotment. I'm sure I mentioned it.'

'No.'

'Oh. Well, I thought it would be wonderful to grow our own vegetables. Peas. Beetroots.'

'But our own garden's running wild . . .'

'It's not the same thing.'

'Maybe not but – Kit, you're going to be late if you don't get a move on.'

'And I can't find my shoes.'

'Lewis, you're nearly eleven. I can't chase around after your clothes every morning.'

'I'm leaving now, Edie.'

'What time will you be home?'

'Not sure. We've got another bloody staff meeting straight after school finishes. I'll call you, OK?'

'Have a good day – oh shit, Jess, watch out. It's all over your jersey.'

'You shouldn't swear at me, that's wrong. You always tell us not to swear. Can I have plaits today?'

'OK. But don't scream at me while I'm doing them.'

'Here's the brush.' Jess climbed on to Edie's lap, knocking Kit's pencil case on to the floor. Pens and crayons rolled across the tiles. A sharpener burst open and scattered pencil shavings everywhere.

'Jess!' said Kit. 'Now look.'

'Sorry,' said Jess blithely. She wriggled hotly in Edie's lap. Golden syrup appeared mysteriously on Edie's shirt.

Edie took a deep breath. 'Just two plaits?' she asked in a tight, calm voice. She'd clear everything up later, after she'd delivered them to school. She didn't have to be at work until eleven. Clear up, have a large cup of tea, go swimming, even walk in the garden, where butterflies shimmered round the shrubs and yellow roses opened to the sun.

They left the house late. Edie carried Jess's school bag and swimming bag, Kit's PE kit, and everyone's lunchboxes. She felt like a pack-horse. Jess pulled on her hand so that the bags kept falling off her shoulder. Kit hung back, feet dragging.

'There's the school bell.'

'Oh God, hurry now, Kit.'

'You're making us late,' complained Lewis. 'Mum, he's making us late.'

'You run on ahead now, OK? Have a lovely day.'

''Bye.'

'Hang on, take your lunch. Kirsty's collecting you, remember? I'll see you about six.'

'Why can't you collect us?' asked Kit.

'Because I'm working.'

'Other mothers don't work.'

She left them at the school gate. Jess ran and joined the line of children who were queuing up outside her class.

''Bye, Kit.'

'Mummy?'

'Yes?'

'Oh – it doesn't matter.'

'You're late.'

'But . . .'

She waited but he didn't add anything. She looked at the purple smudges under his brown eyes. Then she leant forward and kissed him on the cheek, quickly so that other boys wouldn't see and sneer at him for being a sissy. 'I love you lots,' she said. He stared at her, then walked slowly towards his classroom.

Edie swam up and down the pool. Forty lengths; one thousand metres. Enough to make her heart pound and her calves ache. She went three or four times a week, more if she could, and was part of a group of regular morning swimmers, most of whom, like her, swam between dropping off children and heading for work. Sometimes she'd see them in the street and hardly recognize them dressed, hair dry. She knew them naked, with circles round their eyes from wearing goggles, wet hair, wet flesh.

Forty minutes before going to the surgery. She washed the breakfast dishes; wiped the table clean of smeared syrup and splashed milk. She swept the floor and threw away the dead flowers. Then poured herself a large mug of tea and turned from the table to look out at the garden, an oasis amid the noise and the dust of London. Everything was bathed in a golden light, and the leaves were a fresh, bright green. It was time for barbecues again. They could sit in the garden in the evening, watching shadows grow longer and house-martins dart in and out from the eaves, while Alex put on his striped apron and turned sausages and his home-made burgers on the grill.

She pushed open the kitchen door, feeling the sun on the nape of her neck. There were golden wallflowers just opening up. Bees hummed in the rosemary bush. She tipped back her head and breathed in the clean air.

'It's going to be a beautiful day,' she said out loud.

Then the phone rang and she ran to get it.

'Hello?'

'Edie.'

'Stella! How are . . . ?'

'It's Louise.'

'What?'

'She's had an accident, Edie. In her car. And . . .'

'Where is she? Is she in hospital?'

There was an odd silence, like the pause you get on an international call, where sense has gone astray somewhere between speaker and listener.

'She's dead.'

Outside, the day glowed. The sky was turquoise, like a bird's egg.

'I don't understand,' said Edie.

'Louise is dead. She died. Apparently she was over the limit . . .'

'Drunk?'

'I don't know. It doesn't matter.'

'Oh,' said Edie.

'I've just heard. I rang as soon as I could.'

'Oh, Stella.'

'I know.'

Edie was having difficulty in making sense of Stella's words. Things kept getting in the way. She looked at the clock on the wall. It was past ten o'clock. She hadn't made up Leah and Gabriel's beds yet. And Lewis hadn't taken his cardboard periscope to school. A bee buzzed uselessly against the pane, then spun off again.

'But she was so young,' she said uselessly.

'Sixty-one.'

'I thought she'd live till ninety.'

'Yes. Listen. I'm going to talk to Jude and then drive up there.'

'Yes,' said Edie. 'Yes, that's the thing to do. Is her body . . . ?'

'In the hospital.'

Edie blinked. She felt as if her vision was blurred. 'I'll come today too,' she said. 'I just need to sort things out – the children. Work. It won't take long.'

'Of course.'

'I'll be there as soon as I can. Where will you be – at the hospital or at Mum's?'

'It depends on the time. Ring me on your mobile when you're on your way.'

'Yes, that'd be best. Stella?'

'Yes?'

'Drive there carefully, won't you?'

'You too.'

'OK. 'Bye. And Stella?'

'Mmm.'

'I love you.'

Afterwards, she stood by the window, waiting to feel that it was true. Her mother was dead. Louise. Mum. Mummy. She tested the words, knowing that what had happened was momentous, yet they carried no impact. Not yet. She wasn't ready.

Two hours later, Edie climbed into her car. Alex bent in and gave her a last hug.

'Thanks for coming back. I know it's hard for you to get away from school.'

'Of course I came back.'

'Remember to give my letters to the children. And say sorry to Leah and Gabriel that I'm not there.'

'I will.'

'And I've left the list of their timetables on the table.'

'I know, Edie. I was there when you wrote it.'

'Tell them I'm sorry to leave without saying goodbye. Tell them I'll be thinking of them.'

'Edie, everything will be all right here.'

'Kit'll be in a state. I know he will. And Jess has to learn her three and four times table by Friday. And if you want to cancel her sleepover . . .'

'Edie. Go!'

'Yes. Thank you. For everything. Take care of them, OK? And yourself. All right, I'm going now. 'Bye. Goodbye.'

He kissed her and then stood back and shut the door. Edie started the engine. Through the window, Alex was mouthing words, but she could no longer hear them. She smiled at him and waved. Then she was driving away at last. In the rear-view mirror she could see him still standing with his hand lifted. He stood there, getting smaller and smaller, and then she rounded the corner and he was gone.

15

Edie had never thought of Louise's house as home. Home was where she had grown up. The kitchen where she had made baked potatoes once a week, apple crumble; where she'd sat every weekday morning in her itchy uniform, eating porridge sprinkled with golden sugar; where she'd been in companionable silence with Vic, podding peas and making raspberry jam. Bowls of satsumas in the winter, and of plums in the autumn. The living-room where all five of them had played charades at Christmas, and Stella had helped her cut out patterns for summer dresses, tissue paper over lime-green cotton; she could almost feel the pins in her mouth and hear the scrunch of scissors. The dim hallway where slatted light fell on summer afternoons. The bedroom where she had lain under the cave of sheets with a torch, reading books and planning what she would do with her life; where, later, she'd stood in front of her mirror, examining her face, looking at herself over her shoulder, waiting to be beautiful. The garden where she had pushed Jude on the swing, learnt to ride her bike with and then without stabilizers, to walk on stilts, to jump on the pogo stick, to do headstands, handstands, cart-wheels. The secret dens – under the stairs, in the thicket of shrubs – where they'd eaten jam sandwiches and handfuls of raisins. The lanes where in the summer the trees made a tunnel of dappled light.

That was home. If she closed her eyes she could see and feel it still – the crack along the stairwell, the nettles in the ditch, the bumpy texture of wood-chip on the wall beside her bed, the smell of vanilla as the rice pudding cooked, the pattern on the plates, the bare patch on the carpet where she swung herself out of bed every morning, the smell of hay in the barn at the end of the road, the yellow dress she'd worn for parties when she was six, with velvet on the hem and at the neck, the bar fire in Louise and Vic's room where she used to dry her hair on Sunday evenings . . .

She had lived in Louise's house for only fifteen months, moving there from Ellen's house when she was nearly into her final year of school, always knowing it was a temporary dwelling, the stepping-stone between the past and future. Of course, she'd visited it many times afterwards, and stayed there in the holidays. But by then she was a guest, and the room that had been briefly hers became the place both she and Stella used on their visits. Her few belongings were gradually cleared away, put into boxes in the attic for when she had a house of her own. Edie had always felt that the new house neutralized memories – old pieces of furniture, or the pictures they'd had for as long as she could remember, held different meanings once they were moved to this compact semi down a cul-de-sac in a new estate on the edge of the town. It was agreeable enough, with large windows, thick carpets, a forty-foot garden that was mostly lawn with a neat strip of bed around it, neighbours on either side who nodded to you over the garden fence. But it had no resonance for Edie – or it had a negative one, reminding her of what it was not. It had always been a place of absence and of forgetting.

She parked the car behind Stella's. They had come in convoy from the hospital, where they had both sat for half an hour beside Louise's body. Edie was professionally used to death, but Stella had never seen a corpse before and she had been visibly shaken by the waxy sternness of the face, the chilly hardness of the flesh. She had bent forward and kissed Louise's cheek, below the two-inch gash and violent bruise on her forehead where she'd hit the windscreen, and gasped.

'She's already so dead,' she said in horrified wonder. 'So completely dead.'

Edie picked up Louise's left hand and held it between her own. She still wore her wedding ring. Her nails were smooth and painted a pearly pink. Her mother's face looked thinner than she remembered; her hair coarser. There were folds under her chin. Her closed mouth looked determined.

'She's beautiful, isn't she?'

'She always was.'

'Like you.'

'Like I used to be, maybe,' said Stella ruefully, touching her face. 'Not any more. That's all gone, since Sam.' Sam was her sixteen-year-old autistic son, in whose service Stella toiled and for whom she had given up her career, her sleep, her youth, her loveliness. Edie looked across at her; she had grown plumper and she wore practical clothes: brown trousers and a baggy oatmeal cardigan. Her hair was losing its glorious apricot colour – soon it would start to turn grey. Her face was middle-aged and kind. Stella had always been kind, thought Edie; kind through and through.

'That's not true at all,' she said firmly.

'It doesn't matter. I wonder if she knew she was dying.'

'Probably not.'

'I hope not. I wish we'd been with her.'

'Yes, I know.'

'She didn't have the life she wanted, did she?'

'No,' said Edie slowly, still holding Louise's cold fingers. 'I don't think she ever got over Daddy.'

'It surprised me at first.'

'I know. She used to be such a flirt when he was alive; but as soon as he was dead and she was free she became almost, well, austere.'

'I almost think she didn't want to get over him. Like she made a decision about it.'

'Maybe,' said Edie cautiously.

'Maybe she felt if she'd been a better wife, he wouldn't have killed himself.'

'You can go mad if you think that way,' said Edie. The conversation filled her with dread. Memories she had dammed up for twenty years could flood over her. Suck her under.

'Now we've got no one ahead of us,' said Stella. 'I don't feel ready for that, do you?'

'I don't think one's ever ready,' said Edie. 'Not even when you're very old.' She looked across at her sister. 'Should we tell Ellen?'

'Why? She wouldn't understand.'

'Or she'd understand then forget, so she'd have to keep on being told, all over again. I have patients like that – in a perpetual state of new bereavement; it's heartbreaking. So should we not tell her? Or is that wrong, somehow?'

'Jude would say we should tell her. She would say it was her right to know, no matter what.'

'When's Jude coming?'

'Late afternoon, early evening. It's a long drive from Glasgow.'

Edie laid Louise's hand back on the bed. 'I haven't cried yet, have you?'

'Not yet. It doesn't feel real.'

'Shall we go?'

'I suppose so. She isn't here.'

So now they were back at the house, parking their cars on the gravel drive. The curtains were still closed; Louise had left last night and not returned. She'd driven off the road, down a bank and into a beech tree. There was alcohol in her blood and she hadn't been wearing a seat-belt.

'I've got my key,' said Edie, fishing around in her voluminous bag among the wax crayons, tissues, hair-bands, pipe-cleaners, Polo mints and miniature plastic animals.

She inserted the key in the lock and pushed the door open. They stepped into the hall, where Louise's coats hung on hooks, and her slippers stood by the bench, ready for her to put on as soon as she came back inside.

It was very quiet and their feet squeaked on the polished boards. Without saying anything, they moved into the kitchen. There were yellow and purple tulips on the table, their petals splayed open and their stems drooping; a folded newspaper; a mug with an inch of black coffee in the bottom, a blue china plate with a knife and orange peel on it. A postcard that Edie had sent a week ago was propped against the vase, and by the side of it was a shopping list, written in Louise's looped writing. Edie picked it up. 'Apples, lemons, lettuce hearts, avocado pears × 2, streaky bacon, spinach, semi-skimmed milk, Cheshire cheese, tomatoes, garlic, Basmati rice, whisky, washing-up liquid, bleach, kitchen towels, face cream, soap (lavender), coffee, matches, A4 batteries . . .' She put the list back on the table.

'Shall I make us some tea?' Stella asked.

'That'd be nice,' said Edie. She didn't know where to begin. There were so many things to do, arrangements to make, emotions to feel – but where to start? She sat down at the kitchen table and propped her chin in her hands. It was nearly four o'clock. Soon, she'd ring the children and make sure they were all right. Then Jude would arrive, with her firm views. It had been a long time since the three of them were together. 'We have to think about the funeral,' she said.

'And the house and everything.'

'I suppose so. We should put it on the market, I guess.'

'And go through all her stuff, decide who'll have what.'

'It seems a bit quick to do all that,' said Edie.

'I know, but if we don't do it now, when are we all going to be together like this again? And anyway, will it feel better if we wait?'

'You're probably right.' She thought of those patients of hers who'd lost spouses: they often said that having to make all the arrangements was helpful. It gave them something to occupy themselves with and took them through the first days. 'And maybe it will be good for us – going through her things, I mean, sorting stuff out. It'll be a way in.'

'A way in to what?'

'To her.'

'It's too late for that.'

'Well, of course, in a way. You always think there'll be a moment when everything will be sorted out. There were so many things I never said to her. After Daddy died, I kept thinking that one day I'd have a proper talk about it all – about what she felt, and what I felt. About him, and them, and her life afterwards. But somehow I never did. It never seemed the right moment. There were so many times I was on the brink of it, and then I didn't. Perhaps because she didn't want me to, I don't know. But I always felt sure that one day we would talk, really talk, and cry and hug each other and open our hearts. Comfort each other. You know. And now we won't. So of course you're right in one way, and it's too late, for us – me and her together – at least. But I can't feel it's all over, just because she's dead. I can't feel that there's a neat line drawn under her – under them – like a sum, and we can add up their lives. There has to be something more to this.'

'More?' said Stella. She was looking into her mug as if she could see answers in it.

'Yes,' said Edie. 'Or maybe that's what I've got to come to terms with. That there isn't any more. This is the end. They're gone, and some things we'll never understand.'

They lapsed into silence. Edie wished Jude would arrive. Then they could begin, although what it was they would begin she couldn't say.

'How's Sam?' she asked.

Stella smiled. 'Huge,' she said. 'He towers over me now; he can put his chin on my head. I hope Bob manages all right with him while I'm away. He can be very bloody-minded.'

'You've been extraordinary, you know.'

'Not really.'

'Your whole life changed, all your plans, and yet I've never once heard you complain.'

'Giving things up wasn't so hard actually,' said Stella. 'I never really knew what I wanted to do anyway – not like you or Jude. I wasn't ambitious for myself. Really, I just wanted to be a wife and mother. That probably appals you. Anyway, now I'm a mother in spades. Maybe it was almost a relief not to have to make decisions about my life; they've all been made for me.'

'You've still been extraordinary.'

'Hmmm.' Stella got up and pulled the fridge door open. There was a bowl of tinned peaches in there, covered with clingfilm, a carton of plain yoghurt, a vacuum-packed smoked mackerel, half a pint of semi-skimmed milk. Nothing else. 'Bob's having an affair,' she said into the fridge, her voice muffled.

'Oh, Stella!'

'He doesn't know I know.'

'How do you know?'

'Oh, the usual things. Him coming home late and having a shower, the smell of someone else's perfume on his clothes, too many Sundays when he had to go and work. And then I followed him.'

'You didn't!'

'Yes. I waited outside his office and followed him.'

'Blimey! And?'

'And he's having an affair,' said Stella flatly. She turned back to the fridge. 'We have to buy stuff to eat,' she said.

'I'm so sorry,' said Edie. 'What are you going to do?'

'Do? Oh, nothing probably.' She shut the door and turned back to face Edie. 'Wait for it to be over.'

'That's it?'

'I'm not surprised really. I mean, we've known each other for ever, haven't we? He hardly had any girlfriends before me, not really. And our life's not much fun for him. I get up two or three times every night, and then I'm up by six, and I spend every day trying to make Sam do things that most people would think were meaningless. Honestly, we make such tiny advances, Edie. And by the time Bob comes home, I'm exhausted. I can't be bothered to make an effort for him. I go to bed at ten – and when I say go to bed, I mean I fall asleep, as if a boulder's been dropped on my head. I can't remember the last time we made love. Plus, he doesn't like being an accountant much, and feels a bit of a failure, stuck in a dead-end job that he was only going to do for a few years – and that was fifteen years ago – and surrounded by people much younger than him. Except they're rising and he's staying still. He probably thinks, is this it then? Is this my life?'

'What about you?' said Edie. 'Don't you think, is this *my* life?'

'I think: this *is* my life. I have no choice.'

'So you won't even talk to him about it?'

'I don't know. I'm not like you,' said Stella slowly. She was still standing with her back against the fridge. 'I don't expect so much. I just like to get by really, muddle along. Not like you. You were always an absolut-ist – all or nothing.'

'Was I?'

'Me and Louise were the pragmatic ones, making do with what we'd got. You and Jude and Vic were the dreamers.'

'Oh,' said Edie. 'I don't think so.'

'Maybe only dreamers kill themselves.'

'That can't be right.' Soon, she would call home and hear Alex's voice.

'Take the way you were with that boy.'

'What boy?' asked Edie, though she knew.

'Ricky.'

'Oh, Ricky.'

There was a crunching of gravel outside.

'Jude,' said Edie with relief.

Jude strode in through the door, her long linen coat flapping behind her, her shoes clicking over the hall floor, her black hair expensively shaggy. Her face was pale and thin, her eyebrows were thick and dark, her lips were painted scarlet. She was carrying a large box.

'There's another of these in the boot,' she said, putting it down on the table. 'I thought we'd need sustenance.' She pulled out three bottles of wine, and put the white one into the fridge. 'I thought we could have pitta bread with marinated chicken tonight. I've got all the ingredients. Something simple.'

'Hello, Jude,' said Edie.

'Hi, Edie, Stella. Just the three of us now,' said Jude and kissed them both. She smelt of a sharp fragrance, almost lemony; her hair glistened and her teeth were white. She took off her coat and slung it over the back of a chair. Edie was struck again by her thinness; the sinews on her arms stood out, her collar-bones were sharp under her shirt. 'Are you all right?'

'We don't know,' said Edie. 'It hasn't sunk in. Are you?'

Jude shrugged. 'Who knows?' she said. 'I'll go and get the other box.'

They helped her in with her luggage and took the food out of the boxes. Then Stella asked, 'Who's going to sleep where then?'

'Jude in her old room, obviously. Then you or me in the spare room. And there's Mum's room. I'll sleep there, if you like.'

'I'll help you change the sheets,' said Stella.

'Funny, isn't it?' said Jude. 'If she was still alive, then changing her sheets wouldn't seem quite so important. But the thought of sleeping on the sheets of a dead woman, well . . .' She shuddered theatrically.

*

Edie took her one bag up to Louise's room. The cat, Smoky, was lying on the bed, and she lifted her off and put her on the floor, gently. Then she stripped the sheets off the bed. There was Louise's nightdress on the pillow: pale blue and long. She held it against her cheek for a moment, breathing in the familiar smell. Soon that smell would be all gone, she thought; clothes would be washed, rooms aired. The perfume would fade: the memory of Louise leaning down towards her with her creamy, fragrant skin; of Louise dabbing it on her wrists, behind her ears; Louise sitting by her bed in the darkness and the sweet drift of her on the air.

She opened the wardrobe and ran her hands through the dresses hanging there. Cotton, velvet, silk, wool. She squatted down and touched the leather shoes, felt their grain.

On the dressing-table was a photograph of Louise and Vic, in a silver frame. It was them on their wedding day; it used to be in the living-room in their old house, but Edie hadn't seen it for ages. She lifted it up and stared at it. Louise's face was smooth; she smiled luminously out at Edie, and looked so young and certain that her daughter, forty years later, felt a pang of protective fear for her. But Vic looked only at Louise, as if she was a miracle. His arm was round her waist and his fingers lost in the white folds of the dress. They looked like children, thought Edie. They'd had no idea.

16

'Mummy?'

'Yes.'

'Can I see her body?'

'I'm not sure that's a good idea, Kit.'

'I want to.'

'Well, I don't know. It's strange, seeing someone you love dead. It's better to remember her as she was when she was alive.'

'I want to,' he repeated.

'I'll think about it. I've talked to Alex and you'll all come on Sunday, the day before the funeral. That's not so long, you know.'

'Why not before? Why not Friday after school?'

'Because – well, I guess because this is for me and Stella and Jude to do.'

'I can help sort things out. I wouldn't get in your way, I promise.'

'No, Kit.'

'Please.'

'It'll only be a few days now.'

'Mummy?'

'Yes.'

'Oh – nothing.'

'Tell me. Is everything all right there?' There was a silence. 'Kit?'

'Fine.'

'Nothing's happened in particular?'

'No. Not really.'

'All-right day at school?'

'Kind of.'

'Listen, why don't you write things down for me? Write me a diary of what you're doing while I'm away. I'd love that — and then all the things that are hard to say out loud, I can read about. How about that?'

'Maybe.'

'You've got that new notebook with stars on the cover I bought you. Write in that. Or if you preferred, you could send it to me in an e-mail every day, then I could e-mail back. I brought my laptop with me specially.'

Kit made an indeterminate noise at the other end. Edie could hear the radio in the background, Alex laughing at something Jess was telling him.

'I'll go now. Have a lovely evening, all right? Alex said he was getting an Indian take-away for everyone.'

'Mmm.'

'That'll be nice. I'll speak to you tomorrow. Put me on to Lewis, OK?'

''Bye,' said Kit in a small voice. He sounded very far away.

Jude cut chicken into chunks and chopped red chilli and spring onions over it. She squeezed a lemon into the dish and added two crushed cloves of garlic. Edie sipped red wine and watched her. They could hear Stella on the phone in the hall; her voice rose and fell soothingly; she was talking to Sam.

'There,' said Jude. 'That just needs half an hour or so.'

She spooned yoghurt into a bowl and added chopped fresh mint and basil, then a spoonful of paprika. Her fingernails were painted a pale brown. She was so elegant, thought Edie, and so thin. It was hard to remember how she'd been as a teenager, overweight and rumpled, hair hanging in clumps over her face, her face heavy and white, dimpled hands. She used to dress in leggings and big tee-shirts, read books for hours in an unaired room, and eat biscuits in the dark. She used to shout at Louise, her face turning shiny and red with rage. Edie watched her thin fingers shredding basil. Jude's anger remained, she thought, though it was controlled now, turned into something abrasive and witty.

'Why are you looking at me like that?' Jude asked, glancing up to meet her sister's gaze.

'I was thinking how beautiful you've become,' Edie answered.

'I know what that means. Everything's going to be about memory while we're here; wall-to-wall nostalgia. I've come prepared. You were remembering what I used to be like, weren't you?'

'Partly, yes.'

'Fat and ugly.'

'Never ugly,' said Edie.

'You're the kind of person who never thinks anyone is ugly. If you love someone, you think they're lovely, don't you?'

'I suppose so.'

'After Dad died,' said Jude, 'I made a decision that I

was going to become a different person. The funny thing was that Mum, who'd spent my whole life telling me how drab I looked and how I needed to go on a diet and put on make-up and start taking an interest in clothes, well, she hated seeing me change.'

'It was a bit dramatic,' said Edie. 'You starved yourself, like a prisoner on hunger strike.' She hadn't been there for most of Jude's punitive re-invention. She'd done her A-levels and fled home, leaving Louise and Jude to fight it out. And now Louise was dead, and Jude was a glamorous academic, teaching philosophy and psychology to besotted students, and writing books with titles like *How to Lie* and *The Deceits of Friendship*. 'Louise was worried sick about you.'

'I changed, but into the wrong person,' said Jude. 'She couldn't like me.'

'Who couldn't like you?' asked Stella, entering the room.

'Oh, nothing,' said Jude brusquely. Edie saw a shadow of hurt chase across Stella's face.

'How's everything at home?'

'Fine. Bob sounded a bit harassed.'

She wandered over to the sink and started washing up their mugs. Edie took another sip of wine. She'd eaten nothing all day and she felt all her edges were softening. I could cry now, she thought. But she didn't know whether she would be crying for Louise.

'When were we last all together?' she asked. 'Just the three of us.'

'Ages ago,' said Stella. 'Years.' She sat down at the table and Edie poured her a glass of wine.

'We should drink to Mummy,' said Edie.

'I never could understand why you persisted in calling her Mummy,' said Jude.

'To Louise then,' said Stella.

'We've all come here with our different expectations, haven't we?' said Jude, sitting up straight as if she were teaching a seminar to her students. 'Stella wants us to be affectionate and comforting, like a proper family. No arguments, no uncomfortable truths. Love and tolerance are the answer to everything. Edie, on the other hand, wants us to talk and cry and gain some new understanding of Mum and Dad and of ourselves. She wants this to be a healing, illuminating, rawly painful experience. In fact, I'd say she's been waiting for this for twenty-two years, without really knowing that she was waiting. Waiting to acknowledge all her feelings of sorrow and loss, once it's too late to do anything about them. Am I right, Edie? Anyway.' She lifted her glass and clinked it against theirs. 'To Mum, Mummy, Louise.'

'And what do you want?'

'Me? To get out unscathed.'

'No, really. Tell me.'

'I am telling you.'

'I don't think so.'

'Oh, Edie, when I'm angry or irritated you always think I must be suffering inside, don't you? That's the trouble with families, they believe they know you better than you know yourself. Well, really, I don't know what I want. That's the truth.' She took another gulp of wine and stirred the chicken round in its dish. 'I can cook this soon. Shall I make a salad to go with it? I brought some in bags.'

'I'll do it,' said Edie. 'And we ought to sort out who's going to do what over the next few days.' The cat was wrapping herself round her legs and she bent down and rubbed her chin until she heard the purr.

'The funeral,' said Stella. 'We've got to arrange it and ring round people. And we should sort out Louise's things, or at least make a start on them. And there's the house. And her money,' she added. 'I'm her executor.'

'And there's Ellen,' said Edie.

'Yes,' said Jude.

'We were thinking,' said Stella. 'Should we tell her?'

'Tell her?' Jude raised her eyebrows.

'About Louise.'

'You mean, you were actually considering *not* telling her?'

'Maybe it would be the kindest thing,' said Stella.

'Kindest – ignorance-is-bliss kindness, you mean?'

'Yes,' said Stella. She sighed. 'I know you can ride rough-shod over me, Jude, and crush me with your arguments. The housewife against the philosopher, hardly fair is it? But I hoped we could just talk about it without quarrelling, and try and decide what's best for Ellen.'

'That's the point: you want to decide *for* her. What gives you that right?'

'It's not a right,' said Edie. 'But she's no longer able to decide for herself.'

'She's not a baby.'

'She's like a baby though, isn't she?' Edie thought again of the teddy bear she was going to buy her grandmother, but decided not to mention it to Jude right now. 'In some ways.'

'She won't understand,' said Stella. 'Or if she does, she'll be heartbroken.'

'Yes,' said Jude. 'Life is heartbreaking. That's what it means to be alive. Would you prefer it if no one had told you about Mum, and then you could go on being happy, because you simply didn't know?'

'It's not the same.'

'OK. How about if Bob was having an affair, would you choose to know or not to know?'

Stella stared at her silently.

'We've drunk too much and not enough,' said Edie. 'I'm going to open another bottle of wine. I'll buy us some more tomorrow.'

'Did I just say something?'

'Never mind,' said Stella. 'I'm going to get my cardigan. I'm cold.'

Edie pulled the cork out of the second bottle. 'She has a hard life,' she said. 'And she was closer to Mummy than any of us. She used to help out with Sam quite a lot, too. It'll be worse for Stella than for us, not having that support any more.'

'OK.' Jude held up her hands. 'Sorry.'

Stella came back into the room and stood at the window. Two white towels hung on the washing-line, and there was a mug and an ashtray on the patio table. 'It's as if she's just popped out, isn't it?' she said. 'Her book was face down on the sofa arm, with her reading glasses on top of it. There are clothes in the laundry basket, waiting to be washed.'

'Have some more wine,' said Edie.

'Thanks.'

Later that evening, Edie checked her mail.

Dearest love, wrote Alex. *We are all missing you here. The house seems very quiet – though Gabriel and Leah are here, and you're the least noisy of all of us. Except Kit, of course, who's spoken about two syllables since he came home: 'yes' and 'no' (he's sent you an e-mail but I wasn't allowed to look at it). But everyone understands why you have to be there, even Jess, who's making you a card right now (all right, I know she should be in bed). Gabriel and Leah send lots of love to you, and said how sorry they were. They are very keen to come to the funeral – I'll speak to Peggy about arrangements and let you know. But what I really wanted to say to you is that you've always been a wonderful daughter. Remember that, even when you're feeling sad and down. Say hello to Stella and Jude – and don't let Jude boss you about too much, will you? Take care of yourself. I'll ring you tomorrow. Axxx*

PS What do you want to grow in the allotment?

And Kit: *Hello, Mummy. You said I should write things down. My typing isn't very good. It takes ages. Today at school Robbie called me freak and someone put my packed lunch into the fish pond. I didn't cry, but I wanted to. I didn't tell anyone about it. It makes things worse. I would have told Lewis but he was with all his friends and he is different with his friends. I wasn't hungry anyway, not after that. I felt a bit sick. So it didn't matter about lunch. We miss you lots. It is like being homesick except I'm still at home. Daddy is being very loud*

and jolly. We had an Indian meal and he told us lots of
knock-knock jokes. Bilbo killed a mouse and brought it to me.
It didn't have a head. Now I am going to bed because it is late.
Love, Kit.

Edie lay down on Louise's bed, still dressed. It was a warm, soft night and she'd drunk too much wine. From where she lay she could see the wedding photograph. How odd, she thought, for Louise to have seen, every morning and every evening, a picture of Vic looking at her younger self with such bemused rapture. It seemed almost like a punishment. She closed her eyes.

17

Edie had met Alex on a skiing holiday in France when she was twenty-five and he nearly ten years older. She was there with three women friends, and he with his two children, aged six and four. It was just a few months after he and his wife had separated. Although he was energetically good-humoured all week, he sometimes seemed bewildered, as if he had wandered into an un-familiar world and didn't know quite what he was doing, sitting night after night at the corner table of the hotel restaurant, cutting up food for his children, putting the cork back into his wine bottle at the end of the meal. Perhaps, thought Edie, that was why she had let herself fall in love with him; there were cracks in his flamboyant cheerfulness. She looked at him with his son and daughter: the way he bent over them with tender solicitude, the way he listened respectfully to what they were saying. He was a large, untidy man and they seemed tiny beside him. She was profoundly touched.

Or perhaps their initial bond was simply their inability to ski. They were all in the same beginners' class at the start of the week, but while everyone else graduated from it after the first day, including Alex's children, Alex and Edie remained there for the whole week. They fell over on nursery slopes, they ploughed into drifts, and once, sharing a chair lift, their legs tangled and they tipped into a heap and slid sideways over the iced tracks. And she suddenly asked him, as they lay on the snow with flakes softly landing and dissolving on their noses and cheeks, why he and his wife had separated. She had expected him to rebuff her, or else tell her ruefully about some infidelity of his. Instead he replied, 'Because she was disappointed by me. I was too ordinary. Not ambitious or dynamic.' He waved one leg in the air, the blade tipping above them. 'I mean, look at me. I'm a maths teacher in a comprehensive and she's on her way to becoming a head. She was always on the fast tracks – she'd be on the black runs by now.'

And Edie had turned her gaze from the thick white sky to look at him. He was wearing a red bobble-hat that was too small, and there were snowflakes on his eyelashes. His cheekbones were sunburnt and his nose shiny. 'Did you mind very much?'

'You're a funny woman,' he said. 'You seem so quiet, but you go straight to the point.'

'So did you?' she persisted.

'Of course.' He gave a laugh, manoeuvred his legs into position and stood up unsteadily, then held out a mittened hand. 'Shall we go then?' He pulled her up beside him and then said, 'You want a confession? I'm terrified of skiing. I stand at the top of the bloody slope and I can't believe the only way off it is down. Anyway, here goes.' He took a breath and an expression of resignation crossed his face. He pushed off vigorously, leant forward into the gathering snow, and she admired his lack of dignity. His skis turned into an asymmetrical snow-plough and he lifted one pole as if he could fend off disaster. Edie watched him as he gathered speed and as he splendidly crashed.

Two years later, when she was pregnant, she asked him, at last, if he had ever been unfaithful to his first wife.

He shook his head. 'I always told myself that if I was tempted, then I'd think of my children's faces. I'd think of them staring at me at the bottom of the bed.'

'You think that works?'

'It's the only thing I can think of that *would* work.'

'I'll remember that.'

He put his hand on the stretched dome of her belly. 'You're not a prime candidate for an affair at the moment,' he said.

'What about you?'

'Oh well, I am, of course. I've read that there are several high danger points for a man. One is when his wife's pregnant. One is after the birth of the second child. Then, his entire forties aren't safe for all sorts of reasons, like boredom and insecurity about virility and fear of death. If he survives all that, then he often buggers off after all the children leave home.'

'That takes up the next twenty or thirty years,' said Edie, and they smiled at each other happily.

She thought of Alex as she left the funeral director's. It was a beautiful morning – one of those blue, breezy days when everything seems washed clean. He'd phoned her that morning. She heard the children in the background – Jess yelling something about a plastic horse free in one of the cereal boxes; Lewis asking Alex where his football boots were. Alex had made mashed banana sandwiches for their packed lunch, but Kit couldn't find his English folder and Jess had announced her school library book was due back that day, and did Edie know where it was? And what temperature should he put the washing-machine on at, because he'd done a wash last night and everything was blue.

'Everything else fine?' she asked.

'Absolutely.'

'The children all right?'

'Yup.'

'Kit?' She tried to sound casual.

'Quiet. He's missing you.'

'I miss him, them. You too.'

'Mmm.' There was the sound of something crashing. 'Oh bugger. I'll call you later.'

Edie walked slowly up the main shopping street. She dawdled outside the windows, looking at jewellery, candles, fishing rods. It occurred to her that it was the first time she'd been on her own like this since Lewis was born, nearly eleven years ago. It gave her a sense of slightly panicky liberation – as if she'd taken heavy boots off. She didn't want to have to think about Kit at school, missing her. Once, a few months ago, she had passed by the school playground on her way back from the surgery and had looked through the railings at where the children were gathered during their lunch hour. She had seen Jess on top of a slide, bellowing orders at a group of girls below her. Then Lewis, kicking a ball with his friends, his face red with furious concentration. Then Kit, standing at the far end of the yard – but she would know him from a mile off; the way his shoulders hunched, his shock of coppery hair. Just standing there by himself, a little figure in trousers that were too long for him. She had jerked away from the fence, as if there was electricity running through it. She didn't want him to see her witnessing his loneliness and shame. After that, she always went home the long way.

In the toyshop, she chose a panda with black eyes and a soft, pouchy body. She tried to imagine Ellen sitting with it in her arms, hugging it. She went back to Louise's house via the deli, where she bought a slice of Brie, a ludicrously expensive seafood salad, some artichoke hearts, coffee beans and pumpkin-filled ravioli. She picked up two bottles of white wine and a bottle of malt whisky at the off-licence and, at the bakery, a loaf of brown bread that was still steaming from the oven.

Stella was phoning people about the funeral when Edie returned. She was half-way through Louise's address book.

'It's weird,' she said when Edie came in. 'Like a site of archaeological interest. This is the same address book she had when we were young. It's held together with Sellotape. Some of the writing is Vic's. Look. It goes back about thirty years. Half the names are crossed out – does that mean they've moved, died, divorced, or that they've just lost touch?'

Edie peered over her shoulder. 'How do you know who to invite?'

'I'm calling all the people I know she still saw. She had quite a few friends round here, you know. I talked to them at the art shop when you were out, and I think they're all coming. They'll just close up for a couple of hours. They seemed very fond of her.'

'That's good. She liked it there.'

'And I think it was important leaving the house every morning and coming back in the evening. Can you imagine if she had moved here and not worked? She'd have gone mad. She was a very gregarious person.'

'Have you noticed?'

'What?'

'We're already talking about her in the past tense.'

'Are we? I suppose we are. Shall I invite Rose's parents do you think?'

'Alison and Simon? Did she still see them? They got divorced you know, years ago now.'

'I think she does. Did. I might as well ask them.'

'I haven't seen them since, oh, I don't know when.'

'How often do you see Rose?'

'Just a few times a year, usually when she's in London. She's just separated from her third husband.'

'Does she have children?'

'No. She wanted to but it never happened. Now, I guess it's too late.'

Edie knocked on Louise's neighbour's door and waited. After a few minutes she heard the sound of footsteps, and saw the shape of a figure through the glass. Then the door opened.

'Yes?' She was a stout, handsome woman, about Louise's age, with pewter-grey hair in even curls all over her head.

'Mrs Lovell? I'm Edie. Louise's daughter. I think we met once, years ago . . .'

'Edie? I didn't recognize you. I was going to come and see you myself, but I didn't want to intrude . . . Come in, please. Excuse the mess.'

Edie followed her into a spotless kitchen.

'I'm so sorry about your mother. What a terrible shock.'

'Yes. Thank you. We wanted to invite you to the funeral. It's on Monday.'

'Well, of course I'll come. We were neighbours for, let's see, thirteen years. Can I get you some tea?'

'Thanks, I'd love some. Did you see much of her?'

'Well, I *saw* her of course. But we didn't meet up so much. I look after my grandchildren a lot – and she worked of course. And . . .' She hesitated.

'Yes?'

'It's not for me to say . . .'

'Please tell me.'

'I don't want to speak ill of the dead . . .'

Edie waited. When people say they don't want to speak ill of the dead, it's a sure sign they're about to.

'Your mother was drinking a fair bit.'

'I never knew that,' said Edie cautiously.

'I like my drink in the evenings,' she continued. 'A glass of wine, maybe a sherry. But your mother – well, I've seen her drinking,' she lowered her voice as if someone might be listening, '*in the mornings.*'

'You mean – really in the mornings? Not just lunch-time?'

'Breakfast.'

'Oh God. I didn't know.'

'You can't blame yourself.' Mrs Lovell pursed her lips. 'But if you ask me, I think she was lonely, you know. Living all by herself and her children so far away. Not like me with my children.'

'We visited her,' said Edie. 'As much as we could. And she came and stayed.' But it sounded false.

'Mmm,' said Mrs Lovell dubiously. 'Sugar in your tea?'

'Granny. Ellen.'

They were in one of the small sitting-rooms at the home. The sun shone directly in through the large windows, and the radiators were still on. Ellen sat holding the panda against her chest, her chin between its ears. She smelt of urine and talcum powder. Her pink scalp showed through her hair. The sisters were grouped around her and Edie held one of her hands in her own; she noticed that her grandmother's nails needed cutting and there were new bruises spreading on her legs, above her swollen feet in their shabby pink slippers.

'When am I going home?' Ellen said. 'Today? I want to go home you know, Louise.'

'I'm not Louise,' said Stella, helplessly. Her eyes filled with tears. 'I'm Stella, your granddaughter.'

'I know who you are. I'm perfectly well now,' said Ellen. 'It's too hot here, and the old people keep making noises at night.'

'Granny,' said Edie. 'Granny, we want to tell you something.' She looked at Jude. After all, Jude had been the one who was so certain it was Ellen's right to know her daughter was dead. But Jude said nothing; her face was pale and expressionless. 'Louise had an accident,' said Edie at last. Her head ached in the stale, warm air. 'A car crash.'

'Car crash,' repeated Ellen softly.

'She died, Gran,' said Stella.

'Louise? Louise died?'

'Yes.'

'My Louise?'

'Your Louise.'

'No.'

'Granny.'

'No,' she said louder. She put her hand on Stella's knee. 'Won't you take me home?' She lifted the panda from her shoulder and looked at it with puzzlement. Then she let it drop on to the floor where it lay looking up at them with its beady black eyes.

'I'm not Louise, Granny. I'm Stella.'

'Stella. Stella.' Ellen said the word as if she was testing it against her tongue, but it was a flat battery. No tingle of recognition showed on her face.

'Louise is dead.' This from Jude, very quietly.

'She said she would take me home. Vic won't mind. He's a kind man when all is said and done, in spite of everything. I'll weed the garden for you, and your house could do with tidying, you know.'

'The funeral is on Monday,' said Edie.

Ellen turned and looked at her, then at Stella. She pursed her mouth shrewdly. 'I always said still waters run deep,' she said. 'I'm not blind, you know.'

'Granny . . .'

'I just want to go home.'

They sat at the garden table, eating Brie sandwiches. Jude was wearing dark glasses, so they couldn't see her expression. She had tied her hair up in one of Louise's old scarves, in preparation for the house-clearing they intended to do that afternoon.

'There are box-loads in the attic,' said Stella. 'I went and looked.'

'I thought she threw almost everything away when she came here,' said Edie, remembering the bonfire in the garden, Louise casting books and papers into the leaping flames.

'Not at all. There are all our old school reports, for a start. Picture books. Bags of clothes.'

'We should just hire a skip and load everything into it,' said Jude. 'Share out jewellery, the silver, the pictures, things like that, decide who should have what bits of furniture and things. Throw everything else out. We don't really want to take chipped plates away with us, do we, just because we remember eating Christmas cake off them when we were six? Or book markers and comb cases we made for her when we were in primary school? Bits of clay with the imprint of our hand in it. Those old school photos, me the one at the end of the row looking like a sack of flour.'

'We can't just throw things away!' said Edie, laying down her sandwich and staring across at Jude. 'Things like that are precious. Everything has a memory to it.'

'Exactly,' said Jude. 'Is that what you want – to sift through all your childhood?'

'Maybe,' said Edie. 'I don't know. But I'm not going to throw it all away. It would seem quite wrong.'

'I agree with Edie. Anyway, I have happy memories.'

'Of course you do,' said Jude. 'Count me out.'

'Come on, Jude. Do it with us,' said Edie.

Jude scowled at her.

'It's not ever going to be like this again,' said Stella. 'We'll leave here and go our separate ways and we'll see each other on and off over the years, but this won't happen again.'

Jude muttered something under her breath.

'What?'

'I said . . . Oh, never mind. Memories are dangerous things.'

'How can someone who's spent eight years in analysis say something like that?'

'That's why I can say it. I'm an expert. Never underestimate the usefulness of denial.'

18

'Do you remember this?' Holding up an ancient tartan blanket, dust falling from its tassels.

'Ah yes.'

Draped over the chairs in the living-room to make a tent, with dolls inside arranged in a circle. Picnics under the plum tree. The itch of the wool and the scratch of grass on bare legs. Sun falling through the latticed branches. Weak milky tea, the cups tipping on the bumpy ground. Chocolate éclairs and jam doughnuts. Those little fairy cakes that Stella made when she was a teenager, with a strawberry on top. Or stopping the car in a lay-by on the way to Wales, climbing through hedges and over fences to lay the blanket in a field, covering up the prickles and the nettles; Marmite rolls and peeled carrots; the moo of cows and buzz of mosquitoes. Or on a beach, sand in the crisps and biscuits, the slap of grey waves, Vic's sunburnt arms as he crouched over rock pools; Louise lying back, her shapely legs glistening with oil, her head tipped back, eyes closed.

'And look!'

'Those were in my bedroom.'

Old curtains, with rusting hooks on the gathered top. Blue-patterned, bleached by the sun and worn with age. Edie lifted a corner to her face and breathed in the moth-balls.

'And these were in mine.'

'God, it seems such a long time ago. I remember choosing them with Louise. At the same time as I got that knobbly yellow counterpane.'

The three of them sat in a circle in the living-room, drinking tea and eating brittle flapjacks that Mrs Lovell had brought round, shortly after Edie's visit. They had taken most of the junk down from the attic. Black bin-bags lay all around them, with their contents spilling through splits in the plastic. Old lamp-shades and deck-chairs were piled up by the door, with the tent that they used to put up in the garden, its bent pegs wrapped inside the groundsheet. It had always leaked, especially if you touched the walls. Edie remembered the sound the rain had made on its canvas at night; and the angry buzz of wasps that got caught in the netted ventilation on its ceiling in the day.

The sun shone in at the window, dust motes floating in its golden rays. Squashy bags full of clothes: Louise's party dresses from thirty years ago, folded carefully. A long black one with lace sleeves; one with zigzag patterns to hurt the eyes; a long, rustling chiffon skirt; something in pink, with silk lining. Those were from the days when Louise and Vic had dinner parties, and Louise would dress up in a way that seemed unimaginable to her daughters now: long dresses, dangling earrings, the good hour in front of her winged mirror; endless overlapping reflections of her face. Perfume, lipstick, hair spray that made Edie sneeze. There was nothing of Vic's, except two ties, coiled inside a small bag.

But they found a few of the clothes they'd worn as

children: a pair of post-box-red corduroy dungarees that Edie had forgotten till now, when it released a vivid flash of recall, a sense of almost being back there again, running into the garden in the rain. That beloved yellow party dress, with a wide netted skirt and a brown velvet trim. A pink suede coat with fake fur trimming that Stella pounced on with a yelp of childish delight. A jersey that Ellen had knitted in red and blue with a shiny little button on the neck. A tie-dye tee-shirt that Jude had made; they all remembered her stirring the plastic tub in the garden, slopping violet liquid over the patio stones. In another bag there was a pair of boots that must have fitted one of them when they had first learnt to walk. There were bibs, a bit stained, a lacy baby's shawl, a tiny white cardigan, a crocheted hat, along with old balding teddies, a doll with eyes that clicked open fiercely when she was upright, a topsy-turvy doll, with a second head hidden under her skirt.

Edie shook out a long rust-coloured dress with a low neckline. A dress she had worn only once, and then put away. She gazed at it for a moment, allowing herself to remember. Then she folded it up and put it back in the bottom of the bag.

'She kept all my shells,' Stella said in a voice that sounded like a moan. 'The ones I used to collect.' Dull, broken razor-shells, spiralled shells that you hold to your ear to hear the sound of the sea, tiny pink shells, like a painted fingernail, that Stella used to stick on to boxes, cowrie shells ... 'I never knew she'd kept all these things.'

She had also kept Edie's glass ornaments, individually

wrapped in tissue paper and placed in a small cardboard box, even the elephant with the broken trunk. And Jude's book of pressed flowers, done when she was about eight, speedwell and celandines and forget-me-nots. Fragments of petals fell to the floor like grains of sand. All the Dr Seuss books, and various anthologies of children's poems, with childish scribbles on some of the pages. There were the school reports, and in the same box they found their old exercise books and sheets of school work, going back to when they were tiny. Stella unrolled a self-portrait that Jude had done when she was three or so, with the legs coming out of the chin, and the eyes huge and lopsided at the very top of the head. The thickly applied green and yellow poster paint was flaking away.

'Just like me,' said Jude sarcastically, but even she was drawn into the nostalgic circle.

'Look,' said Stella.

'Oh no, photos,' said Jude. 'Now we've really had it. We'll never leave here. We'll stay here until we're old, remembering when we were young.'

The photos were in a series of shoe-boxes. Vic must have been behind the camera in most of them, but there were all the rest of them: the three girls and Louise, growing up and getting older. Black-and-white gave way to colour. Them as babies, as little girls, as teenagers. Louise with back-combed hair and skirts with cinched waists, Louise in a bathing suit, crouched on a rock. So many of Louise, as if Vic couldn't stop looking at her, even when he was looking at her through the lens. And she smiled at him, knowing she was beautiful. The sisters thumbed through the glossy images: posing, grinning, glancing up in surprise, looking away, blurred, bleached out, obscured by an errant thumb, caught unawares.

'We all look so happy,' said Stella.

'Well, that's the thing with family pictures,' said Jude. 'Everyone's always smiling in them. You don't find many albums where people are crying, do you? You've got to be jolly when you pose for memories. Anyway, I don't think I look very happy, do you?'

'Here are Rose Scott's parents,' said Stella, picking up an over-exposed shot of Louise with her arms around Alison and Simon. 'I remember that day. They came and had a barbecue.'

'Yes,' said Jude. 'And Dad burnt the meat and Louise shouted at him. See? That's the real story behind the photo.'

'And here's one of Daddy,' said Edie. 'This must have been shortly before . . .'

He was smiling, that puzzled smile of his, and his black hair hung down over one eye. His hand was half-raised, as if he was about to wave, or put his hand in front of his face. He was looking straight at them.

'I think it's time to open a bottle of wine,' said Jude, standing up abruptly.

'It's not six yet.'

'So? I'll give you special dispensation, Stella. After your mother dies, you're allowed to drink at any time of the day or night for, what? Ten days. OK?'

'OK.'

Jude disappeared off to the kitchen and reappeared a few moments later, carrying a tray.

'Here,' she said, pouring wine into three glasses.

'I bought some cigarettes as well,' said Edie, surprising herself. She'd thought she was going to smoke them in secret, in some inadequate return to her teenage days. 'Who wants one?'

'Why not?' said Stella. She took one and put it defiantly in her mouth. 'Bob would kill me.'

'I used to smoke roll-ups,' said Jude. 'That's one of my abiding memories of being here, when you lot had gone and left, and it was just me and Mum. Sneaking out and making roll-ups; the way the end would catch fire when you lit it, and the way flakes of tobacco stuck to your lips. God, it's been years.' She inhaled deeply and grinned. 'Then of course I stopped sneaking out and smoked in front of Mum, just to annoy her. This patient, sad look would come over her face, and she'd get up and open a window wide.'

Stella started coughing. 'I never smoked,' she said.

'I only smoked roll-ups,' continued Jude. 'Because he did.' She lifted up her glass, looked at Edie defiantly, then drank. Her hair was coming unloose and curling round her hollowed cheeks.

'Who?'

'You know. Ricky.'

'Oh,' said Edie faintly. She felt a bit dizzy. She knocked ash into a saucer and took a sip of white wine.

'I completely adored him. Head over heels.'

'I didn't know,' said Edie, wondering if this was the truth.

'God, I was hit hard. I don't think I've ever felt anything like it since. Not even with Euan. Or Robbie.

Or poor Derek. Sad, isn't it? I was a fat fifteen-year-old and he was besotted with my older sister, and yet I couldn't think of anything else. I couldn't sleep for thinking about him, and when I did, the dreams I used to have.' She gave a laugh. 'First love is agony, isn't it? When we get older, we forget what it's like when you're young.'

'You played chess with him. And discussed *Lord of the Rings*. I remember.'

'I've still got that chess set. It was almost like a sacred object to me. I would have done anything, you know, no hesitation,' said Jude. 'Anything to get him away from you. But he never even looked at me. Why am I telling you all this now?'

'You poor thing,' said Stella softly. She was still mussing through the photographs that lay scattered on the carpet. Faces shuffled before their eyes.

'He liked you,' said Edie. She looked out of the window at the sun on the neat lawn: the photographs, the wine and cigarettes, and now this. The tips of their cigarettes brightened and faded with each puff.

'That almost made it worse. I wrote to him, you know. After we left and you wouldn't see him.'

'Did he reply?' This from Stella. Edie didn't really want to know. She didn't want to see him standing at the end of the lane, waiting for her, with a hopeful look on his face.

'I told him I would always be there for him. Like the Carole King song. I said even in ten, twenty years, I'd be there for him. I thought you were so unbelievably stupid and hard-hearted,' she said. 'I had contempt for you. No, he never replied.'

'I don't really want . . .'

'Of course, I understood as well, later at least. Sex and death: they must have tangled up in your head.'

'Yes,' said Edie. She stubbed out her cigarette. 'They did.' She noticed with surprise that she'd finished her wine. 'I couldn't look at him or even think about him without feeling sick.'

'His letters are still here,' said Stella. 'There's a box of your stuff still in the attic that we haven't brought down yet, and I saw them. Just one,' she added hastily. 'I didn't read them.'

'It doesn't matter now,' said Edie. 'It was such a long time ago. I wasn't even seventeen, you know.' She made up her mind. 'The thing is,' she said. 'I sometimes think if it hadn't been for me and Ricky, Vic wouldn't have killed himself.'

'That's just ridiculous,' said Stella warmly.

'Not to say narcissistic,' added Jude.

'Maybe.'

'What makes you think that?'

'I wasn't particularly nice to him,' began Edie. 'I was cruel. Just before . . .'

She closed her eyes and remembered. Ricky's head heavy against her breasts, and Vic staring at her through the opened door. His hang-dog face. She could almost hear her spiteful voice. '*Vic*,' she had said, like someone spitting venom.

'So you've been going around for the last twenty-two years thinking you were to blame, just because you weren't nice to him.'

'Not exactly. I just can't forget how he looked so very

hurt.' As if she'd slapped him, she thought; a stinging blow across his face. 'I'll always remember. And then the next day . . .'

'He always looked hurt,' said Stella. 'Even when he was playing Monopoly.'

'How many times a day are your children rude or unkind to you?' asked Jude. 'You don't kill yourself, do you?'

'It's not the same . . .'

'He'd lost his job. He was depressed. Those are real reasons,' insisted Stella.

'What strikes me is how powerful you must think yourself,' said Jude, 'if you believe that a brief argument with your father – who had two other daughters, remember – could be so murderous.' She sounded so angry that Edie held up her hands.

'You're probably quite right, and I'm being stupid and egotistic, but didn't either of you ever think like that?'

'I thought I shouldn't have left home,' said Stella. 'For a long time, I thought if I had stayed, it wouldn't have happened.'

'Well, of course we all thought things like that. It was suicide, after all: that's what happens. Guilt crashes in.' Jude's voice was still tight with anger. 'For instance, what if I hadn't been fat and unhappy, the cuckoo in the nest? You should grow out of thoughts like that, Edie. Cause and effect isn't that childishly simple.'

'Well,' said Edie, stung, 'are you saying you don't think like that sometimes, or are you so very rational? You became anorexic, didn't you? You starved yourself nearly to death. That must have been connected.'

'Of course it was bloody connected. I'm like a text-book case.'

'So . . .'

'I'm just saying that you can't go around thinking Vic wouldn't have killed himself if you'd behaved differently. Anyway, isn't this all topsy-turvy?'

'How do you mean?'

'Usually children feel that they're the products of their parents' fuck-ups, not the other way round.'

'I don't feel either of those things,' said Stella. She had taken off her sandals and the evening sunlight was in her hair and on her skin, giving her a softness, like a bloom.

'I'm going to phone home,' said Edie, standing up. She needed to hear Alex's voice, the bicker and clatter of children in the background – a reminder of the normal life to which she would soon return.

19

They ate outside that evening. Edie had made a cold watercress soup, and Stella a spinach and feta pie. Everyone was quiet. Afterwards, although it was still dusk and the house was filled with the baked warmth of the day, they each went to their separate rooms.

Edie stood in Louise's bedroom. She wasn't tired. Indeed, she felt alert and restless. Sleep seemed to be receding as night drew in. She didn't want to read, or have a bath, or watch the small TV in the corner of the room. She stood for a moment by the window and looked out at the tidy garden. She picked up the wedding photograph and stared at it. She opened the wardrobe but closed it again; they would sort Louise's clothes tomorrow. Then she sat on the bed and plugged her laptop into the phone connection beside the bed to check her e-mail.

Darling Edie. I've just spoken to you and so I've got no news. I just wanted to say good night to you. Alex.
PS Do you have any idea where Lewis's calculator might be? And Kit's asthma seems to have come back. Any idea where you put that old inhaler?

Mummy. I miss you lots. Today I was wishing a lot I was someone else, but it is hard to think about that. It makes your head feel like a bomb.

Edie unplugged her computer and put it on the floor, next to the TV. She went and ran herself a full bath, pouring a generous splash of Louise's lavender oil under the taps. She lay in the scalding water for twenty minutes while the air filled with steam and the mirror misted over. Then she put on her dressing-gown and went into the hall. Both Jude's and Stella's doors were closed. She fetched the torch from the kitchen and then went up the stairs to the landing and as quietly as she could, pulled down the attic ladder. She climbed the rungs and shone the torch into the darkness. There were several boxes at the end, under the beams with the rolled-up foam mattresses and the Christmas decorations, that they hadn't yet looked through. She shone the beam into them. In one were Jude's animal magazines and posters, and several board games with battered covers. In another, records, both LPs and singles. Many of them were out of their sleeves and were scratched. And then there was a box half-filled with things that used to belong to Edie. She bent down and saw letters, post-cards, birthday cards, even Christmas cards, as well as swimming certificates and old school folders with the subject on the top in her writing.

And there was the small wooden box. She opened the lid and the smell of lavender filled her nostrils, from the muslin bag she'd placed there so long ago. There was something else: the crumbled remains of a yellow leaf. Stupid, to remember so clearly.

She picked up the box and carried it down to Louise's room, pushing the ladder back in place, and shutting the bedroom door with a faint click behind her. She dusted off her gritty feet and climbed under the duvet, with the box beside her.

She glanced through the postcards first, just to steady herself. Some were from people whom she no longer remembered. Who were Annette and Elaine? The Christmas cards she would throw away without even looking at them; the birthday cards too. She had no idea why she had ever kept them. The letters looked more interesting. She picked out an envelope at random; the letter inside was from a girl called Carol who'd been her friend at junior school and then, when she was ten, gone to live in America. For several years, she and Edie had managed to stay in touch, but the gap between letters had grown larger, the letters themselves shorter, and at last they'd dwindled away. There was a letter from Vic, she saw, with his spidery handwriting across a creased white envelope. He had sent it to her when she was fourteen and staying in France on an exchange the school had arranged, miserably tongue-tied and home-sick. It was a brief, reticent note: he'd told her about Jude's swollen glands, Louise working hard at the shop, a house he'd sold that day, the unusual number of butterflies in the garden. He ended by saying they were all looking forward to seeing her and signed himself 'Daddy', with a single crooked kiss.

Edie laid aside the letter. She turned to the box that smelt of lavender. On the top of the pile was a postcard whose picture – a black-and-white photograph of a man in a doorway – made her gulp with memory. And the handwriting when she turned it over, the spiked letters and the sharply looped 'y'; the flamboyant 'R' of his name.

She picked up another letter and saw it was the last one that he'd written to her before she left, in which he'd told her how lonely he was without her. She remembered the letter; she remembered all of them. And she remembered how she'd felt, reading them, re-reading them. Some she had put under her pillow at night, or carried around with her. Even the polite first letter, when he'd simply given her his address and signed himself, 'Love' – even that null little note she had pored over, traced his name with her finger.

In one note, he had written, '*I see you in my dreams.*' That was from a song, although she hadn't known it at the time. Maybe he'd quoted lots of songs to her, and she had thought they were his own words. He'd once said to her: 'I'd follow you anywhere, even through solid air.' She'd laughed at him; it didn't make sense. And then, years later, sitting in a car with a colleague on the way to a conference, she had heard the same words in a song on the radio and it was as if everything around her had receded into the distance and all that was present was the past; his warm breath in her ear, the feeling of being young and in love and the future bright before her. Jude was right, she told herself; there's nothing to match the longed-for agony of first love. She had had dreams about Ricky for twenty-two years.

Edie shut the lid sharply and pushed the box away from her. She thought about the children, who would all be asleep now, each in their own dark forest of sleep. She filled her mind up with their solemn, closed faces. She thought of Alex, guarding them for her while she was away. Then she riffled, without much curiosity, through the rest of the letters in the box, taking them out at random. A party invitation. A thank-you note. A Valentine card. Several letters from Rose. Probably she would throw them all away. There was a single white page without an envelope, whose writing she didn't recognize, and she picked it up. '*My Darling*,' she read. '*I've got to see you. I'm going mad without you here. Please ring me.*'

She read the note twice. It wasn't signed, but she was quite sure no one had ever written it to her. Maybe it was to Stella, and had got into the wrong box. Or Jude, though that seemed unlikely. Or maybe it was to Louise and had been sent to her by some admirer of her widowed years, somehow ending up in the wrong box in the attic. But the letter filled Edie with anxiety.

There was a date on it. Tuesday, 16 September, written in an abbreviated scrawl, but no year, so that didn't help. She laid it back in the box, then put the box on the floor beside her. She turned off the light and closed her eyes, and another memory came to her unbidden. The morning the first letter from Ricky had arrived, when Vic had driven his car into the milk float. She had walked over to the gawping postman and taken the letters out of his hand. There'd been bills for Vic; something for Stella, she thought; and a letter for Louise. Yes, and the writing was like this writing, she was sure, a bold blue careless scrawl. The memory is very mysterious, she thought. It stores away things that even at the time you didn't know you had noticed.

She turned the light back on and looked through Ricky's letters again, until she came to that first one. But there was no date on it, and the postmark on the envelope was illegible. All she knew was that it had been sent to her in the middle of September, in 1980. She rubbed her eyes. She was probably making wrong connections, joining up dots that should be kept far apart, making a picture where there was none.

It occurred to her that her electronic diary might show her old years and she got out of bed once more, went into the hall where her bag was stashed under the table, and took it up to the bedroom. And, pressing the leadless pencil against the miniature screen and clicking back two decades, she discovered that 16 September fell on a Tuesday in 1997, 1986 and 1980.

Edie was sure now. Actually, she had been sure before. As soon as she had read the letter, it was as if a light had come on in her mind. Things that had lain in shadows and dark corners sprang illuminated into view. Louise in the pub, on the night of the party, laying her hand over Simon's, leaning forward to puff on his cigarette; Louise in their garden in a summer dress, laughing with Simon, while the smell of meat burning on the barbecue filled the air. She lay back in bed in the dark and put one hand on her heart.

'Oh God,' she said out loud. 'Oh, poor things.'

20

At half past six the next morning, when Stella and Jude were still sound asleep and the leaves and window panes sparkled with dew, Edie left a note on the kitchen table saying she'd gone out to do a few errands, but she'd be back before long. She made herself a cup of strong coffee and drank it in the garden, the dew seeping in through her sandals. Then she got into the car and drove away as quietly as she could.

It was less than an hour's drive, but she had never been back to Baylham. Louise had returned there. Stella had gone back several times in the first few years, visiting old schoolfriends. And even Jude had told her how once, driving home from a conference, she had suddenly found herself on the newly built bypass that ran just above the town. On an impulse, she had turned off and driven along the main street, past their old school, then over the bridge and up the lane to their house. But she hadn't stopped, she'd just gone straight by, craning her neck to see the chimney-pots and the red roof-tiles. But Edie had always avoided it, and even the countryside around it, as if in her mind she had drawn a great circle around the area and hung a no entry sign on it.

Just before she arrived, she pulled over into a lay-by and phoned home on her mobile. Alex was distracted.

Lewis had just announced he hadn't done his homework; Kit said he felt ill and wouldn't get out of bed; Jess was crying because everyone else was shouting and no one was listening to her. And he hadn't prepared his lessons. And needed to get to work on time, for once.

'I'm sorry,' said Edie, but coolly. She meant, I won't feel guilty, I'm here because my mother's just died; and she also meant, now you know what it's like for me every morning of my life.

At first, Edie was struck by the unfamiliarity of the town, after more than twenty years' absence. It had extended in every direction. There was a new housing estate as she turned off the bypass, where there had once been fields. Shops had sprung up around it. Whole areas had been cleared to make way for roundabouts and a dual carriageway into the town centre. There were half-completed office blocks ahead of her, with empty windows and concrete beams. But then, gradually, old landmarks appeared. The row of Victorian houses near the station; the church, stained almost black by age and pollution; the stationery shop where they used to get their ink cartridges and ruled paper; the pet shop where they'd bought cat food once a week.

It was all one-way systems now, though, and it took several false turns to find the road that led past their school. She stopped the car for a moment, letting the engine idle. The giant chestnut tree still stood outside the grey 1930s building that Louise used to say looked like an Eastern bloc interrogation centre. But there were new red-brick buildings to one side now, with large windows. As she sat in her car, a coach drew up behind her and children spilt off it, carrying rucksacks, musical instruments, sports bags. They passed her in groups and singly, chattering and jostling each other.

She watched them as they disappeared behind the building, where other children were gathering. The girls seemed more orderly; they talked to each other, laughed. Their hair was tied back in plaits and smooth pony-tails. But the boys ran and slouched, pushed against each other. Some of them seemed huge, others tiny. One of them shoved another so that he stumbled backwards, dropping his bag. Books and pieces of paper scattered over the tarmac; the wind lifted a sheet and blew it a few paces away from where the boy stood. People were sniggering round him, hands shoved in pockets, and Edie saw his face. He was trying to pretend he didn't care, but the way he was blinking too rapidly gave him away. He fooled no one. She thought of Kit, miles away: he'd be just going into school himself now, a last glance back over his shoulder at Alex.

She drove on and found herself by the swimming-pool. From the outside it looked just the same – but perhaps inside it had been turned into a leisure centre. No more cramped cubicles, and plasters bobbing along on the turquoise tiles at the bottom, and swimmers doing lengths, with the broken clock on the grimy wall and the fluorescent strip-light blinking.

But she was near now, and the closer she got the more familiar everything seemed, as if the years were peeling away, like bark from a twig, until at last it's white and sappy and new again. Past the library where Jude had gone every Saturday morning, taking out six books to last her through the week, and reading a seventh on the spot; past the bakery where they bought Chelsea buns for Sunday breakfasts; the second-hand clothes shop; the triangle of green where winos sat among the flowers in the evening, with their bottles of cider. Now the houses and shops were petering out. A field full of cows; an ancient oak tree with a hollow chamber in its trunk; a small nursery where they sold bedding plants and climbing roses. A lane to the left, leading up a hill away from town.

She pulled over and parked the car. Her mobile phone started ringing, but she switched it off and put it into the glove compartment. She put on her dark glasses, climbed out of the car and started walking up the lane. There was a small avenue of beeches and the sun shone down through their new leaves, dappling the ground beneath her feet. They used to bike down this road with a picnic in their panniers. Stella could bike without any hands – Edie remembered her sitting upright, her legs pumping steadily up and down, her arms held straight out away from her body, as if she was flying, her apricot hair streaming behind her. They'd never worn helmets in those days.

Here was the chestnut tree, shading the road, light rippling in its leaves. She stopped for a moment and took off her dark glasses. Her throat was hurting and there was a heaviness behind her eyes. Her sinuses ached. She walked on, round the corner, waiting for her first sight. But when it came it was oddly anti-climactic. The house was smaller and squarer than she had remembered, less rambling and mysteriously ramshackle. It had been painted white, the door blue, and there was a new conservatory against the side, glinting in the sunlight, with smart wicker chairs and a glass table in it. She stood and gazed at it. Everything looked so neat: the pale pea shingle on the drive; the terracotta pots on either side of the front door, the expertly trimmed hedge running along the side of the house. There was no car outside, but that didn't mean no one was in. She hesitated, then drew nearer, until she was standing outside the window of the living-room.

She pressed her face to the window and squinted through the glass. There was no longer a scuffed green carpet, but sanded boards, with a rug thrown over them. The walls were painted yellow and there was a mustard-yellow sofa against the wall, under two framed botanical prints. Everything looked very tidy. Edie wondered if any children lived here.

With some nervousness, she went to the front door and rang the bell, hearing it chime its three-note melody in the hall. She waited a few moments, then peered in through the letter-box, but saw only a strip of floorboard and the first step of the stairs. No one was in, but she wasn't ready to leave just yet. She glanced around to make sure nobody was looking, then walked swiftly down the path that ran round the side of the house, past the new conservatory. Her feet scrunched loudly on the gravel.

But what was this? As she came through a wrought-iron gate that looked charmingly old but hadn't been there in her day, she stopped in her tracks. Nothing was as she remembered. Even the shape of the garden, now marked out by a tall wooden fence, seemed different. The wavy lines had all gone, the sense of wilder nature surging in from outside, defeating all Vic's sweaty attempts at order. They'd put a path through the length of the garden, with an arched trellis of wisteria. There was a small ornamental pond, where Edie could see the golden glint of fish among the lily pads. Outside the kitchen, several pots of herbs, and a large table with a tall, folded sunshade stood in the middle of a wide area of paved stones. A miniature bike with stabilizers leant against the wall under the kitchen window, and at the other side, where the thick bushes used to be a place to hide, was a carousel washing-line with several baby-gros hanging from it.

In a daze, Edie went up the garden path. All she could see was what wasn't there. The old shed had gone and in its place was a gleaming all-in-one swing, slide and climbing-frame. No old swing with fraying rope and mossy seat. No disintegrating wall, so no climbing roses with thick branches, sharp thorns, blowsy flowers. No ancient lilac trees, with their cool shadows. No beds overrun by mint and the horseradish she used to grate when they had roast beef; her shaved knuckles and stinging eyes.

And no plum tree. An irrational anger crackled through her. She stepped off the path and on to the grass, still wet with dew. Nobody would even know that it had been here. The grass had grown over the place where it had stood, dropping its plump fruit to the ground. She thought of Vic with his outstretched hands full of plums. She stood on the spot where Ricky had pressed her up against its trunk and kissed her, where Vic's ashes had been scattered.

Or maybe it hadn't been exactly here. She could no longer remember. Everything shifted and slid in her mind. Memories that had been clear and bright were queasy and uncertain. The well-tended, sunlit garden took on a nightmarish quality. She pressed her fingers to her temples, trying to clear her thoughts. Images of the past slid over the landscape, so that she was seeing double. Barbecues in the garden, and Louise in a thin dress with her hair falling round her face and her golden skin, laughing, face open like a flower. Louise laying her arm on Vic's shoulder and bending down towards him, and his face looking blindly up at her. The sloping words on grainy paper – *I've got to see you. I'm going mad without you here.* Vic's silence, deepening through the house. Vic's face when he had watched her through her bedroom door and she had spat out his name.

Vic had lost his job and he had lost his wife to someone else. His eldest daughter had left home and his middle one – the one who had always been biddable and sweet to him – had turned on him. His youngest daughter stuffed herself with junk food in the dark. And the trees were bare, the wind sharp, the light drab. Winter was coming. So he'd walked up the arched bridge and jumped off, because he didn't know what else to do.

Edie stumbled to the path but her limbs felt impossibly heavy and were trembling. She made it to the bench

185

on the paved area and collapsed on to it. She put a hand up to her face and found her cheeks were wet. She put her head in her hands and at last she let herself cry until she was snotty and puffy and her skin stung, her throat felt raw. Her sobs came out in spasms and her whole body shook. She couldn't stop, except to catch breath. There was a groan and she realized it came from her. She put her face on the table and felt the rough grain of wood against her cheek. Then a shadow fell across her vision.

'What on earth . . . ?'

Edie looked up, still weeping uncontrollably. She made out the blurred shape of a woman with a buggy by her side. Young, surprised, a bit scared.

'I'm so very sorry,' she said between sobs. 'I'm so sorry.'

'Who are you?' The woman's voice was sharp with fear, and she put a hand instinctively on the baby's buggy, as if to protect it.

'You must think I'm mad.'

'What are you doing in our garden?'

'I used to live here. I just wanted to see . . .' Edie couldn't finish.

'I don't understand.'

The woman took a step forward. Edie pushed her hair behind her ears and wiped her face with her hands, but the tears kept sliding down her cheeks in sheets, and her breath came in hiccups. She pictured how she must look: a red-eyed, swollen-faced, middle-aged woman, crying like a three-year-old.

'I'll wake your baby,' she said at last.

'Who are you?' the woman said again.

'My name's Edie Jennings. Doctor Jennings,' she added ludicrously, as if her title would give her respectability, make her seem less mad.

'And you say you lived here?'

'Twenty-two years ago. Oh, sorry. Sorry. I don't know how to stop crying.'

'Here.' The woman stepped forward and handed her a wodge of tissues.

'Thanks.' Edie mopped her cheeks and blew her nose loudly. 'It's all changed. Even the plum tree.' More sobs gathered in her throat. She pressed the sodden tissues against her eyes.

'Do you want something? A glass of water, or tea or something?'

'Maybe some water.'

The woman hesitated a moment, then said, 'Look, why don't you come inside? Wash your face, calm down a bit.'

'Got to go,' said Edie, struggling to her feet. The world swam around her.

'You can't go anywhere like this,' the woman pointed out. 'Come on.' She smiled suddenly. 'Then you can snoop round the house as well.'

There was a downstairs toilet where the tall cupboard had been. Edie splashed cold water over her face, then leant forward to stare at herself. She touched the crêpey skin under her eyes and grimaced. Her skin was blotchy with tears. She looked scraggy and old. Careworn, that was the word.

'I made us tea,' said the woman when she came out. 'I'm Caroline, by the way. Caroline Revel. And this,' she pointed at the baby asleep in the buggy, 'is Angela.'

'You're reacting very well, I must say. I don't usually behave like this.'

'It was a bit of a shock at first, that's all. How long did you live here?'

'All my childhood. Well, almost.'

'It must have changed a lot then?'

'Yes,' said Edie, looking around the kitchen, which had been opened up to include the poky old scullery. Gleaming pans hung in rows above a huge oven. The work surfaces were clear. Seeing her gaze, Caroline wiped an imaginary crumb off the table. 'Lots.' She took a sip of tea.

'We've been here seven years now. Do you want to see the rest of the house then?'

'Oh, I don't think . . .'

'Go on. Now you're here.'

'Do I even want to?'

'Well, do as you please.' Caroline seemed almost offended.

'Just a quick peep then.'

Edie stood up. She felt frail and sad and very tired. The stairs seemed steeper than she had remembered. She hesitated on the landing, then went to the door of her bedroom. She pushed it open and stood on the threshold. It was painted sky-blue, with stencilled clouds on the ceiling, and blue-and-white curtains. A young child's room. The duvet had fish all over it. She went over to the window and looked out at the garden.

Nothing was the same. Every crack had been plastered and papered; every view had been rearranged.

'Thanks for the tea and tissues.'

'That's all right.' Caroline seemed to be waiting for something else.

'You've done the house very nicely,' Edie managed.

'Well, we like it. It was very run-down when we bought it. Down-at-heel, you could say.'

'Yes,' said Edie. She just wanted to be gone.

Edie had three messages on her mobile. One was from Alex, saying he was sorry he'd snapped when she'd called before. One was from Jude: she and Stella were going out to make last-minute arrangements for the funeral, and had she forgotten the estate agent was going to come round later? And one was from Rose, saying she was so sorry to have heard about Louise from her mother. And she was going to stay with her mother in Birmingham at the weekend, so was hoping she could come to the funeral with her on Monday. Maybe they could even meet before that. Edie switched the mobile off, put on her dark glasses and drove the car slowly back towards the river, and a pay-and-display car park that hadn't been there before.

She sat in the car for a moment, closing her eyes in the warmth. She felt as if her body had suddenly lost any resilience. Her hands trembled, her eyes throbbed, there were butterflies in her stomach. Apprehension dried her mouth. She was about to do something stupid.

She got out of the car at last, paid her £2 for a ticket to stick to the window, and then made her way down the stone steps on to the river bank. Although it was not yet ten in the morning, there were already lots of people, brought out by the soft warmth and the cloudless sky. They wore bright dresses, cotton shirts open at the neck, sandals, even brimmed hats against the glare, and they walked with a spring in their step. On the river, there were canoes and little rowing-boats, and a group of brutal swans harassing the mallard ducks. Mothers handed their small children crusts of bread to toss into the water.

Edie walked along the path, and very quickly the crowds thinned out, so that there was no one in sight ahead of her except for the receding figure of a jogger and his dog. Here, everything was familiar. The river was the same as it always had been: brown and swollen, carrying half-submerged objects. She paused for a moment and stood looking at its murky flow, listening to the a-rhythmic slap of its ripples against the bank.

There was a bench just behind her and as she was about to sit down on it, she read the inscription, and as she read it remembered it from all those years ago: 'In memory of beloved Gareth, 1949–1970, who fears no more the heat of the sun'. The tears that she had been holding back since leaving the house started again. She made no effort to wipe her face. This time the warm flood of tears was oddly soothing. She knew she was not just crying for Vic, or Louise, but also for Ellen sitting in a clean square room dreaming of home; for Alex and his eagerness and trust; for Ricky with his cheap clothes and bad haircut and young romantic soul; for herself, the girl she had been then, and the woman she had become; for her children, who would have to go through all these things in their time.

A couple of hundred yards further on, the river curved to the east and she saw the bridge. It took her fifteen more minutes to reach it, for she was walking slowly, and then she left the river bank and scrambled back on to the road. Here, Vic had parked his car, leaving his keys tucked safely under the flap of the passenger mirror. She took a breath, and began walking up the bridge. It had a waist-high barrier, and then there were spiked railings. There was a warning sign to parents not to let their children climb up. She didn't know, of course, but she had always imagined that Vic had jumped from the highest point, into the deepest part of the river, where the current was strongest. She pressed her face to the railings and even though she knew she was in no danger, the drop made her shiver and step back a few inches.

It wouldn't have been easy to climb up and over. He would have had to put the tip of his foot on the barrier, pull himself up, holding on to the railings, and then clamber over the spikes somehow, the way one climbs over a barbed-wire fence. At each point, he would have to have made a particular effort – right until he was perched on the wrong side of the barrier. Then the hard thing would have been to return, the simplest thing to let go and fall.

She seized the railings in both hands, and stretched her right foot up against the barrier. She pulled herself up, her arms aching with the effort. Now the upper barrier reached only to her hips. If she leant forward, the water was right beneath her. A bit of uprooted tree bobbed along in its path, its branches like arms reaching up. Up here, the wind licked Edie's face and her hair blew across her eyes, half-blinding her. From this point it would be simple enough, she could see now, to climb over. Just stand on tiptoe and scissor her legs over –

and of course, Vic had been taller than her. She lifted a leg, just to test it. Now she was straddling the railings. If she looked down, her stomach lurched and her head swam and fear flooded every cranny of her body. But if she looked up, past the bridge's struts which seemed to be forever tilting towards her, up at the soft, inhuman sky with that faint mackerel cloud on the horizon, she no longer felt afraid. Even her sadness was painless. Perhaps this is what Vic had finally felt, here in the wind, with the sky around him and the world far below, people shrunk to matchbox size, the brown river wrinkling, and all the hopeless tangles of his life irrelevant. Unafraid.

'Jesus! Jesus, don't do it. Lady, stop now.'

Edie looked back, bewildered. A tall man with a brick-red face and hair like a shock of dry straw seized hold of her road-side leg in both his big hands.

'I'm not going to let you,' he said. 'No way.' He was wearing a thick tweed coat in spite of the balmy weather and it billowed behind him.

'It's all right. I'm not going to jump. I just wanted to see what it was like.'

'Just step back over. Step back over, darling. Easy does it. I'll keep hold of you. There, there. Now jump down, I'll catch you.'

'I can manage perfectly well. I wasn't going to do anything stupid, you know.'

She half-jumped off the barrier, stumbling as she landed, and he caught her in his arms. She caught a thick reek of alcohol and cigarettes and stale sweat.

'Got you!' he said. 'Sweet Jesus! Never mind you, you nearly gave me a heart attack.'

'You misunderstood,' said Edie. 'I was never . . .'

'Don't cry, you're all right now, I saved you, darling.'

'I'm not crying.' But she put her hand up to her cheek and found that she still was, after all.

'Come on,' he said, and started tugging her arm. 'We've got to get you off the bridge.'

'I'm all right,' she insisted. 'My car's parked up the river.'

'I'll walk with you.'

'Don't worry.'

'"Don't worry," she says.' He gave a chesty laugh. 'I just saved your life, and you say not to worry. It's not every day you save a life.' He glared at her suspiciously. 'You'll not try again, will you now?'

'But I . . .' She gave up. 'Thank you,' she said meekly. 'No. I'm quite all right now.'

He insisted on walking her back to the car. She tried to give him some money, but he wouldn't hear of it. 'No, no, it wouldn't be right,' he said. 'Not for saving a life. Maybe I'll have good luck from it.' But he took the half-packet of cigarettes and pushed it into his coat pocket.

'Was it a man?' he said, as she put the key in the ignition and reached out to shut the door.

'A man?'

'That made you want to end it.'

'Oh, that.' She looked at him, his caved-in chest and the unnatural red of his face; his grubby clothes. 'Kind of,' she said.

And he nodded, as if satisfied. 'I thought so,' he said. 'Love.'

*

194

Even then, Edie didn't go straight back, although until she turned right on to the bypass rather than left, she had thought she was going to. Instead, she drove to a small corridor town called Kelsey, and although she'd only been there once in her life, she found Beckett Road immediately. Some of the council flats had been knocked down, but this estate remained. She didn't give herself time to think. She got out of the car and knocked at the door of number 19. Of course she knew it was absurd; they would have moved years ago. So even when a meagre woman with the lined face of a smoker stood in the doorway, looking at her inquiringly, she didn't allow herself to think of what she was doing.

'Yes?'

'Sorry to disturb you. I was looking for Mrs Penrose.'

'Yes?'

'I mean – are *you* Mrs Penrose?'

'Yes.'

'Ricky's mother.'

'That's right. Do I know you?'

And only then did the fact of what she was doing overwhelm Edie. She felt her face burn like a sixteen-year-old's.

'I – I –' she stammered.

'Who are you?'

'I used to know Ricky,' Edie said at last, in a croak. All she wanted was to be gone from here. 'A long time ago. And I was in the area, and I suddenly thought, well, I thought I'd call on the off-chance.'

'He doesn't live here, you know. Not for years and years and years.'

'No, I suppose not. Look, I'd better go.'

'What's your name?'

'Edie Jennings. Doctor,' she added, realizing as soon as she did so that it made her sound even madder. 'My mother died,' she said foolishly, feeling tears start to well up in her eyes again. 'That's why I came back here. I was staying in her house in Shrimpley, not so far from here you know, just forty minutes' drive really, and – oh well, all the memories, suddenly . . . you know how it is.'

Ricky's mother looked at her through narrowed eyes. She had dark grey hair scraped back in a bun, and was wearing slippers. Her hands were red and chapped, and her nails were bitten to the quick; there were discontented lines around her mouth. Edie suddenly understood how very poor Ricky had been. She hadn't known at the time, not really. There were so many things that she hadn't known.

'There used to be an Edie,' Mrs Penrose said at last.

'I've got to go.'

'But that was a long time ago.'

'I shouldn't have disturbed you. It was a mistake.'

'Shall I tell . . . ?'

'No! No really! I'm sorry. Sorry.'

She turned, clammy with shame. At the car she turned, raising her hand in an apologetic wave to Lesley Penrose, Ricky's mother, still standing in the doorway staring after her.

22

'*Dear Mummy,*' Kit wrote, typing painstakingly with one finger, '*I am . . .*' He stopped and chewed his lip. He didn't know what to write. Edie had told him to put down what he was feeling, but he didn't know what he was feeling. Wrong, that was the only word he could find for it. He was feeling all wrong. As if his chest was hollow and his head full of ugly, buzzing thoughts. As if everything had come off its hinges inside him. '. . . *fine,*' he wrote. He stared at the lie.

He couldn't tell Edie what he was feeling. If she was here, may be he would be able to. But if she was here, he wouldn't need to tell her. She would look at him and dismay would cross her face before she banished it and knelt down beside him, gathering his hands in hers and staring into his eyes and telling him everything would be all right. Insisting on it. She had this special voice, just for when he was feeling bad, and sometimes it made him feel worse because she sounded a bit scared. Like she thought maybe everything wouldn't be all right. Anyway, if she was here, maybe he wouldn't be feeling like this.

'Kit, here, I made you a sandwich. You didn't eat any tea.' Alex crouched beside him, holding out a plate. 'Ham and cucumber.'

Kit shook his head.

'Not hungry?' Alex waited, but Kit didn't reply, just gave another shake. 'Are you writing to Edie?' he asked with forced jollity. Then he took hold of one of Kit's cold hands and said, 'Why don't you tell me what's up? You haven't spoken a single word since you came out of school. Did something happen? Someone did something to you? You can tell me, you know. You can tell me anything. As soon as you say it out loud, it'll start to get better.' This was what he often said to his pupils, the ones who stumbled into his classroom at playtime, their faces full of fear and shame. It had always made him so angry, the shame that a victim feels. 'Or is it because of Granny dying so suddenly, and Edie having to rush off?'

Kit shrugged and looked down at his lap. Adults always thought there was a reason for everything, and if you found out the reason then you could make things better. He could say, 'Ken locked me in the toilets,' and they'd rush off once again to see the head teacher and make a complaint and for a few days Ken would kept in at break. Or he could say, 'I feel different from everyone,' and Alex would tell him how difference was a good thing, but people didn't know how to deal with it, and it made them scared and hostile, but they were proud of him. Perhaps he would tell the story from his schooldays about a boy called Peter who had tormented him. Or if he said, 'I miss Mummy,' then Alex would lean forward and hug him and tell him that Mummy missed him too, and they'd see her soon. Just a few days now.

But what if all these things were true, but they still

didn't add up to this feeling? Rather – he wrestled with the thought until he felt dizzy – the feeling made the other things true? He kicked his heels against the chair legs and stared at the computer screen. '*Dear Mummy, I am fine.*'

'Tell you what,' said Alex, smoothing Kit's hair back, noticing how his face had become thinner, and there were hectic spots on his cheeks, 'you look all done in. Send your message and get into your pyjamas. I'm going to make you a cup of hot chocolate and you can drink it in bed. Listen to your tapes. You can have supper in bed as well. And you don't need to worry about cleaning your teeth. Except don't tell Edie I said that. And then tomorrow you can take the day off school. Read, watch telly, play on your computer. I'll get Kirsty to come in for the day, OK?'

Kit nodded.

'Marshmallows in your hot chocolate, for a special treat?'

Kit looked at him. He nearly smiled, then opened his mouth. 'Thank you, Daddy.'

Stella and Edie were making cakes for after the funeral: a sharp lemon drizzle cake, oat biscuits, a ginger cake dark with molasses and spice. Jude was preparing fresh mayonnaise for their supper, to go with grilled prawns. She had crossly insisted on it being home-made, although they were trying to empty the fridge and store cupboard rather than fill it up. Now she was separating eggs in her hands, letting the gloop of egg-whites slide through her fingers, cradling yolks in her long fingers. The smell of baking filled the kitchen. The low sun shone through the window. The clock ticked, the washing-machine chugged consolingly and somewhere in the distance they could hear the sound of a lawn-mower. Edie, hollow with fatigue, let herself be comforted by the placid domesticity of the scene.

She had got back at lunch, white-faced and puffy-eyed, with hands that shook when she made tea for them. Stella and Jude hadn't asked her about her morning, beyond inquiring if she was all right. Edie just nodded and said it was a strange time. They had gone together to the home to see Ellen, then rushed back in time for the estate agent, who seemed as young as a schoolboy to Edie. Now she grated lemon zest into the sifted flour and let her agitated mind settle. She had thought to tell them about the letter she had found last night, the love letter to Louise, but couldn't find the moment. The words stuck in her throat. She couldn't bear to see the hurt disbelief in Stella's face when she heard, or the contempt in Jude's. And she hadn't mentioned going back to their old house, sitting in the neat garden, walking the bridge. Not yet, not while everything was so raw. She would tell Alex when she rang him. But when she thought about Alex, big, dishevelled, kind, trusting Alex, she flinched with guilt. For she wouldn't tell him about her visit to Ricky's mother: not now, not ever. No one ever thought she was the kind of woman who would have secrets and hidden desires.

The phone rang and Stella went to answer it, but she returned almost at once, shrugging. 'Nobody,' she said.

'Did you try one four seven one?'

'"The caller withheld their number."'

'I always find that creepy,' said Jude. She was steadily dripping olive oil into her egg yolks while whisking the mixture vigorously; her face was tight with concentration.

'I agree,' said Stella. She seemed to make her mind up about something. 'I wanted to tell you,' she said to Jude abruptly. 'I told Edie before, and I thought – well, anyway, Bob's having an affair.'

For a moment, Jude simply carried on whisking. The sinews on her forearm rippled; her lower lip was caught between her teeth. Then she said lightly, 'You poor thing.'

Stella stared at her, waiting, but Jude said nothing else.

'Soon,' said Stella after an heavy pause, 'we'll all be gone from here, back to our lives. We'll never be together like this again; you won't have to bother about us. I just thought I should . . .' She trailed off, and picking up a wooden spoon, stared down at the mound of flour and ground ginger in the mixing-bowl. Her face looked slack with unhappiness.

Jude put down her whisk. She dipped the tip of her little finger into the mayonnaise and licked it, nodding appreciatively. 'OK,' she said. 'I'm having an affair too. With a married man. So you see, you're the abandoned wife, and I'm the wicked other woman.' She grinned mirthlessly. 'Once again.'

'Oh,' said Stella, slowly. 'Well, that's your business, of course. But I don't see why that means you have to be dismissive of what's happening to me – it should be the reverse, if anything. You should at least be able to imagine what it must be like.'

'Look,' said Edie, startled by the sudden change in the room. 'You're both going through traumatic experiences, and then Mummy . . .' She put a hand on Stella's arm, the one that was holding the wooden spoon suspended over the bowl, and a puff of flour rose in the air and scattered on the work surface. 'So you feel bad, Jude, when you hear about Stella, because you're the other woman. But on the other hand . . .'

'Oh, for goodness sake, why do you always have to put yourself in the middle?' snapped Jude. 'Why can you never take sides? It's always "On the one hand this, on the other hand that." Just tell me I'm being a bitch. It's true, after all. But you have to imagine what it feels like for everyone. You have to feel their pain. How can you live like that? It must drive you crazy.'

'I don't know how not to,' retorted Edie. 'That's what I am. But this was about Stella, not me.'

'Oh, it doesn't matter,' said Stella. 'Don't let's quarrel. Not now.'

'When then?' Jude clicked across the kitchen and put her mixing-bowl in the sink. 'Tomorrow? Next year? Anytime but now?'

'You must be very unhappy,' said Stella. 'To be like this.'

'Oh, fuck off,' said Jude. 'What do you know?'

'Who do you really care about, apart from yourself?' Stella went on, standing up very straight and pointing the spoon at Jude.

'Just fuck off,' Jude repeated in a deliberately vulgar

voice. Then she began giggling. She put her hand across her mouth. 'Sorry,' she said in a choked voice from behind it. 'But look at us. Three grown-up women squabbling like little girls in our dead mother's kitchen.'

'I'm not squabbling,' said Stella primly.

Jude went on giggling. Her eyes were watering. 'I'm not squabbling,' she mimicked.

'Don't,' said Stella in a strangled voice. 'Stop it.'

She sat down at the table. Her shoulders were shaking and there were tears in her eyes. Edie couldn't tell if she was laughing or crying. Jude sat down weakly next to her and put an arm around her shoulders and kissed her on the crown of her head.

'Of course I'm unhappy,' she said through her snorts. 'As Edie put it, that's what I am. I don't know how to be anything else. But don't cry. I'm sorry about Bob. Sorry about everything.'

Edie watched them. She felt oddly left out, but there were no tears left inside her. She went to the oven and took out the oat biscuits, golden-brown and curling at the edges. She pressed a finger on the top of the lemon cake. It needed a few more minutes before it would be ready. She wiped the flour from the surfaces.

'I'm going to ring Alex,' she said.

They didn't look up as she left the room. She used the phone in Louise's room and lay on the bed, listening to the dialling tone.

'Hello, who is it?' Jess said.

'It's me. Hello, poppet.'

'Mummy? Guess what? We had a practice for sports day today and I won the skipping race *and* I'm going to do the three-legged race with Kelly, unless she says she's going to do it with Chloë, and Mrs Friar says will you run in the parents' race?'

'OK, as long as you don't mind me losing?'

'Will you lose?'

'I won't win. Some of the mothers are about half my age.'

'But you won't fall over?'

'Fall over? I don't think so.'

'I wouldn't like you to fall over.'

'So you're well?'

But there was no reply. Jess had obviously wandered off. In the distance, Edie could hear her shouting for Alex. She lay back against the pillow and closed her eyes, waiting for his voice.

'Edie?' He sounded so glad to hear her.

'Hello? Are you all OK?'

'We're fine. I'm making them supper, Jess is drawing a picture for you. Lewis is out playing football. The house is a bit of a mess, I'm afraid. Well, more than a bit.'

'That doesn't matter a jot. Is Kit all right?'

'He's, you know . . .'

'What? What's happened?'

'Nothing's happened. He's just upset today. He's not talking.'

'Well, he never talks much.'

'No, I mean he's not talking. Maybe ten words today.'

Edie pressed the receiver against her forehead. She was shivery, as if she was coming down with something. Her skin felt bruised and tender.

'Edie, are you still there?'

'Yes. Shall I have a word with him?'

'He's having a boiled egg in bed. I said he needn't go to school tomorrow.'

'But . . .'

'I'm taking care of it. You'll be back soon, then we'll talk properly.'

'Alex.'

'Yes.'

'You're a very nice man, you know.'

'No, no,' he protested, half-laughing.

'And I love you very much.'

She would tell him about everything another day.

She clicked on her mail. '*Dear Mummy, I am fine,*' she read. That was all.

She phoned Rose at her mother's house and got her at once.

'I'm so sorry,' said Rose.

'Thanks.'

'She always seemed so young.'

'I know.'

'It makes you think . . .' said Rose. 'It can happen any time. Just like that.' Her voice became earnest. 'We have to make the most of every single day, don't we?'

'Yes,' said Edie, embarrassed.

They arranged to meet the next day. Rose would drive over for coffee at eleven.

Jude had put candles on the table and floated a single rose in a vase. She had placed small bowls of warm water in front of each of them, so they could clean their hands after peeling the prawns.

'This is nice,' said Edie. Stella was in the hall, talking to Sam.

'I'm making amends.' Jude's tone was dry.

She put six giant prawns into a hot pan and turned them in the garlic-and-chilli butter, watching as they changed colour to a dark pink. They could hear Stella's voice change from solicitous to anxiously bossy: she was talking to Bob now.

'Do you cook every night?'

'When I'm all alone, you mean?' Jude said. 'No. When I'm alone I starve myself.' She looked at Edie. 'You're the one who's all right, aren't you? Out of us three, I mean. You've turned out the happy one.'

'Oh well, happy . . .' said Edie nervously.

'I always thought it would be Stella,' said Jude. 'Because she didn't expect so much.'

Stella came back into the kitchen.

'Time for wine, I think,' she said. And then she said vaguely, as if she was thinking out loud, 'Perhaps I should leave him.'

'We were just waiting for you.' Edie poured three glasses of white wine and they raised them to one another. She thought, I'll tell them about the letter. If I know, they should too. Especially now. She took a sip of wine and cleared her throat. 'Have you ever wondered . . . ?' she began.

Then the phone rang.

'Your turn to answer,' said Jude to Edie. 'We've been

on the phone half the day. It's probably someone about Monday.'

Half-relieved, Edie went out into the hall and lifted the phone to her ear.

'Hello?' she said.

There was silence, except for the faint sound of breathing.

'Hello?' she repeated.

'Edie.'

'Yes. Who is this?' As if she hadn't known at once. As if she hadn't been waiting.

'Ricky.'

23

'Ricky,' she said. She glanced towards the kitchen. The door was slightly ajar and she could hear the sound of Stella and Jude talking, the sizzling of the prawns.

'My mother told me you went to her house.'

'Yes.'

'Why?'

'I don't know,' she said in a small voice. 'My mother died suddenly and it was a shock, and I was driving near your house, and I suppose I just thought . . .' She stopped. 'I don't know. How did you get this number?'

'Directory. What did you want?'

'Nothing. It was very stupid. I'm sorry.' She paused and then added, 'I suppose I just wanted to know that you were all right. I think about you sometimes, and I hope you're all right.' There was a nose like a stifled snort at the other end. She took a gulp of her wine. The cord of the phone was all twisted up. When this conversation was over, she'd straighten it out, and then she'd go and sit down and eat prawns. 'So are you all right?'

'Fine,' he said in a polite, disgusted voice.

'OK. I'll go then. Sorry. Goodbye.'

'Hang on.'

'Yes?'

'Do you want to meet then?' He sounded dismissive, showing her he didn't care.

'That's not what I meant.'

'So, do you want to meet?'

'I don't think so.'

'All right. But anyway, I live in Kingley, between you and Baylham. There's a pub called The Bell. I'll be there after nine.'

'I don't think there's any point,' repeated Edie, almost whispering.

'Fine. Whatever.' And he put the phone down.

'Who was it?' asked Jude. She was sliding the prawns on to a serving dish and scattering segments of lemon over them.

'Rose.' Edie sat down. 'She's down for the weekend and might stay over for the funeral. She's coming here tomorrow for coffee.'

'I haven't seen her for years,' said Stella. 'What's she up to?'

'I'm not even sure,' said Edie. 'She's always changing jobs.'

'Is she still married to what's-his-name?'

'Richard? No. They split up a couple of years ago.'

'So, she's alone?'

'Yes,' said Edie abstractedly.

She took a prawn and bent its spine back until it cracked, then peeled off its carapace. The flesh was pale pink and steaming. She dipped it into the yellow mayonnaise. She glanced up at the clock on the wall. It was five minutes to eight, and outside the sky was darkening.

They talked about the order of the service. None of

them had decided what to read. Stella had an anthology of poems about mourning that she had bought from the bookshop in town that morning, and she thumbed through it, leaving smudges of grease on the margins. Jude said she didn't think they ought to wear black. Stella disagreed: they should definitely wear black. She'd brought her black suit with her, and a hat that went with it nicely. Edie didn't know; she didn't think it really mattered one way or the other.

'Well, of course it doesn't *really* matter,' said Jude. 'Not to Louise.'

'Something dark at least,' said Stella anxiously.

'In India, they wear white.'

'This isn't India. Lots of her more traditional friends are coming. What will they think if they see you drifting around in white?'

'I'm not planning to wear white – I don't have anything white, anyway. Nor do I drift. I just meant, why conform to . . . ?'

'I don't think it's about conforming,' interrupted Edie. 'It's about ritual, isn't it?' She glanced at the clock again.

It was nearly nine when they cleared away the plates. Edie went upstairs to Louise's bedroom and stood in front of the mirror. She stared at herself: her thin shoulders, her brown hair, the lines that marked her face: laughter-lines, furrows of anxiety, and the brackets by the side of her mouth. The tired skin under her eyes. She leant into the mirror and saw the grey hair in her eyebrows. She thought about the fillings in her mouth, the scar on her stomach, the stretch marks on her breasts.

In a few months' time, she would be forty. She had always said that she didn't mind, but she suddenly realized this wasn't true. The girl she had been at sixteen – so hopeful, so unmarked, travelling so light – had gone, and in her place was a stranger with a face like a map and half her life behind her. Soon, she thought, she'd be old. Her children would be grown-up and gone. They'd ring up every few days to ask her kindly how she was. They'd come home for weekends perhaps, with flowers wrapped in paper and photographs of their holidays, and then on Sunday afternoon pack their small suitcases and be gone back to their own lives. The house would be tidy and silent and full of ghosts.

'It goes so quickly,' she said out loud. 'How does it go so quickly?'

'I'm going for a walk,' Edie said, coming downstairs with her jacket over her arm. 'It's such a glorious evening.' She waited for one of them to offer to come with her, half-hoping that they would. But Jude was marking essays and Stella was still looking for a suitable poem, so she went out alone and stood for a moment, indecisively, on the pavement. She looked at her watch. It was twenty past nine.

She got into her car, telling herself it was just a matter of curiosity, and by the time she had got to Kingley, Ricky would be gone anyway, so what was the harm? She looked at the map to work out the route and then drove slowly, giving him time to leave.

The Bell was crowded, hot and full of smoke and the smell of beer. People were crammed in corners and had spilt out into the small garden at the back. The hubbub was deafening. Edie pushed her way through, searching. He wasn't by the bar, nor at a table, nor playing snooker in the back room. He wasn't outside, in the crowded darkness. Probably it was just as well for she wasn't feeling herself today. She turned to go, and then she saw him, sitting at a table. He had a glass of beer in front of him, half-finished, and was rolling a cigarette in one expert hand. Her eyes must have passed over him before, but she hadn't recognized him. In her imagination, he had been taller, more solid, more handsome, younger. Not this slight man with thinning hair and several days of stubble on his cheeks, who'd never managed to leave after all, in spite of his dreams, but who was sitting in a pub on a Friday evening, a few miles from the place where he'd been born, sipping beer. Staring at him, at the thin white neck above his tee-shirt, the flecks of foam on his upper lip, she felt dazed. She hesitated, then half-turned to go.

But he looked up and it was too late. His eyes were deep brown under thick brows. He stood up, picked up the coat on the back of his chair, and squeezed past the other drinkers at the table, saying nothing.

'Hello,' she said, longing for home.

'Hello.' He looked down at her and didn't smile.

'It's been a long time.'

'Yes.'

'Um . . .' There was nothing at all she could say to this man.

'Do you want a drink?' he asked at last, putting his hand into his pocket and jingling change.

She could hardly hear what he was saying in the din. 'No. I'm not staying.'

'You mean, you'll just have a quick look at me and then rush off? So what do you think then? A bit of a disappointment? I'm not looking so good, am I? Bit shabby for you, I reckon.'

'No,' she protested. 'It's just that this was very foolish of me. I don't know what I'm doing here.'

'What's that?'

'*I don't know what I'm doing here*,' she repeated loudly.

Someone bumped into her from behind and she felt a splash of beer on her shoulder.

'Come on,' he said, and took her tightly by the arm, just above the elbow, and led her to the door. His fingers dug into her flesh.

'Where are we going?'

'Just out of here.'

'I don't think —'

'What?' he said too loudly. 'What don't you think?'

She looked at him in alarm. A blue vein pulsed in his temple; his eyes were slightly bloodshot.

'I made a mistake,' she said softly.

They were out in the cold air and he still had her by the arm. He started pulling her along the street, past the betting shop, the post office, the hardware store with army knives in its window.

'Twenty-two years,' he said.

'Yes.'

'You haven't changed much.'

Edie put a hand up to her face. 'I hope that's not true.'

'I was sitting there thinking, what will she look like? Will I recognize her? Every time a woman came in I thought, maybe that's her, that fat one with greasy hair, that scraggy blonde one, or that one that looks about fifty, or that one with dyed red hair and loads of make-up. I thought, maybe she's completely different now, not a trace left. But here you are. Thin, brown-haired Edie. Here you are and here I am, and what shall we do now?'

'Where are we going?' She pulled at her arm but he kept a tight hold of her.

'What about me? I've changed, haven't I? I saw the way you looked at me. You were going to turn around and leave, weren't you? Am I that bad?'

'It's not that,' she said, stopping in her tracks and turning to him. There were no more street lamps, and she felt uneasy in the darkness. She took a breath. 'Ricky.' She said his name to know that this was real. 'The reason I wanted to see you is because I behaved wrongly. I've thought about you a lot, probably because I felt bad about you.' She didn't tell him that she had dreamed about him at least once a week for the last twenty-two years – distressing erotic dreams, from which she'd jerk awake, reaching out to touch Alex's broad, warm back, waiting for the images to fade.

'So you're here to say sorry?' His voice was neutral. He sounded almost bored again.

'I suppose so.' She ploughed on: 'This makes me feel very stupid. Here we are, two more or less middle-aged people, and I know you probably haven't thought about me at all for years and years.' She waited a beat but he said nothing. 'But for me it's always been like unfinished business. My life just went all wrong and I couldn't see my way through it. I felt ill with misery and guilt. I thought everything was my fault.'

'As you say, it was a long time ago,' he said after a pause. 'We were kids. It's more like a dream than anything.'

'It's odd. I remember it as if it was yesterday.' Edie gave a small laugh. 'I even remember the clothes you wore, the words you said to me.' She knew she shouldn't be saying things like that, and she swallowed hard. 'I still have all the letters you wrote to me,' she said.

'I was just a stupid boy. A dreamer.' He took a tin of tobacco out of his pocket and started rolling himself a cigarette in the dim light. 'I thought my life could be different. Ridiculous, wasn't it? I had this idea I could change things. You wouldn't understand that, would you? It's not the same for people like you, the ones in big houses at the edge of the town. You were always going to leave and be a doctor or something – is that what you are? Yes? You see. And I was always going to stay, whatever I thought.'

'I'm sorry.' There was nothing else to say.

He handed her a thin cigarette and she took it, leaning forward to the match that flared in the half-darkness. She pulled the acrid smoke into her lungs.

'Anyway,' she said. 'You probably want to get back to your friends.'

'Not particularly.' He sucked on his cigarette and the

tip glowed brightly. 'Of course I thought about you, Edie. I hated you. You betrayed me. I blamed you for everything that happened after that, all the things that went wrong for me. I thought you were timid and weak and sentimental. A coward, not worth bothering about. I had contempt for you, and for me, because I'd believed you. All your fine words of love had meant nothing.'

'They didn't mean nothing,' she said. 'They didn't.' It seemed very important that he should know that. She put her hand on his shoulder and repeated it a third time. 'They didn't.'

'It doesn't matter now anyway. It's all history, isn't it? I don't miss you at all.'

'I must get back,' she said, dropping her hand. She shivered, suddenly cold.

He shrugged. 'OK.'

'My car's outside the pub.'

'I'll come with you. I could do with another drink.'

They walked in silence. A group of teenagers passed them from the other direction, talking and laughing loudly, passing at last out of hearing.

'What do you do?' she asked. The pub was in sight at last.

'I work for a central heating firm.'

'Oh.'

'You don't know what to say to that, do you?'

'No,' she admitted.

'Not like being a film director. Then you could have said, how brilliant, how interesting, would I have seen anything you've directed, things like that. Mmm? But working for a central heating company near Birmingham, well, it's a bit of a conversation-stopper for you.'

'Here's my car,' she said with relief. She pulled her keys out of her jacket pocket and unlocked it.

'She never liked me much, did she?'

'Who?'

'Your mum, Louise.'

'I think she worried,' said Edie. She got into the car.

'Quite right too. A boy like me. Low life.'

'Goodbye, Ricky.'

'Goodbye then,' he said, but then he put a hand on the door as she was about to pull it shut. 'Edie?'

'Yes?'

'Just – oh, I don't know. It's odd, isn't it?'

'Yes,' she said in a soft voice. She reached up and touched his stubbly cheek with her hand. 'It's odd.'

'Can I sit in your car and have a last cigarette? I don't feel like the pub after all, or like going home. Not yet.'

'All right.'

She reached across the car and opened the door for him and he climbed in beside her. He rolled another two cigarettes for them without asking her, just as he'd always done in the past, and put one into her mouth. Lit a match and in the sudden flare she saw his face as it had been when he was young, and her heart rose in her throat as it always used to.

'Nothing turns out how you think,' he said. 'Suddenly, it's too late. You realize you've missed the last train out. But you only know when it's too late to do anything,'

'Surely it's never too late?' she said inadequately.

'Oh Jesus,' he said, and closed his eyes and rested his head back against the car seat. 'Jesus.'

She made the first move. Afterwards, she wouldn't even have the comfort of saying it was him. She took the cigarette out of his mouth and reached across the gear-stick and put her free hand behind his head and kissed him on the lips. She remembered the way he felt and the way he tasted. Tobacco and beer. His stubble scratched her cheek. The cigarettes burnt down between her fingers. The years disappeared like smoke.

A long time ago. Alex had told her how if he was ever tempted to be unfaithful he would think of his children, picture their faces watching him. Edie thought of her children. She closed her eyes and let their faces fill her mind. Lewis. Kit. Jess. They would be asleep now, lips slightly parted, eyes flickering, tugged in the river of dreams. And Alex, too, would probably be lying in bed, with her empty space beside him. And Louise, in the Chapel of Rest, eyes closed and hands folded together, as if she was praying. She saw them as she lay back in the car seat and let Ricky unbutton her shirt and put his head against her breasts.

24

'What have I done?' she whispered to herself as she lay on Louise's bed and waited for morning. Slowly the sky was lightening outside, from charcoal to navy to a dull grey-blue, and birds were suddenly singing, first just individual notes and trills testing the silence, and then the full joyful chorus. She could smell tobacco on her skin, and taste it inside her mouth. Her head ached dully, though she'd only had one glass of wine at supper last night.

Why had she done it? Not out of simple desire, nor for any dramatic pleasure. Not because she was drunk. Not because she was dissatisfied with Alex – she had never felt so tenderly towards him as now. Was it for something as paltry as nostalgia? Was fidelity as precarious as that? You go along, year after year, being faithful, and you think you're making a choice, exercising will, making love work, but it turns out it's just a habit after all. Every day you come back to your home, to your husband and your children; and you think: this is the life I've made for myself. You have a routine that's rarely broken. You wake up beside him; you cook meals together; you walk in the park on a Sunday; you cook cakes and he makes curries. Every other weekend and each Wednesday evening, his children from his first marriage come to stay and you put flowers in their room and try to make them feel this is their home too. You tell each other about problems with your jobs. You discuss other couples. Every so often you have an argument and it's always about the same few things; it's just part of the pattern you've established. You have stories you tell as a couple, and you often finish each other's sentences. He rubs your back when it aches and you cut the hairs at the back of his neck and iron his shirts for him. He loads the dishwasher; you sort the children's clothes. One of you drinks and the other drives. You take it in turns to clean the children's teeth. Every so often, you go out separately with friends, but you always go to bed together at the end of the day and often enough you make love, turning to each other in the darkness, knowing what gives the other pleasure by now. You have a joint bank account and a shared memory bank. You build a life, brick by brick.

Then one day someone you've dreamed about sits beside you in a car. You're far from home, you've swallowed your anchor, and you lean over and kiss him on his mouth, softly, and he closes his eyes just like he used to do. Blindly, he opens your shirt and kisses your breasts. He pulls down your jeans. His hands are cold on your body and his face is white and thin. And though he's so familiar, he's a stranger, and that makes you into a stranger too, and like two desperate teenagers, you have sex there across the front seats, with your clothes like straitjackets, and the gear-stick jabbing you in the ribs, and the steering-wheel trapping you, and the door handle pressing into the crown of your head, and the moon watching you through the smeary windscreen. In less than five minutes, you have wreaked havoc on your constructed world.

Edie sat up in bed. She could put it in the passive tense: it was something that had happened to her, like a landslide, madness, or the weather. She had heard people say that often enough. 'I couldn't help myself, it just happened, I went crazy for a while . . .' And it was true that she had been under stress. Her mother had died suddenly, she had been newly haunted by thoughts of her father's suicide, two decades ago. For a brief time, she hadn't been herself. But she had always thought such excuses were precisely that: excuses, made by people who couldn't bear to take responsibility for their mistakes.

Edie swung her legs out of bed. It was half past five and light. This morning, the skip they had ordered would arrive, and a friend of Louise's was coming round with his truck to take several loads of unwanted belongings to the dump. They had to go through Louise's clothes. They had to collect the flowers and the drink. And Rose was coming at eleven. She had a quick shower, pulled on her jeans and a tee-shirt, and went downstairs, through the hall stacked with bin-bags and boxes, its walls now bare of paintings. In the kitchen, most of the cupboards were empty – just a few pots and pans, and enough plates and cutlery to last them over the next couple of days. Cardboard boxes full of cheese graters, lemon squeezers, wooden spoons, toasted-sandwich makers, pastry cutters, tupperwares and flan dishes stood by the door. They'd divided up who was going to take what. Stella had claimed the porcelain blackbird that Louise used to put in the centre of an apple pie, to hold up the pastry like a tent; Edie the large mug she'd found, pushed to the back of a deep cupboard, that Vic always drank tea from.

She put the kettle on to boil and ground up coffee beans that Jude insisted on keeping in the freezer compartment, for freshness. There was very little left in the fridge: just milk and butter, four eggs, a bunch of spring onions and some tomatoes. Today she'd have to buy food for dinner – the last dinner for the three sisters by themselves – and for tomorrow, when Alex and the children would be here. Her heart flipped. What was she going to say to Alex? He'd bound towards the house, the children's sleeping-bags spilling out of his arms, an eager smile on his face, but how would she meet his frank and wholehearted gaze?

The kettle boiled. She made the coffee strong, almost thick; then she toasted a slice of brown bread and spread it with bitter, chunky marmalade. She felt hollowed out but shakily nauseous as well. She wrapped her hands around the mug and leant over the steam. She should tell him, but the thought of doing so made her stomach scramble with dread and her mouth go dry. She knew how he would look. His expression wouldn't change, but it would be like a light going out. Then his face would slacken and his broad shoulders slump. She'd seen him like that sometimes when his older children turned on him. 'What do you know?' Gabriel had once shouted, his adolescent voice piping then breaking over the words. 'You're just a slob and a failure!' Edie had crossed over to Alex and put a hand on his shoulder to comfort him, and he'd turned and given her a grateful look. But now it would be she who was hurting him, and there'd be nobody to comfort him. Perhaps she shouldn't tell him, after all? It would be her secret. They would talk about which of their friends they were sure were faithful to each other, and when they were half-drunk or sentimental they'd tell each other how there'd never be anyone else, and she'd feel her skin prickling and her heart hammering. But she'd say nothing and gradually – how long did these things take? – the guilt would fade and it would just be a stupid thing she'd done long ago.

She finished her coffee. It was quarter past six. The sky was a pale clear blue and already the chill in the air was lifting. Edie took a couple of empty boxes to the tall food cupboard in the corner and started to sort out the tins of beans, sweetcorn, tuna, the bags of risotto rice, noodles and flour. Half of it was past its sell-by date, so Edie chucked it straight in a bin-bag, which she put with all the other bags by the side of the overflowing wheelie bin. Next, she moved on to the books, stacking the ones Jude and Stella had wanted into piles, heaping hers into the box with Vic's mug and a food mixer, putting the rest into boxes to take to a charity shop. She bubble-wrapped the pictures and rolled glasses in sheets of old newspaper.

At eight o'clock, when Stella was still asleep and Jude was, by the sound of the gurgling tank, in the bath, the skip arrived and Edie started carrying things out to it. She worked steadily, without stopping, glad of the knots in her arms, the ache in her back and the sweat that gathered on her forehead and trickled down between her breasts.

'Can I have the wedding photo of Mummy and Daddy?' she asked later, when they were all drinking coffee in the garden and the skip outside was piled high. 'The one in the bedroom.'

She knew she wasn't going to tell them about the letter to Louise. Not now. It was Louise's secret, one that she wished she didn't know herself.

They went through Louise's clothes. It didn't take long. Some they put in bags to take to the charity shop in Shrimpley. But Stella kept her good black coat, her long blue velvet dress, the orange shirt, a linen suit and several pairs of shoes. Edie kept a yellow cardigan that she thought she remembered Louise wearing back in Baylham, though she knew she would never wear it herself, several scarves, and a black cloche hat. Jude took nothing. Every time a garment was held up for her to inspect she would shake her head and look away.

'I went back to our old house yesterday morning,' said Edie, folding tee-shirts.

'My God! So that's where you were while we were slaving away. Why? And why didn't you mention it before?'

'Sorry. I just – well, everything felt a bit much for me yesterday.'

'What was it like?'

'Different. Modernized. Nice, probably, but it felt so very strange.'

'I bet.'

'I met the woman who lives there now and she let me inside.'

'I wish I'd been with you.'

'Me too,' said Edie. 'I should never have gone alone. I wasn't feeling myself.'

Not feeling myself, she repeated to herself. That's the way to think of it. Hang on to that. It wasn't me, not really. Not me in the car, with his mouth on mine, his hands on my breasts, his tears running down my neck, his smell of loneliness. And in the middle of her guilt, terrible desire snaked through her.

'Here,' she said. 'What about this jacket? Jude?'

Rose arrived just after eleven. She climbed out of her car carrying a massive bouquet of flowers. She was wearing tight leather trousers and a bright white cotton shirt, her streaky yellow hair piled artfully on the top of her head. She had put on make-up – foundation to cover up her wrinkles, eye-liner, mascara, blusher on her cheeks, lipstick – and perfume as well. Edie was still in her old tee-shirt and her jeans that had become shapeless with wear. She'd taken off her shoes and there was a hole in the toe of her sock. Her hair was pinned crookedly back from her face and she was grimy from her morning's work.

'Look at us!' she said with a rueful laugh. 'It's as if you're about to go to a party and I've been sleeping rough for a week. Honestly, Rose, you're more gorgeous than ever! How do you do it?'

'Don't be daft,' said Rose, but she looked pleased.

She placed the scarlet tip of one finger on her cheek. 'It's all fake. Every morning I put my face on; nobody ever sees my real face. Underneath this, I'm disintegrating.'

'I don't believe a word of it,' said Edie fondly. 'You were always the prettiest girl in the class. I felt invisible beside you. Come on, let's have coffee and you can tell me what's going on in your life.'

'If only something was going on. I'm a lady-in-waiting.'

They sat in the garden. Rose turned to the sun and sighed.

'Blissful, this time of year,' she said. 'It makes me feel so full of life and hope. Like I'm about to fall in love again. Or at least buy a wonderful new dress. Nothing can be so bad, if there's sun on your bare skin.'

'I don't know. I always feel a bit anxious in the spring, as if it's about to disappear on me. It goes so fast it brings on a mild panic.'

'God, you don't change! Listen to you, you can even be melancholy about spring! Go on, say it's like life passing, and it reminds you of mortality, and then I'll believe we're both sixteen again and you're about to quote some bit of poetry I won't understand.'

Edie laughed. 'Sorry.'

'I like it. It's nice some things stay the same. Do you remember how we used to get the giggles in assembly?'

'Yes. I've not giggled like that for ages, so that it hurt.'

'Mmm.' Rose sipped her coffee, leaving a semi-circle of red on the rim of the mug. Edie saw, out here in the harsh sunlight, that beneath her make-up, underneath her glossy hair, she looked tired and worn. 'Anyway, I'm really sorry about your mother.'

'Thanks.'

'She was always so nice to me. She used to be my role model, you know – always beautiful and full of life. That's why I wanted to come to the funeral, though I haven't seen her for years and years. I can't believe she's dead. Are you all right about it?'

'I've been better,' said Edie carefully. 'I wasn't ready for this. Perhaps you never are though. You always think when you get older you'll become stoical and wise, and things won't matter so much. But suddenly I don't have a mother any more. It's ridiculous, but perhaps it's the first time I've properly understood I'm not a child.'

'I can't imagine it,' said Rose.

'We had our problems. After Daddy died, I mean. She seemed to shut herself off from us all. It was worst for Jude of course, she was there for longer, all on her own, fighting every inch of the way. But for Mummy, it must have been like her nice, ordinary existence suddenly turned into a nightmare. We never talked to each other about it. It was like an unwritten agreement. I always thought we would eventually. It's too late now.'

'I'm sure you did all right really,' said Rose. 'No relationship's perfect, is it? I mean, when people die, everyone always goes on about all the things that they did wrong, but maybe they ought to think more about what they did right.'

'Probably that's true. You know, Rose, I just feel so sorry for her.'

They drank their coffee and Rose lit a cigarette and sat back with a small sigh. 'How's Alex?'

'Fine,' said Edie warily.

'You've done all right, you two, haven't you? You always seem very good together. You're actually nice to each other, after all these years. I don't know how you do it.'

For a moment, Edie was choked by a sense of panic. 'We get by,' she managed to say, with a grim sense of her fraudulence.

'Come on, he adores you. Anyone can see that.'

'I'm lucky,' said Edie. She took her dark glasses from the table and put them on.

'I mean, look at me. I'm fine in the first stages of a relationship, but I can't seem to get beyond the five-year mark. Oh well.' Rose blew smoke into the air. 'I blame my parents, for arguing through my childhood then divorcing. They probably think they did well to wait till I was nearly grown up. I bloody wish they'd done it earlier and spared me the screams in the night. Or maybe I'm saying that so I don't feel so bad about my own divorces.'

'Why did they eventually separate?' asked Edie.

'Apart from not getting on with each other? Oh God, who knows?'

'Was there anyone else involved?'

'You mean, was either of them having an affair? Well, my mum wouldn't have been. Or maybe she would. You never know what goes on in people's lives. But I can't imagine it, can you? I don't know about Dad, though it's more likely. I don't think I want to know, even now that I'm nearly forty and they're approaching their seventies. You're never quite grown-up where your parents are concerned, are you? And you *certainly* don't want to think about their sex lives.'

'No,' said Edie. 'That's true. Can I?' She reached out and took one of Rose's cigarettes, lighting it with the lighter on the table.

'I didn't think you smoked.'

'I don't. Everything's an exception while I'm here. Are both your parents coming to the funeral?'

'I think so. They don't mind being in the same room or anything like that. And they were all good friends for a bit, weren't they?'

'Mmmm.' Edie concentrated on smoking the cigarette. The conversation seemed so obvious to her that it was like asking Rose to add two and two. 'I went back to our old house yesterday,' she said to change the subject.

'You didn't! Was it the first time?'

'Yes. Twenty-two years.'

'Did you go inside?'

'Yes. Nothing's like I remembered it. But maybe if they'd changed nothing at all, it still wouldn't be how I remembered it.'

'God, we had nice times there, though. I still think about those days. Do you remember the party we had?'

'Of course I do.'

'Matt, that was his name.' She giggled like a teenager. 'And you were with that Ricky.'

'Yes,' said Edie. She closed her eyes behind her dark glasses and sucked smoke into her lungs. 'That's right.'

'And now we're nearly middle-aged.'

'Yes.'

'I preferred being seventeen,' said Rose. 'I think that's my real age. Seventeen. Or sixteen was even better. Do you know, I can't believe that'll never come again.'

25

Dear Mummy, wrote Kit with his single finger. *I had a dream about you and you were not going to come back ever again. And I tried to find you but I looked and looked but couldn't see you anywhere. I woke up . . .*

He stopped for a moment and frowned. He wouldn't tell her about the wet sheets, or the way Lewis, meeting him in the bathroom as he peeled off his pyjamas, had wrinkled his nose in disgust.

For ages after it still felt like real life, not just a dream. Daddy and I just worked out that it was 22 hours and 20 minutes till we set out to see you. Which is 1,320 minutes. That sounds long and short at the same time. But Lewis says it is longer because Daddy is always at least an hour late. I love you and I am glad it was just a dream. Kitxxxx

Edie saw him as she waved Rose off. Standing at the far end of the street, hands in his pockets, watching. She looked away sharply, and gave Rose a final wave. The car pulled away from the kerb and she went on standing there. Nothing seemed real. The way the sunlight glinted on the cars and bounced back from windows. The way the trees cast their shadows, so the road was geometrically stripped. The day was suddenly too bright, and she felt exposed.

She looked up again and he was still there. He raised a hand. She looked back and the door of the house was half-open. Inside it was shaded and cool. Jude was filling rolls with Parma ham. Stella was unpacking the glasses that had been delivered, wiping each one with a soft cloth. Edie hesitated, then walked down the street towards him in her grubby clothes, with her schoolgirl's pony-tail.

'Hello,' he said.

'Hello.'

He was wearing the same clothes as last night. She noticed his fingers were stained and his teeth were discoloured.

'What are you doing here?'

He shrugged and pushed his hands into his pockets. She saw clearly how thin he was, almost undernourished. His skin was white, as if he never went outside, and his neck scrawny, with its prominent Adam's apple. He looked at her from under his thick brows.

'Shall we walk a bit?'

'All right,' she said, brimful with the sense of calamity. 'Just a couple of minutes though. I've got to get back.'

They went away from the direction of the house. The heat beat down, oppressive; the tarmac shimmered.

'It was a mistake,' she said at last. 'I don't understand why it happened, but it was a huge mistake.'

'A mistake,' he repeated, as if it was a foreign word that he couldn't get his tongue around.

'I've got a husband. Children.'

'Yes,' he said.

'Well, what about you?'

'Not any more. Not with me.'

'I've ruined things,' she said, more to herself than him. She was limp and tired out, and stumbled on a crack in the pavement, feeling suddenly that she couldn't walk any further. He put an arm out to steady her and she let him. They walked slowly along the road towards the fields on the town's outskirts.

'When are you going back?' he asked.

'Tuesday, I think. The funeral's on Monday.'

'And when's your family coming?'

'Tomorrow.'

'Will you tell him?'

'I don't know. Probably.'

'What for?'

'Trust?'

He glanced at her, then ahead again. 'It's good to have secrets sometimes. Honesty can be just a fancy word for being cruel.'

'Maybe.' She paused. 'I should go back now, Ricky. Jude and Stella will be wondering where I've got to.'

'All right.'

But they walked on until the houses petered out, and when he stopped by a field, she stopped too. Waited. And when he put his hand at the back of her head, where it was hot from the sun, she let him. And she knew she didn't want him to touch her, she mustn't allow him, and yet she did. He opened the wooden gate that was held shut with a loop of orange string, shut it carefully behind them, and led her along the side of the hedge until they were hidden from cars.

'I will never forgive myself,' she said out loud, and he kissed her hard on her mouth while she was speaking the words. 'Don't,' she said. But she let him push her on to the grass and tug down her trousers and then he was on top of her, his mouth against her mouth, teeth clashing, his chest against her breasts, his body bucking against hers, thistles on her bare thighs and a stinging nettle burning her forearm, and the sun hammering down and her eyeballs burning in the light.

She stood up and did up her jeans and pulled her shirt down and picked the grass out of her hair while he watched her, saying nothing. Then she turned and walked away from him and this time she didn't look back, not once, she just kept walking up the road, over the brow of the hill and into the cul-de-sac to her mother's house, where the front door was still ajar and her sisters were in the garden waiting for her, not even realizing that she'd been away.

They had their final meal together – a take-away from the Indian restaurant in the centre of town because Edie had failed to buy anything. Lumps of meat in orange, oily sauces; whole chillies in a sludge of spinach; slimy okra and flecked rice. Two bottles of red wine. They ate slowly. In the candlelight, their faces shone with heat and grease; their foreheads were damp with sweat.

Edie looked at her two sisters. Stella had braided her hair into a single thick plait, just as she had done all those years ago when she was young and full of ease.

She wore a pink cotton shirt, open at the throat. Her skin was smooth and creamy. She looked the way she used to, when she wandered downstairs from her deep, hot bath, flushed with health and youth. And she looked the way Louise used to look, when she leant towards Vic, laying a hand on his arm, and her breasts pushed against the thin fabric of her dress and her red lips smiled. Jude was like a sculpture. Her neck was long, her forehead high, her cheeks carved. Her eyes glistened in the dim room. But when she threw back her head and laughed, Edie caught a flash of the gawky, clumsy, scowling girl she'd been.

'A toast,' Edie said, picking up her glass and holding it high, so it caught the candlelight. 'To us.'

'I'll drink to that,' said Jude, with hardly a trace of irony in her voice.

'And Vic and Louise,' said Stella beseechingly. 'To the family.'

'To the family.'

They chinked their three glasses together and drank.

Darling Edie, it doesn't feel like days but weeks since you left. But I'll see you tomorrow. Goodnight my love, and sleep well. Alex.

26

'Granny.'

Ellen did not move. She sat in the armchair in her overheated room, clutching her panda, with her back to the window. Edie had brought in sweet peas from Louise's garden and put them on the table; a damp pastel mass of colours.

'Ellen.'

She turned her head, looked at Edie.

'Yes?'

'I want to tell you something. You're the only one I can talk to. You would have understood. I'm sure you would.'

She picked up her grandmother's hand. The gold ring on her wedding finger was loose on the thin finger, but the swollen knuckle stopped it from falling off. Her skin was baggy and slid on her bones, like an ill-fitting glove. Ellen let her hand rest in Edie's for a few moments, then pulled it away, frowning.

'Don't do that,' she said in a sharp voice that sounded so like the crisp, organized Ellen of old that Edie was momentarily stopped in her tracks. She stared into the cloudy eyes. What if behind that vague face, inside that folding body, Ellen knew exactly what was going on? What if she was trapped in her own disintegration, while stupid people talked to her in loud baby voices and fed her sloppy baby food and put nappies on her and thrust soft toys into her arms.

'I don't know where to begin,' she said.

'It's a story,' said Ellen hopefully.

'Yes, I suppose it's a story.'

A story about a shy man, about ordinary people making mistakes in their lives and being cruelly punished for them. About lies, betrayal, love gone wrong and the past refusing to fade into bearable history. A story about patterns being repeated down the generations.

She started with Louise and Vic falling in love. She described their wedding day: how Louise had looked, cocooned in her white dress. How stunned by joy Vic had been, because he knew he was a dull, plain, timid man with few expectations, yet here he was, his arm around a princess, his fingers sinking into her gown's satin folds, his nostrils filled with her fragrance. How they'd bought an old house and filled its rooms with daughters. But life isn't like a children's story. Vic had a job he hated and couldn't do. They were always worried about money. Louise became discontented with her role as wife and mother, and with her introverted, silent husband. She saw Vic as a failure. Gradually disappointment had seeped into the house, spreading like damp.

Ellen rested her chin on her panda's head and said nothing. Edie talked, imagining what she did not know. She described Louise's affair, stretching through the summer and into autumn. The snatched meetings, the lies she told to Vic, the excitement of subterfuge. She knew she had to end it but she couldn't. She was cruel to Vic, because she felt guilty. She almost hated him, because she saw how much she was hurting him.

Edie talked about her family, her silent middle son with eyes like Vic's. She moved on to what had happened between her and Ricky. She listened to the sound of her own voice, precise and undramatic. It took half an hour to tell the whole story. When she'd finished, she sat for a few moments in silence. Then she added, 'Alex and the children are arriving soon. What shall I do?'

Ellen didn't reply. She stared out at the lawn, where a woman in a wheelchair was being slowly pushed over the mown grass by her overweight, middle-aged son. Her legs hung down like pink sausages; sweat trickled down his red forehead.

'I just want to go home,' she said. 'Take me home.'

'We can't leave her there.'

'What are you suggesting, then?'

'I don't know. I'm not suggesting anything, just saying we can't leave her there. She hates it. She's unhappy.'

'I can't look after her, not with Sam.'

'I don't think she should actually live with anyone. She needs round-the-clock nursing. But if she stays where she is, who'll visit her? Nobody, except one of us, a couple of times a year. She'll just sit in her room day after day, staring out of the window.'

'It doesn't mean anything to her when we do visit her,' said Stella. 'She doesn't know we're there, not really, and as soon as we walk out of the door she's forgotten us.'

'So are you saying that it doesn't matter? That nothing about her life matters any more?'

'No,' said Stella. 'You know I'm not. Except maybe it matters more to us than to her — she makes us feel guilty.'

'What do you think?' Edie turned to Jude, who had said nothing, just chewed her lower lip.

'Oh, I agree with you,' said Jude heavily. 'I was just plucking up the courage to say I'd take her.'

'You!'

'I don't see why you should be quite so surprised. Why not?' Jude raised her eyebrows at Edie. 'I've been pondering it ever since Mum died.'

'But how would she fit into your life? I mean . . .'

'I'm not talking about installing her into my flat and giving up work to feed her and lift her on to the lavatory. I'm just saying that if she's going to move to be nearer one of us, it should be me. I don't have other responsibilities, like you two have.'

'But you're always railing against family responsibilities.'

'So now I'd have something to rail against and blame everything on.'

'I don't know,' said Stella. 'It doesn't seem fair that just one of us has to take the burden.'

'Maybe it won't be such a burden,' said Jude. 'And if I'm not going to have children — it doesn't seem likely, does it? Not the way things are looking at the moment — then at least I can have a granny to take care of. And I won't have to do nappies and bedsores and toenails and things. I don't think I'd be very good at that.'

Edie looked at her. She was wearing a short-sleeved, low-waisted yellow dress and her glossy hair was tucked behind her ears. Her slim legs were stretched out, feet in light sandals, toenails painted brown. She looked like a member of a different species.

'What about your freedom?' she asked. 'Your spontaneity?'

'Oh, I think freedom's overrated,' said Jude carelessly. And she added, 'Anyway, she'll not live long, will she?'

'Jude!' Stella looked shocked.

'What? She's a frail old woman with diabetes and a heart murmur and bad circulation. She'll die in the next few years. And I'll be left feeling noble and virtuous. An unusual emotion for me.'

Edie giggled. 'OK,' she said. 'If it would make you feel good.'

Jude stretched in her chair, then checked her watch. She looked over at Edie. 'Alex'll be arriving soon.'

'In about half an hour, if he leaves when he said he would. Which he won't.' Edie got to her feet. 'I'm going to have a quick shower. Then I'll put things out for lunch. I picked up some cheese and cold cuts on the way back from Granny's, and salad stuff.'

After her shower, Edie dressed with more care than usual, putting on a thin, patterned skirt that reached just below her knees and a loose blue shirt that Alex had bought her. She dried her hair and tied it back, then put studs into her ears and a dab of perfume on her wrists. For the first time since Louise had died, she applied make-up – not enough to be noticeable, but enough to make her feel she was in control of the way she looked. She stood back from the long mirror that Stella was going to take with her when she left, and examined herself. She looked quite normal: a fresh, neat, brown-haired woman approaching her forties. She didn't seem like the sort of woman to cry at night, to feel panic sluicing through her body, to betray her husband, to have sex in a field with her jeans round her ankles and the road a few feet away. She stepped close up to the mirror, meeting her own gaze, but her eyes gave nothing away.

They arrived at two, spilling out from the hot, cramped car, cheeks flushed, clothes full of crumbs. There were circles of sweat under Alex's arms and his forehead was damp.

'You don't want to come too close,' he said to Edie, beaming at her.

'Oh, but I do,' she replied, and took his face between her hands and kissed him on the lips. 'Hello.' She felt self-conscious under his gaze.

She gathered the children into her arms. Lewis half-resisted her hugs, but Jess and Kit leaned into her with their warm, sticky bodies, their silky heads. They wrapped their arms round her neck and pulled her towards them, rubbing flushed cheeks against hers.

'I've missed you so much,' she said, feeling the weight of their demands at once, understanding how their love pressed down on her, insistent. 'Jess, you've lost a tooth!'

'And the bloody tooth fairy kept forgetting to give her a pound,' said Alex. 'Here, I'll take our stuff into the house. I even remembered your clothes for the funeral.'

'We're in Louise's room. The children are sleeping on the living-room floor. It's just for one night, so we can dump their sleeping-bags and clothes in there. Was your journey all right?' She was talking too fast, smiling too much. He'd guess.

'Oh, you know. Jess needed a pee about three minutes after we set off. Kit spilt Coke on Lewis's lap. Lewis hit him. I shouted at Lewis. Jess started to cry. Same as usual.'

'When are Leah and Gabriel arriving?'

'Tomorrow, at eleven-thirty. Is that OK? The funeral's not till two, is it?'

'That's fine. I don't think there's much to do for it. We're just having people back here, if they want to come. We'll have tea and sparkling wine and there are crisps and cakes.'

They went into the house together, through the empty echoing hall, and upstairs into Louise's bedroom.

'It seems ages since I saw you,' said Alex. 'But I already wrote that, didn't I?' He put his arms round her from behind and kissed the top of her head.

'Mmm.' Edie leant back against him. She could hear the children in the garden and when she looked out of the window she saw Lewis kicking his football through the sweet peas.

'Has it been a terrible week for you?'

'Not terrible. Strange. Good for us as sisters, I guess. There's so much I've got to tell you. Things I couldn't really say over the phone.'

She turned round in his arms and met his candid gaze. She could say it now. Hit him with it straight away.

He smiled at her and tucked a stray wisp of hair behind her ear. 'We've got plenty of time.'

''Mummy!' Kit's voice was tremulous. 'Mummy, where are you?'

'Coming,' she called. She stepped out of Alex's embrace. 'You must all be starving. There are lunch things on the table. I'll get the children.'

'I'll have a quick shower. Then I'll be able to hug you properly.'

Edie sat on the sofa in the living-room with a book and Jess plumped on her lap, inside the circle of her arms, with her hair tickling Edie's cheeks. Her breath was warm. She kept shifting and wriggling. Kit sat beside them. He let his head rest against Edie's shoulder, his leg pressed against hers. His eyes were closed; he wasn't listening to the story at all, just letting his thoughts drift in the sleepy afternoon. But every so often he would open his eyes and glance up, to make sure she was really there. There was a blade of grass in her hair and a faint rash on her arm. She smelt different than he remembered. As if she'd been standing by a bonfire. And she was wearing a perfume that she usually only wore in the evenings, when she and Alex were going out together. Outside, Lewis and Alex were playing football on the small lawn. He could hear their voices every so often: a cheer, a shout of protest. Jude and Stella were upstairs, sorting out what to wear for the funeral.

Kit wanted never to move from here. He wanted to lie, half-slumbering, on his mother's shoulder and hear her voice in his ear. And when he opened his eyes, she would smile at him, maybe push his hair off his hot forehead, or plant a swift kiss on his cheek.

'Kit?'

He looked up.

'Why don't you go and play football in the garden? Get some fresh air after being cooped up all morning in the car.'

He shook his head and closed his eyes again. Edie's voice resumed the story. Somewhere, a bee buzzed against a window pane. The sound of distant laughter, the smell of toast from lunch still hanging in the heavy air. If he didn't move, if he stayed here like this with his mother solid against him, then he was safe. Nothing could harm him ever again.

'Mummy was having an affair.'

'Well, good for her, I guess.' They were in the bedroom, in the early evening. Alex was putting on clean clothes before dinner and Edie was sorting Louise's jewellery into three gleaming heaps. She hesitated over a moonstone ring they all wanted. How she had loved it as a child, bold on her mother's finger. Then she dropped it into Jude's heap.

'No, I mean, when Daddy died.'

'Oh.' Alex frowned, letting the implications sink in. 'How do you know?'

'I found a love letter.'

'But are you sure . . . ?'

'The dates work. It all works, and makes horrible sense when I look back. And if Vic discovered . . .'

'I see.'

'It makes everything seem different.'

'Of course.'

'You think you understand the past, then you suddenly realize there are hundreds of ways to see it. Everything shifts, all the time.'

'Does it change the way you feel about Louise – are you angry with her?'

'I don't know. She's dead now. They're both dead. All that franticness is over. And it happened so long ago. I mainly feel terribly sorry for her, for both of them.' She picked up a silver bracelet and fiddled with the clasp.

'It's a bit of a brutal punishment, isn't it?'

'Him killing himself, you mean?'

'Yes. How could she ever forgive herself, after that?'

'Or forgive him, for that matter?'

'That too. Strange for you, to discover after she died. Now you'll never be able to find out what it all meant. Like a fragment of a story, and you don't know the ending.'

'It is strange. Very unsettling.'

'What do Jude and Stella say?'

'I haven't told them.'

'Why not?'

'I thought – oh, I don't know. I was going to, and then I thought it was her secret to tell, not mine. And she never revealed it, not for twenty-two years. Perhaps she never told anyone. Do I have the right to tell the others?'

'I don't know,' said Alex slowly. 'If you gave them the choice, they'd choose to know. Especially Jude.'

'Of course. Almost everyone wants to know. If I say . . .' she swallowed hard and continued. 'If I say, I've got a secret and you won't like it but do you want to know what it is, what would you say?'

She had imagined having this conversation with Alex when she first discovered the letter – the eager examination of implications; the relief of sharing the knowledge with someone who would understand. But now every word felt fraudulent, and thorny with dangers. She tried to imagine what she would have said, if nothing had happened with Ricky, and then to repeat those words, but she was like an actor who had learnt her lines imperfectly and was now trapped on stage, stammering.

'I don't know.'

'You'd say, tell me, wouldn't you? Surely.'

'I don't know if I would. There are some things you shouldn't know.'

'Oh,' said Edie doubtfully.

'Say,' continued Alex cheerfully, 'say for instance that you had an affair.'

'Yes?' She smiled at him, feeling as if her knees were buckling underneath her and reminding herself that they often said this to each other – imagine how you would feel, how I would feel.

'Would I want to know? If I had to choose between knowing and not knowing, and the not knowing included forgetting that I ever had been in the position to find out, if you see what I mean . . .'

'Yes.'

'Then maybe I'd be wise to choose that. You know,

I sometimes think that in relationships there are maybe two types of people – the ones who don't want to know enough about their partner's life, and the ones who want to know too much, who want to know everything. The indifferent and the obsessed. You could go mad if you started wanting to find out exactly what went on in your loved one's head.'

'That's not the same – you don't want to know what's going through my head all the time, but what about my life . . . ?'

'Anyway, luckily for me it's academic because I know you're not having an affair. I wouldn't be so rational then. I think I'd go mad.'

Edie tried to smile at him. 'Anyway, we're getting off the point, which is Louise.' She was amazed at how natural her voice sounded.

'The older I get,' said Alex, 'the more I feel that judging people is irrelevant. You just have to understand them. You just have to feel pity for your parents, don't you, caught in their own tragedy?'

'Yes,' said Edie. 'I guess you're right.'

'Come on.' He took her hand and pulled her off Louise's bed to her feet. 'Let's go and cook supper. I'll get drinks for everyone. Then you're going to bed early. You look exhausted.'

'Do I?'

'Done in.'

She woke at one and lay for a while, listening to Alex breathing. She stared at the darkness outside. Then she got out of bed, very quietly so as not to wake him, and stood by the window, looking out at the dim shape of the garden, the massed black of the trees.

She was thirsty, so she padded to the bathroom, listening out for any children as she did so, but everything was quiet. She drank a tumbler of water, then looked out at the street. For one moment she thought she saw a figure standing there, near the street lamp, but when she looked again there was nobody. She was just imagining things. She crept back along the corridor and climbed into bed. She closed her eyes and waited for the morning.

27

Alex insisted on making everyone a cooked breakfast the next morning, even though Jude wrinkled her nose at the idea and Stella protested that they'd only just finished clearing out the fridge and now he was going to be filling it up again.

'You'll not be eating lunch before the funeral,' he said firmly. 'And grease is very good for big emotions, I find.'

He was back from the shops by eight and laying out the streaky bacon, eggs, pork and garlic sausages, flat mushrooms, tomatoes, and even – he produced this with a flourish of triumph – black pudding.

'Timing's the secret,' he said.

He enlisted Lewis and Kit to help him. Soon the kitchen was filled with the smell of frying and the scoured surfaces were spotted with oil. Lewis turned the bacon and the sausages, Kit poured freshly squeezed orange juice into seven tumblers and counted out knives and forks. Alex ground coffee, sliced tomatoes and scattered them with herbs, toasted brown bread, sizzled black pudding in the pan. He broke eggs expertly, basted them with the fat from the bacon.

'Perfect!' he said. 'Come on; you have to eat it piping hot.' He shovelled food on to plates.

Edie broke the yolk with a crust of bread and watched it run, sticky and yellow, over the plate. She cut a small piece of bacon and dipped it into the yolk, then put it into her mouth. She wasn't hungry. She took a sip of coffee to swallow down the food. She felt very far away, in a dream of her own making. Tomorrow, she would be gone from here. They would all be gone and scattered, with no further need to come together again. It would just be a memory, like a snapshot, gradually yellowing with age. She'd remember it the way you remember family holidays: glowing images, and around them fog and silence. She speared a slice of sausage. A letter. A house. A bridge. A stranger from long ago.

She flinched and looked round the table. Everyone was silent, concentrating on their breakfast. Kit had shadows under his eyes. Lewis's hair stuck up like an owl's. Jess's lips were a greedy yellow; there were dimples on her wrists, the last traces of her toddler years. Jude was still in her dressing-gown. Her collar-bones were sharp and face pale, and she fiddled with her breakfast. Stella ate peacefully; she looked younger and prettier than she had done a week ago. And Alex – Alex was methodically piling sausage, bacon, black pudding and mushroom on to his fork and covering it with yolk. Jess said something to him and he bent towards her respectfully, fork half-way towards his mouth. Then he must have felt Edie's gaze because he looked up at her and gave her a half-smile.

'Eat up,' he ordered her. 'And you, Jude! I'm here to get you all through the day.'

The house was full of arrivals and departures. Alex, who had cleared all the breakfast things and mowed the lawn, hurtled out of the house late to collect Leah and Gabriel from the station. He returned with them half an hour later. Edie had first met them when they were tiny, but now they were practically adults. Gabriel was through the stage of teenage spots, gangly limbs, a voice which broke in mid-sentence. He was taller than Alex, with sloe-eyes and a shaved head. Leah had smooth skin and long dark hair that she wore in artfully mussed styles. Now she was complaining about the black skirt her mother had insisted she should wear, the ugly shoes that pinched her toes. She hugged Edie. Gabriel was plugged into his portable CD player. When he kissed her on both cheeks, she could hear the tinny beat of its music.

Then Bob and Sam arrived. Stella was right, Sam had become a tall, bulky young man with an offside stare and a shuffling gait. Beside him, Bob looked small. Edie watched them greet one another at the door. Stella seemed cool and self-possessed. She turned her head away from Bob's kiss, so that his lips brushed her cheek.

Then she and Jude went to pick up Ellen from the home. They had said she would be ready, but when they arrived, they found her in a stained woollen skirt and an ugly brown cardigan with several buttons missing. She was wearing thick laddered support tights and pink mules and she smelt of urine.

'She must be boiling,' said Edie.

'And she looks awful. As if nobody could be bothered.'

Jude started rummaging through the wardrobe. There were only a few clothes there and they were all old and shapeless: thick skirts and dreary dresses in browns, dark blues, dark greys.

'Fuck this,' said Jude disgustedly. 'It's as if they're trying to make her even more invisible than she already is.'

She pulled out a dun-coloured shift and held it up. 'Who'd choose to wear something like this? I'm surprised Mum allowed it.'

'How about this?' Edie pulled a light pink shirt out of a drawer. 'This is more like it.'

'Anyway, listen to us,' said Jude. 'We're behaving as if she didn't exist as well.' She knelt down in front of Ellen and held up the shirt. 'What do you reckon, Gran? Will this do?'

Ellen put out one hand and touched the cotton. 'Pink,' she said.

'Right. So, will it do for you?'

Ellen didn't reply and Jude tossed the shirt on to the bed.

'How about trousers, not a boring old skirt with thick orangey tights? Yes? Look, these black slack things will do. And we can give you a black jacket of Louise's when we get there. I put it in the charity bag. It'll be like a trouser suit. You'll look fab.' She put a hand on Ellen's arm. 'Gran? Trousers?'

'Trousers,' Ellen repeated, and Jude took this for agreement.

They pulled off her scratchy cardigan and her thin shirt. Underneath she was wearing a grubby, silky vest. Her arms were thin and loose flesh hung off them.

'We'll put on a new vest, all right? Lift up your arms. That's right.'

It felt somehow indecent to be looking at her shrunken body, her shrivelled breasts. Ellen must have felt so too, because she crossed her arms over her naked chest.

'OK, on with this.'

They pulled a vest over her head, then buttoned her into the pink shirt.

'Do you want to stand up, Granny?'

They pulled her to her feet and took off her skirt; peeled off her thick tights. She looked bewildered. Her skinny legs were veined; her ankles were swollen, her feet were a purplish colour, with yellow toenails. Edie thought of Jess's lustrous body and her clean smell.

'I'm going to wash her,' she said.

She filled the basin with lukewarm water and wiped her between the legs with a warm flannel.

'And we should put her in a nappy for the service.'

'Is that really necessary?'

'Yes. I'll do it now. Pass it here. Then those huge knickers.'

'It's treating her like a baby.'

'It's better like this. And we'll take a couple of spares.'

'Trousers,' said Jude. 'That's it. Step in.'

They buttoned the trousers over her padded buttocks and her pot-belly and put her feet into slip-on shoes. Edie brushed her thin hair and Jude whisked a bottle of perfume from her bag and put some on her wrists and behind her ears.

'Look at you!' said Jude, standing her in front of the half-mirror.

They steered her down the stairs and through the front door. She smiled as she felt the fresh air on her face.

'Are we going home?'

'You're spending the day with us,' said Edie. She paused, then added: 'It's Louise's funeral.'

'Funeral?'

'Louise is dead, Gran,' said Jude.

'My little girl Louise?'

'Yes, your little girl. She died in an accident. We're burying her today; saying goodbye to her.'

'No. No, that's not true. I can see you now.'

'Come on, here's the car. Mind your head.'

She sat in the front, beside Jude, and they strapped the safety-belt round her.

'Home,' she said again.

'I'm not a daughter any more. All my life I've been a daughter. Now I'm just a mother. So many things behind me, which will never come again.'

'A mother. A wife. A sister. A friend. You're lots of things to lots of people.'

'I went back to the house.'

'Did you? I wondered if you would.'

'And the bridge where, you know . . .'

'Yes.'

'It all seemed so far off and yet so near as well. Raw like yesterday. I realized I'd never got over it all.'

'Oh Edie,' Alex said tenderly.

It was no good. She couldn't speak now. She saw how he'd missed a patch when shaving, how his shirt was only half tucked in, and there was a smear of dirt on his cuff. His shoes were battered and scuffed. She stood up and crossed over to him. She put her arms round his neck and kissed him on his eyelids, the pulse of his neck, his lips. She ran her hands through his soft hair.

'I've never loved anyone the way I love you,' she said. 'You're the one.'

'Am I?'

'I don't deserve you.'

'Don't say that.'

He put his arms round her and they held on to each other tightly. Downstairs, Lewis shouted for her, but she didn't move, just held Alex tighter.

28

A few tears rolled down Stella's face, but only Jude cried properly. She sat quite straight in the pew, her hands plaited together in her lap, Louise's moonstone ring on her finger, a jaunty beret on her coarse black hair. Her eyes were dry, the expression on her face barely altered, but her body shuddered spasmodically. Edie put a hand on her shoulder. She was all bone and sinew and muscle, nothing soft or pliable about her. Grief gripped and shook her, but she looked ahead, silent, and gradually her dry sobs subsided and she was still again.

Edie had thought she would weep, and indeed the sight of the coffin made her throat ache. But for the most part she remained calm. She was drained after the last few days, exhausted as an addict recovering from a binge. She wanted to go home. She let herself think what it would be like, to wake up in the morning with Jess wedged in between her and Alex. Or to sit at the kitchen table with Lewis, watching him dunk biscuits into his tea and then suck off the soggy portion while he told her about his day. Cycling down the road with Kit to buy doughnuts, with the evening sun behind them. Alex coming in from work and pouring them both a glass of wine. Going from room to room together, kissing the children goodnight or standing in the door-way to watch them while they slept.

She made a decision. She would take Kit out of school at once and find him a place somewhere else. It didn't matter how long it took. She wasn't going to force him to walk through those school gates a single day more, seeing the dread in his face, feeling his whole frame shudder, all in the name of sticking it out. He had to begin again, in a place where boys didn't call him 'poof' and lock him into the toilets at break, and where failure didn't stick to him like a bad smell. She twisted her head to the pew behind and caught his eye. She smiled and he smiled back gravely. There'd been too much unhappiness. She had a choice.

Stella stood up and walked to the front of the church. The book she held was trembling in her hands, but she lifted up her head and read clearly. After hours of agonizing, she had chosen a poem that people always read at funerals. Her low, pleasant voice filled the church. 'When I am dead, my dearest,' she began, and a stifled hush fell over the congregation. This is what they had come for. Someone gave a sob. But Edie hardly heard the words of the poem Stella had chosen. They pulled her under, like a withdrawing tide.

In a few months, Edie would turn forty. She was the same age as Louise had been when Vic killed himself. The second phase, that's what some people called it. Or the middle years, sandwiched between the beginning and the end. In her job, they often called them the danger years – men hurtling off their track, falling for a young woman, ditching the life they'd made; women silently and invisibly breaking down, as if a rust of sadness was corroding them from within. Men do it outside-in, women inside-out – that's what they'd said, and Edie had agreed, complacently ignorant of the emotional blizzard she was about to enter. Vic and Louise had both been wrecked at the beginning of their middle years; one sinking to the bottom of the ocean, the other holed and splintered, listing on through to her sixties. Now it was her turn. Part Two.

Stella finished and sat down again. Edie stood and turned to face the pews. In front of her were row upon row of people she knew and half-knew; people she'd forgotten, or who'd been changed by the years, so that only the way they smiled up at her brought them flooding back. Old friends of her parents, some of whom she had last seen at Vic's funeral. People she'd never met. Work colleagues, neighbours, distant relatives she hadn't thought about from one year to the next. Rose was here, sitting next to her mother; she wore a long black dress and a chunky amber necklace, and her lips were scarlet. Tears ran in rivers down her cheeks, leaving tracks in her make-up. At funerals, people cry for their own lives; all the wrecked hopes. At the back of the church, far from his ex-wife, was Rose's father, with silver hair and the over-tanned face of a heavy drinker; a gin-and-tonic man.

'This is in memory of Mummy and Daddy,' she heard herself say. 'Because once they told me that they learnt it together when they first met, and when we were children we all knew it off by heart as well. It was one of those family things. And because I thought we should remember the happy times, as well as the sad ones. So . . .'

She caught Alex's gaze and held it for a few seconds before looking away. Her eyes slid over Lewis, Kit, Jess, then rested on the faces of her two sisters; Stella looked smooth and warm, Jude raw-boned and lonely as a crow. Beside her, Ellen had fallen asleep; her head lolled forward. Edie felt big and heavy with love, weighed down with it, like a ship with too much cargo, sinking beneath its Plimsoll line. She smiled at them all.

'The owl and the pussy cat went to sea,' she began, 'in a beautiful pea-green boat . . .'

She knew it off by heart. She often read it out loud to all her children as well, passing it on. That's what you did in families, she thought, as she recited the familiar words. You repeat things and you pass them on, all the rituals and customs; the deep structures of life, underneath belief and common sense and will. All the stories that define you; the tyrannical, tender, undignified anecdotes that keep you in your place. All the lies and the secrets. You think you're an individual, freshly minted, radical and alone, and then you discover that you're a link in the chain after all. Even the struggle to be free is part of the pattern that binds you.

'They sailed away for a year and a day . . .' She heard Vic's voice under her own. For a shy man, he had been surprisingly theatrical, reciting passages in an out-thrown voice, acting charades recklessly, tossing his arms in operatic gestures, as if he could momentarily forget himself and become someone else. Louise had always been more self-conscious. She had loved being looked at and being desired, but she minded dreadfully how she appeared to others. Her life had been full of mirrors. Edie remembered how she would always stop in the hall, on the way to the front door, to check her appearance; how she would turn the rear-view mirror to stare at her reflection before stepping from the car, or glance at herself appraisingly in shop windows. She needed to control the image she was presenting to the world. Her beauty had an element of fear in it, thought Edie. She was always scared of losing it, and of no longer being lovable. Perhaps that was why she had had an affair with a man like Rose's father. Being desired can be the most potent of all forms of seduction, bringing you back to life again.

'They dined on mince, and slices of quince, which they ate with a runcible spoon . . .'

She thought of Ricky as he used to be, a romantic, who was sure that love was the answer, the ladder out of his life. And now he worked for a central heating firm, with a failed marriage, a bitter laugh, a shrug that said he never really expected anything else. Or Rose even, sitting a few pews away from her with the face that she put on hopefully each morning, mopping her eyes so the mascara smudged in rings round them: she'd been the most adored girl in the school, with yellow hair and a giggle like a shallow brook.

Kit watched his mother. She looked different, though he couldn't say how. Perhaps it was just the stained light and her unfamiliar clothes: the black silk shirt over a black skirt, her brown hair coiled tightly on top of her head. Her face was pale, and seemed smaller than usual, while her eyes were big and bright. There was a glow about her. He didn't know if he liked her like this, standing straight as a staff while everyone looked at her, and she looked through them all at something else that they couldn't see.

He stared at the coffin. He tried not to imagine his granny lying inside there, dead for six days. What would she look like? He mustn't think about that. He tried to remember what she had looked like before, but found that he couldn't, not properly. How could that happen? She had only just died and already she was beginning to blur and fade, like his dreams did when he woke in the morning and tried to recall them. He closed his eyes and tried to force her back into his mind: bright hair, with grey in it, a nice smell when she hugged him, sad eyes, soft skin, powder and lipstick. If his mother died, would he forget her like this, and let her sink under the waters, drifting down to the bottom? No! He opened his eyes and stared fiercely up at her once more, and her figure shimmered through his tears. Her voice was softening. She was reaching the end.

'And hand in hand on the edge of the sand, they danced by the light of the moon.'

'They danced by the light of the moon,' said Ellen, lifting her head suddenly. 'The moon, the moon, the moon.'

29

The sun poured down, and people spilt out of the kitchen and living-room on to the lawn Alex had mowed that morning. They took off their black jackets, their brimmed hats; the men loosened their ties and rolled up their shirt-sleeves. Stiletto heels dug into the baked earth. Matches flared under cupped hands. The children carried round trays of drinks and bowls of crisps. The hum of voices, booms and trills of laughter; corks popping, glasses chinking. It was a party.

Edie went from group to group. She'd taken off her hot black clothes in favour of her thin blue skirt and tee-shirt. Her feet were in sandals; her hair had come unpinned and hung in damp tendrils down her cheek. She took a cautious sip of sparkling wine. Her head fizzed. The light glared against her eyeballs, which felt raw. A mild ache corkscrewed into her temple. She wished she were in jeans and an old tee-shirt, walking alone over the green fields, wind in her face. She checked on Ellen, who was sitting by the garden door, then stopped by Rose and her mother.

'Thank you both for coming,' she said.

Rose hugged her. 'I wouldn't have missed it for the world,' she said, and started crying again, luxuriously big tears rolling down her face. 'Sorry. I'm hopeless at things like this.'

Alison took Edie's hand. 'I'm sorry for your loss,' she said formally.

Edie looked at her. It had been many years since they had last met, and she was smaller than she remembered, with stiff shoulders and a pinched and anxious face.

'It was a shock,' she acknowledged. 'I don't think it's really sunk in yet.' She swallowed another mouthful of her drink.

'You read beautifully,' said Rose emotionally. She wrapped an arm around Edie's waist. 'Are you OK?'

'Yes, fine.'

'Fine! And you didn't cry, did you? Are you always so controlled?'

'I don't think so. I don't feel controlled, anyway.'

'She was always the nicest of my schoolfriends, wasn't she, Mum?' Rose was on her way to being quite drunk.

'You were a quiet, very polite girl, that's what I remember most.' Rose's mother allowed herself a smile.

'I was shy, I think. That's not the same really.'

'Come on, Edie! You were goody two-shoes.'

'That makes me sound dreadful.'

'No, we all thought you were so innocent.'

'I was. We all were.'

'Edie!'

Edie turned to see a face she didn't recognize. She smiled vaguely.

'It's Ken – don't you remember? We lived next door to you but one. Such a lovely woman, your mother . . . We couldn't miss coming today.'

A warm hand crept into hers and she looked down. It was Kit, still in his funeral gear, sweat on his brow.

'Go and get into some shorts, honey.'

'I want to go with you.'

'Kit . . .'

'I'm not going anywhere. I want to be wherever you are.'

'I would have known you anywhere.'

'Would you?'

'You've hardly changed. Well, of course, you've grown older. We've all grown older, haven't we?' Simon Scott sighed gustily. Edie could smell alcohol on his breath, and something minty, like mouthwash. 'Look at me. Every hair on my head's grey; I have to get out of bed three or four times to pee. And see this.' He held a hand out and they both watched his fingers tremble. 'We had good times together though, didn't we? Me and Alison, Louise and Vic, you and Rose. It only seems like yesterday and now here we are. Vic and Louise dead, me and Alison not speaking to each other. Everyone gone or scattered. Who'd have thought it, eh?'

Edie muttered something incoherent.

'Your mother was a wonderful woman,' he continued sentimentally. 'Not many women like her.'

She stared at him. If she said now: you had an affair with my mother, and then my father killed himself, what would he do? Bluster? Weep? We all have an immense ability to forgive ourselves, she thought. Time grows over the past like a skin, gradually thickening, until it's just a crooked scar, a story you can track by running your fingers over its pale ridge. She opened her mouth to speak, but then couldn't. I have forfeited my right to judge anyone, she thought. Or anyone except myself.

'She was very beautiful,' she agreed.

'She never got over Vic's death.'

'How could she?'

'Such a waste.'

'Yes. Excuse me. I have to go now. So many people . . .'

Jude was alone in the corner of the garden, with a cigarette in one hand and a glass of sparkling wine in the other. She'd taken off her long jacket and her high shoes; the hem of her shimmery grey skirt dragged on the ground. In her sleeveless black top, her arms looked thin and white; her collar-bones jutted out. Her lipstick had worn off. Without it, her face looked exposed. Edie crossed over to her.

'Are you OK?'

Jude turned. Her face was a blank. 'After my crying jag, you mean?'

'Are you?'

She shrugged her bony shoulders.

'Jude?'

'A bit drunk maybe.' She drained the wine in her glass to prove her point and sucked on her cigarette until her cheeks were hollow.

'Well, why not?'

'I killed them both, you know.'

'What?'

'I killed them.'

'Jude, what on earth are you talking about?'

'Him and her.'

'Jude, darling Jude, you're talking nonsense.'

'No.' Jude dropped her cigarette end on to Louise's neat lawn and ground her heel into it fiercely. 'No, I'm not. I told him, you see.'

'No, I don't see. Told who? Told what?'

'About Mum and that poncey jackass.' Jude jerked her head savagely in the direction of Simon. 'The day before he disappeared. So. You can quit worrying about once being a little bit nasty to him.'

'Hello, you two.' Alex put an arm round each of them. 'I was watching you. Are you all right?'

'Yes.'

'No.'

'Well, that sounds about right on a day like today. Can I get you anything? Drink? Tea?'

'No,' Jude said brusquely.

'I'm fine,' said Edie. 'Are the children all right?'

'Yes – they're inside, watching telly. Bob's with Sam.' Edie turned to Jude. 'You're wrong.'

'You knew about it too? You knew! How long for?' Her expression suddenly changed. 'Jesus! Am I seeing things, or is it who I think?' she said, staring over Edie's shoulder. 'Oh Lord, it is!' She gave a grating chuckle. 'All we need.'

'What is it?'

But Edie knew already, before turning her head to follow Jude's gaze. Dread rippled over her skin like icy water. Alex's hand felt very heavy on her shoulder.

'What the fuck is he doing here?' continued Jude, loudly, so that heads turned towards them.

He looked as if he'd just got out of bed, and put on any clothes that lay to hand: jeans with a tear across one knee, a creased tee-shirt with 'Why me?' written across the chest in pink, scuffed trainers. He was standing by the kitchen door staring around with a lopsided grin on his face. He looked drunk.

'Who?' asked Alex. 'Who are you talking about?'

'Someone we used to know,' said Jude. 'Didn't we, Edie?' She was looking at Edie now; her eyes were bright.

'It's Ricky,' Edie said to Alex in a low voice. 'You know, the boy . . .'

'Your old flame?'

'Yes.'

'How did he know about this?'

'I don't know,' said Edie. She couldn't understand how she was still standing upright, mouthing words that made sense. Her face felt pulled tight, and full of tics and twitches. 'He must have met someone who . . . I'd better just go and, um . . .'

'Mummy.'

It was Kit again. He took hold of her hand with his sweaty fingers. 'Mummy. I couldn't find you.'

'Here I am,' she said.

Ricky had seen them now, but he didn't move, just kept on smiling his lopsided grin. Bob came up behind him and handed him a glass of sparkling wine and he drank it down like water, then grabbed another. People were looking at him – a scruffy stranger with torn trousers. For Edie, it was as if she was transfixed in the golden light of early evening, frozen in place by the stares of Alex, Jude, Ricky – and now Stella as well, her mouth open, recognition gathering in her face.

Then she stirred herself. 'I'll just . . . shall I . . . ?' she said, as casually as she could manage.

She pulled her hand from Kit's, but he grabbed a fold in her skirt and trailed after her, tripping on her heels. She could unpick his fingers, run away, down the path, through the house, out on to the road, into her car. And drive, with the window open and wind whipping through her hair. Foot hard down and never mind where she was going – drive and drive and drive, away from the stares. Or she could scream: sit on the path and hold her head in her hands and howl till her throat hurt and someone led her inside, to a cool, quiet room and a mouthful of sedatives and darkness seeping through her at last.

'Hello, Ricky.' Still that crazy little grin. 'I certainly didn't expect to see you here,' she said formally, and held out her hand. He took it in his and held it for a moment, pressing her fingers in his. His bitten fingernails. 'This is my son, Kit,' she said. 'My second child.'

'Hello,' said Ricky.

Kit ducked his head and moved even closer to Edie, who put a hand on his head. His hair was soft and hot. Out of the corner of her eye, she could see people talking to each other, lifting glasses to their mouths. They were behaving as if everything was normal. She turned her head and saw Jude and Alex, still at the end of the garden, both watching her.

'I don't know what to say,' she said at last.

'Don't worry,' said Ricky. 'Why do you need to talk at all?'

'But . . .' She glanced down at Kit, then said quietly, 'What are you doing here?'

'I couldn't tell you, really. I left work at lunch, had a few drinks and – well, it seemed like a good idea at the time. Is there more wine?'

'People are about to leave.'

'That's all right.'

Oh God, he really was drunk.

'I have to say goodbye to them.'

'Go on then.'

'Ricky, please.'

'What?'

'You know.'

'Edie, we were about to . . .' Rose appeared at Ricky's side, teetering on her high heels. When she saw Ricky her mouth opened into a smudged 'o'. 'But what are you doing here? I mean, I didn't know you and Edie still knew each . . .'

'We don't,' said Edie.

'I came to pay my respects,' said Ricky.

'Oh,' said Rose uncertainly.

'Hello, Ricky.'

Edie looked up. Jude was standing a few feet away.

'Mmm?' said Ricky.

'Don't you recognize me?'

'I can't say I do . . . Hang on, it's Edie's little sister. Jude Jennings. Jesus, you've changed. What happened to you?'

Jude gave a snort. 'Life, Ricky. What are you doing here?'

'Well now.' His glance slid over to Edie, who felt her

skin prickle with fear. 'Who knows?' he said. 'Old times. Any more drink going?'

Edie looked up the garden, which was beginning to empty of people. Alex was standing on his own. He looked big and hot and lonely. 'I'll leave you to it,' she said, and walked towards him, Kit still attached to her skirt. Every so often she stopped to say goodbye to people, but she reached him at last. Her heart was pounding, her mouth was dry. She tried to smile at him.

'Hello,' he said.

She slid an arm through his, but he felt inert. 'Hi.'

They stood in silence for a few moments.

'I just want us to be home now,' she said. Kit fidgeted beside her. 'Us and the children.'

He didn't reply, just stared back down the garden that was striped by the long shadows of evening. Ricky was rolling a cigarette. Jude, Stella and Bob were standing beside him.

'He's just a ghost from the past.'

He turned to look at her then. 'So you haven't seen him for twenty years?'

'Twenty-two,' she corrected him. She looked straight into his honourable face, his clear eyes. 'No. Of course I haven't.'

30

'Goodbye.'

'Take care.'

'Keep in touch.'

'I'm so sorry.'

'If you're ever in this neighbourhood again . . .'

'Goodbye,' said Stella, Edie, Jude. 'Thank you. We will.' They stood together by the door. 'Drive carefully,' they said to the people who'd drunk more than they should have done.

Only a few visitors were left now. Alex was going round the garden with a bin-bag, collecting crisp packets, cigarette ends, half-eaten wedges of cake. Bob was washing glasses in the kitchen, with his eye on the clock. He and Stella were meant to be going by eight, leaving Jude and Edie to clear the last of the mess and close up the house. Gabriel was in the spare room, crouched over Edie's laptop; Leah was sending text messages on her mobile. The rest of the children, even Kit, were on their second video in Louise's bedroom. Jess was asleep in front of it, her thumb in her mouth and her fingers spread over her face. Sam was humming gently to himself.

In the garden, Ricky was sitting next to Ellen and Ken – their old next-door neighbour but one – on the old bench. Every so often, Edie glanced at him, hoping he was about to leave, but he showed no sign of moving. Yet nothing had happened. There'd been no scene. The earth hadn't opened up; the sky hadn't fallen on her head.

'What are we going to do about them?' asked Jude at last.

'Maybe you can run Ellen back to the home,' said Edie.

'And Ricky?'

'I'll call him a cab. He can't drive.'

'I think that's a good idea,' said Jude briskly. 'Why don't I phone the local minicab firm now, while you tell him he's got to go.'

'Jude . . .'

'We can talk later – after everyone's gone. What time is Alex leaving?'

'About eight, like Bob, after a quick supper. He's got to get Leah and Gabriel back to their mother's before too late. The children can all sleep in the car.'

'Right. Come on then.'

Jude led Ellen off. She had chocolate smears all over her pink shirt and somehow Louise's black jacket had a rip along its sleeve.

'Where am I going?' she asked, as she was steered round the side of the house towards the car. 'I don't want to go.'

Ken stood up, looking round the empty lawn as if realizing for the first time that all the other guests should leave. 'Well,' he said, awkwardly. 'I'll be making a move too. After my trip down memory lane.'

'It's been nice seeing you again,' said Edie politely. She turned to Ricky. 'Come on. Time for you to go, too.'

'I suppose it is,' said Ricky. He got unsteadily to his feet and looked down at her. 'Weird, eh?' he said.

'Yes. We've ordered a taxi for you. You can collect your car later.'

Ricky lifted her left hand and fiddled with the gold wedding band on her finger. She knew Alex was watching, but for a few seconds she let him hold her hand, his head bent. There was a scattering of dandruff in his hair, and a pink bald patch, the size of a five-penny coin, on his crown. Edie felt a lurch of tenderness and disgust.

'I'll walk you to the road,' she said. 'Come on.'

'Edie.'

'Come on.' She could hear the drunken nostalgia in his voice.

'Nothing turns out the way you think.' There were footsteps behind them, and Edie looked up to see Alex was standing a few feet away. Ricky stared at him, still clutching Edie's hand. 'I was just saying, nothing turns out the way you think.'

'That's true,' said Alex.

'I knew Edie when she was just a young girl,' continued Ricky. 'Not even seventeen.'

'I know.'

'Come on, Ricky, let's go and wait for your taxi.' Edie pulled her hand free.

'You're a lucky man,' said Ricky. 'She left me, you know.'

'Ricky.'

'When her father killed himself. Just left.'

'I know,' said Alex.

'It was a long time ago, but you remember things like that. They don't seem to get further away. Sometimes they even seem to come closer, as if they're following you. You can run and run but they're still biting at your heels. Have you ever felt like that?'

'I don't know. Maybe.' Alex bent down and picked up a cigarette end at his feet. He dropped it into the bin-bag. 'I'll be leaving in an hour and a half, Edie.'

'Yes.'

'Have you seen the children?'

'No. I'll go and check on them in a minute.'

'Or at least,' continued Ricky, 'they get brighter, if you see what I mean. They have a kind of glow. Memory's a funny thing, isn't it?'

'I'll go and pack,' said Alex, but he didn't move.

'Some things I just forget. There are parts of my life that are blank. Whole swathes. I wonder who I was then; it's as if I've erased myself. You'd probably say that was all the drugs I've taken when I was younger, or the drink. I drink a lot nowadays. Never in the day though. Or hardly ever, except on days like today. I'd be on a downward slide then. But I don't think it's only that. There are things that just get lost. Whole years. People I used to know. Sometimes people come up to me in the street and say, you're Ricky Penrose, aren't you? And I look at them and have no idea who they are, or what bit of my life they belong to. Sometimes that worries me – that people remember me and I don't remember them. I wonder which me they're remembering. Maybe they know things about me that I've forgotten. Because that's another thing I often think: there are lots of people you can become, in the beginning. When we're young, I mean – we can go in so many directions, can't we? Which door do you push, which girl do you fuck – or love, for that matter? Which girl do you love and which girl loves you? So many ghost-lives. All those shut doors. I chose all the wrong things, but I never used to think that mattered much. I always thought I would be able to go back and undo things and start all over again. But you don't, do you? Go back.' He stared at Edie and gave a bark of laughter. 'Or not really you don't. It's a one-way street. And when you really want to, it's too late. So here I am. A failure.'

'Please, Ricky,' said Edie.

'Mmm? Where was I? Yes. So there are things I forget as if there's a hole in my brain where they fall through. But other things I remember like yesterday. Or rather,' his face creased up in an effort to be accurate. 'I *see* them, like photos in one of those albums you probably have at your house, that you all look at as a family together; we never had one of those. But anyway, every detail is there. Every leaf on the tree. Edie is in a lot of those photos in my mind.' He squinted. 'She wore a brown dress.'

'I see,' said Alex. He stared down at the bin-bag that he was holding.

'When I met her I felt sick with love. For weeks and weeks, I just felt sick all the time. I remember that. What? Don't you like me telling him that, Edie? I shouldn't have drunk so much. I can hear myself saying things to you and part of me is thinking, uh-oh, I shouldn't be saying them, but the other half is – well, saying them, I suppose. If you get me. It's all very odd. I work as a product manager for a central heating firm, you know.'

'I didn't know.'

'Of course you don't. Why would you?'

'Why don't you do that packing, Alex?' said Edie. 'I'll be with you in a few moments.'

'Yes,' said Alex, but he still didn't move.

'I thought I would be a film director, or a writer, something like that. Instead I'm in middle management. And I thought I'd travel, but here I am. Five miles from where I grew up. Edie moved. Edie did what she always said she was going to. That's the professional middle classes for you, though. Middle-class children say: I'm going to be a doctor, a lawyer, a teacher, whatever, and that's what happens. But when I said, I'm going to be a film director, well, that was stupid, wasn't it? There's a big gap between central heating and films, you know.'

'It's time for you to go,' said Alex.

'What do you do, then? Let me guess. College lecturer maybe? No? Something in the BBC? Or a lawyer? Or a teacher, maybe? Aha, yes! So you're a teacher. A doctor and a teacher. Very appropriate. Doctor and product manager in a medium-sized West Midlands central heating firm wouldn't have sounded quite right, would it?'

'Ricky.'

'Two nice incomes. A child-minder and a cleaner. Theatre once a fortnight. Am I right? Dinner parties maybe. Red wine you take out of the cellar and – what do they say? Leave to breathe? Hmm?'

Edie took Ricky by his arm and pulled. 'It's late and you're drunk. You've got to go now. Sorry,' she said over her shoulder to Alex as she tugged Ricky towards the door. 'I'll be with you in a minute.'

She led Ricky through the house, passing Stella in the hallway.

'Goodbye, Ricky,' said Stella kindly. She put a hand on his arm. 'Take care of yourself, won't you?'

Tears welled up in Ricky's eyes. 'Oh shit,' he said.

They stood on the pavement together.

'Sorry,' said Ricky.

'No,' said Edie dully. 'It's my fault.'

'I get so fucking depressed. Sometimes I sit in my kitchen and drink neat gin till my tongue's numb. Like sailors used to do. Life's a vandal, isn't it?'

'I think that's your cab now.'

'I had plans.'

'It'll be all right.'

'No.'

Edie waved her hand at the cab and it drew up beside them. She opened the door. 'Do you have enough money for the journey? You have to collect your car tomorrow morning, before you go to work. OK?'

'It won't be all right.'

'I'm sorry,' she said helplessly.

'Oh well. Nothing to be done.'

'Goodbye, Ricky.'

'Is this it, then? Just, goodbye?'

'Yes. I really am sorry. About everything. Everything I've done.'

'You've got a grey hair in your eyebrow,' he said, and clambered into the back seat of the car. 'Time goes by. What's that from? Some song. A kiss is just a kiss. That's not true, is it? It wasn't true with you and me.'

''Bye.'

'Oh God, Edie. I just get so bloody lonely. I've always been lonely.' Maudlin tears welled up in his eyes again. Edie leant in and put her hand at the back of his head. She kissed him on his lips until she saw him close his eyes. A kiss is never just a kiss. Then she stood up and shut the door. He put his face to the window. She smiled and lifted her hand in a wave but he didn't respond, just stared at her through the glass that separated them. His face was broken up by her own reflection, but she could still see the tears.

Jude, arriving back from dropping off Ellen, saw Edie standing on the pavement. She was staring down the road, which was empty of traffic. She looked suddenly older, her face tired and creased. Jude got out of her car and walked over to her.

'How long have you been standing here?'

'What? Oh, just a few moments.'

'Is he gone then?'

'Yes. Solid gone.'

31

Kit sat in the hall, next to the closed door of Louise's bedroom. He shut his eyes and tried to hear what they were saying inside, but he could hardly make out any of the words, just the rise and fall of voices, his and then hers. They didn't seem to be cross with each other, but neither were they jolly. Mostly, he thought, they just sounded tired.

Edie had walked up the stairs and he'd tried to stop her, but she'd stroked his head and said, 'In a minute,' and had gone in to Alex, shutting the door behind her. She'd looked funny. There were flushed spots on her cheeks, like Jess got when she had a temperature. She looked older and younger than usual, at the same time.

He'd seen her. He'd watched them out of the bathroom window, his mother and that strange man who'd sat on the bench with Ellen and mumbled things into his drink. He didn't like him. He had watery eyes and he'd held his mother's hand just like the beggar did once near their house, grabbing Edie's fingers as she walked past and refusing to let go. So he'd shut the door and locked it and stood at the window and watched them on the pavement together, and the man kept staring at his mother and she looked at him the way she sometimes looked at them, when they were hurt or in trouble. It was her private face.

Then the man had got into the car, and he'd seen her kiss him. She didn't hold him by the shoulders and kiss him on both cheeks the way she did with other friends, men and women. This was different. She held his head and kissed him on the mouth and it wasn't just a quick kiss. It lasted long enough to make him wonder how they were breathing. Did they do it through their noses while they were kissing, or just hold their breath till it started to hurt, the way he did sometimes when he was testing himself, saying: everything will be all right if I can last for a whole minute, or until a red car comes past?

He'd seen his parents kiss of course. Once on a beach when he and Lewis were swimming and Jess was asleep on the rug, he'd seen them sitting together by the rocks, their faces squashed together and their lips all rubbery. They seemed like strangers, and he'd looked away and counted to sixty, and when he looked back they'd stopped and were just holding hands, and Edie had her head on Alex's shoulder. And sometimes he came into their bedroom and they were all tangled up in the darkness, but they'd move apart when they saw him and he'd climb between them.

For a moment, he thought his mother was going to drive off with the man she was kissing. But then she stood up and shut the door and waved to him. She went on waving after the car had disappeared, or at least holding her hand up in the air. Even after she dropped it, she went on standing there, looking at where the car had gone.

Kit turned away from the window and unlocked the bathroom door. Alex was coming along the hall with a tight expression on his face, as if he'd sucked on something sour. When he saw Kit, he tried to smile, but Kit knew it wasn't a real smile – more like turning his mouth up at the corners.

'Hello, Kit.'

Kit opened his mouth and tried to say something but words wouldn't come out. He felt odd, a bit like he did in dreams when he was falling fast through space and all his heart was in his mouth.

'Kit?'

'Daddy,' he managed to whisper.

Alex took his hand. 'Come on, let's go and see what the others are doing.'

So now he was sitting listening to them, inside Granny's bedroom with the door firmly shut. Just the burr of voices. Then, quite clearly, his mother saying, 'Oh, my love.' He clasped his hands together and waited, but there was just silence.

Edie sat beside Alex on the bed and undid the buttons on his shirt. He watched her, not helping. Her fingers were trembling. She pushed him back against the pillow and leant over him.

'We'll talk tomorrow,' she said. 'Not now. There's not time.'

'We don't need to talk at all,' he said. 'I just got stupidly jealous. But I trust you.'

'Oh, Alex,' she said. 'Oh, my love.'

'You've forgotten this last box, the one with all the flan dishes and stuff in.'

'Thanks. I'll put it in the back. Then I'm full up. Sam's travelling with me, so the rest will have to go in Bob's car. What about your stuff – aren't you going to send any of it with Alex?'

'I'll take most of it tomorrow. There's not that much.'

Everyone was ready to leave. They'd eaten their bacon sandwiches, made with the leftovers from Alex's cooked breakfast. The younger children were in their night-clothes, teeth brushed, so they could fall asleep in the car and be lifted into their beds the other end. Jess had been taken inside for her last visit to the lavatory. Leah was already sitting in the front, wearing the headphones and jigging one knee slightly to the music no one else could hear.

'I'll be back in time to collect them from school tomorrow,' Edie said to Alex.

He nodded.

Everyone kissed everyone else; hugged each other and repeated the things they'd already said over supper. Promises to keep in touch over arrangements, to meet very soon, to take care.

Edie hugged Stella hard. 'Let me know what happens,' Stella whispered.

'I will.'

Then she turned to the children, kissing Leah and Gabriel, scooping Lewis up and holding his bony little body against hers, cuddling Jess who was sticky with heat, her eyes already closing. She put her arm on Alex's shoulder as he was about to get in the car. 'See you tomorrow,' she said.

'No,' said Kit as she turned to him, her arms already stretched out. 'No.'

'Kit?'

'No,' he repeated.

'I'll be back tomorrow. I've already said that you don't need to go to school. Alex will call Kirsty and sort it out.'

'*What*? How come *he* doesn't need to go to school and I do?'

'Lewis . . .'

'It's not fair.'

'Look . . .'

'No,' said Kit once more. 'I want to be with you.'

'But all I'm going to do is . . .'

'I want to be with you. If I'm with you . . .' He stopped.

'What?'

'Then you'll have to come home.'

'Oh, God!' She stared at him, appalled. 'Of course I'm coming home. It's all I want.'

Kit stared back. 'I'm not leaving,' he said mutinously. 'You can't force me.'

'Then stay,' said Edie suddenly, making up her mind. 'Stay and help me here.' She bent down and lifted Kit into her arms. He was getting too big for her; his weight sagged against her.

'*Mum!*'

'Lewis, please help me here.'

'It's not fair.'

'Yes it is,' said Alex, turning the key in the ignition. 'Fair doesn't mean exactly the same, you know.'

He and Edie smiled at each other.

'Drive carefully,' she said.

'Of course.'

'Thanks.'

'Tomorrow then.'

Edie lay on the bed beside Kit, with her arm around him and his hair tickling her face. His skin smelt of soap. Every so often he shifted against her, to get closer. Smoky lay at his feet. Outside, the sky was nearly dark and the first stars were shining through the window.

'What do you say to taking the cat back with us?'

'Really?'

'Yes, why not? Company for Tangle.'

'I'd like that. I like cats. Sometimes I think it would be nice to be one; the way they lie asleep in the sun. Or a duck. They look happy too.'

'Good, that's settled then. Now go to sleep,' she said. 'Turn your brain off.'

'That's hard to do, isn't it?'

'You're right, it is.'

'Mummy?'

'Mmm.'

'What was Grandpa like?'

'Grandpa? Well.' Edie stared up at the ceiling. 'He was a very kind man. And quiet, too – he only spoke when he had something to say. He was shy, really. Shy and sweet and a bit clumsy. Always dropping things and falling off ladders and spilling soup down his tie and walking into beams. He drove into a milk float once. He

had eyes just like yours, and black hair, like Jude does.'
She stopped and lay still, seeing Vic's face, his stricken
expression.

'Go on.'

'Um. He loved birds and flowers and animals, things
like that. He noticed things other people didn't. He
knew the names of the stars, too.'

'Was he a funny man, like Daddy?'

'No, I don't think he was funny. He didn't really get
jokes. That could make him rather hard to live with,
I think. You know, though, I believe he was a good
man.' Edie was speaking half to herself. 'He never
wished anyone any harm. You can't say that about many
people.'

'But why did he . . . ?' Kit trailed off. 'You know.'

'Kill himself?'

'Yes. Why did he?'

'Life just got a bit too much for him, I guess. Have
you ever heard people talk about tipping points?'

'No.'

'Or last straws? The straw that broke the camel's
back?'

'I think so.'

'There were probably lots of things and they all came
together and one day he just thought: I can't cope. He
should have shared things with the people who loved
him. Like you always will, won't you, Kit? If you feel
upset about things, I mean, you'll always talk about
them, won't you?'

'So there wasn't anything, kind of, wrong with him?'

'How do you mean?'

'He wasn't sick in his head?'

'Who said that to you?'

'People.'

'Kit, who said that?'

'Boys at school, they said I was sick in my head like Grandpa.'

'Where did they get that from?'

'Lewis maybe,' he said in a small voice.

'Listen to me now. He wasn't sick and nor are you. He was sometimes sad – really sad, not sad in the way that they use the word at your school. And some people get sadder than other people.'

'So there's not something wrong with me?' he asked.

'There's nothing wrong with you. You couldn't be righter. It's other people who are stupid, ignorant, cruel. People often are, in groups.'

'Mummy.'

'Mmm.'

'Were you very sad when Grandpa died?'

'Very. I still am sometimes. It takes me by surprise. You can go on missing people for a long time, you know. You can miss them for ever.'

'I don't want you to die.'

'Well, I'm not going to for a long time.'

'Because where will you be then?'

They lay in silence for a few moments, then he added: 'That man?'

'Yes.'

'You kissed him.'

'I used to know him a long time ago, when I wasn't much more than a girl. That was all. I was saying good-bye. It was only a kiss.'

32

'Right,' said Jude.

She plonked two tumblers on the table and chucked ice cubes into each. She unscrewed the top of the whisky bottle and glugged several fingers of amber liquid into each. She put a cigarette into her mouth, passed one to Edie and lit both from the same match. They inhaled, then Jude lifted her glass and clinked it against Edie's.

Edie swallowed a fiery mouthful, pulled smoke into her lungs.

'What a week,' she said eventually.

'You've been a fucking idiot.'

'Jude!'

'Haven't you?'

Edie put a hand over her sore eyes. 'Yes.'

'You slept with him, didn't you?'

'Yes.'

'Jesus! Why?'

'I don't know.'

'What do you mean, you don't know?'

'I don't know.' She took her hand away from her eyes and lifted her glass. 'I can't explain.'

'God, Edie.' Jude sounded disgusted.

'You're hardly the one to take the moral high ground.'

'I'm not taking the fucking moral high ground! I just think you're unbelievably stupid. You're the one person

I know who's got a good marriage to a lovely man who thinks you're wonderful, and you go and do this, out of the blue, as if you wanted to lay waste to everything.'

'I know,' said Edie. She ground her cigarette out in the saucer and took another one.

'Maybe that's why,' Jude went on. 'Maybe it's because it's all so safe and you've always been so good and obedient, doing what everyone else wanted you to do, that you go and wreck it now. Just like you did when you left Ricky all those years ago. Running away from happiness.'

'Can I have some more whisky?'

'Here. So does Alex know?'

'I don't know – I don't know what he thinks. He trusts me.'

'Don't tell him.'

'Do you think?'

'Just don't, Edie.' Jude glared at her. 'Oh, bloody hell, you're going to, aren't you?'

'I'm trying not to,' said Edie.

'You're not going to see him again, are you?'

'No! Never.'

'So bury it. If you tell Alex, things will never be the same again.'

'If I don't tell him, things will never be the same again either – but he won't know.'

'Exactly.'

'You're the one who thinks people have the right to know.'

'Listen, don't make an epic thing out of this. You behaved madly. Just don't do it again.'

'He thinks he can trust me.'

'So don't go and . . .'

'And he can – at least, he can trust me to tell him the truth. I lied to him today and it felt awful. Secrets fester. Look at Mummy and Daddy, for God's sake. Don't you see, Jude? It'll be there between us if I don't tell.'

'And if you do.'

'And there between us if I do. I know. But that's what I've done, isn't it? Changed everything.'

'So why the fuck did you?'

'I can't describe it. I don't want to make excuses. It wasn't a moment of blind passion or anything. All the time, I kept thinking about Alex – and the kids, too, what they'd think if they could see me. It was just – well, it was something I did, that's all.' Edie paused and took another gulp of whisky. 'I felt sorry for him,' she said.

'Oh, Jesus!'

'I know. So stupid. But feeling sorry for him was almost like, well, it was as strong as overwhelming desire. Stronger. I felt I was dissolving.'

Jude snorted something and stood up.

'Where are you going?'

'Nowhere. I was going to make us something to eat. I haven't eaten anything since yesterday evening, apart from one mouthful of Alex's black pudding, and this whisky's making my head swim. Anyway, I hid away a last supper for us.' She extracted a squidgy plastic bag from the empty fridge. 'Scallops,' she said triumphantly. 'With garlic and white wine, I think, and the last of that crusty bread.' She took out four plump scallops and laid them on the chopping-board.

'I'm not sure I could eat anything.'

'It's only a taste really.' Jude picked up a sharp knife and cut away the corals. She fumbled in her cardboard box of packed kitchen things and extracted a garlic crusher.

Edie sighed and leant her head in her hands. 'I wish,' she said. 'I just wish.'

'What?'

'You know. Just wish. I feel sick.'

'I can imagine,' said Jude.

'I always thought of myself as someone who wouldn't do this. Betray him.'

'You're not a monster, you know. You haven't crossed some kind of line between being a good person and being a bad one.'

'I feel I have. That's precisely what I feel.' She lifted her head and stared at Jude, who was crushing a garlic clove into sizzling butter. 'Now I know what Louise must have felt.'

'Mmmm.' Jude sliced the scallops in half and dropped them into the pan. 'Well, maybe that's why you did it.'

'Maybe,' said Edie drearily. 'Which brings us to what you were saying in the garden this afternoon.'

'Wait.' Jude put the corals in with the scallops and turned them deftly. Then she added a slug of white wine to the hissing pan. 'Pass me two plates, will you, and cut some bread. Here, we may as well finish the wine off, now I've opened it.'

'I've drunk too much already,' said Edie. But she poured the wine anyway, and took a sip. 'What did you mean?'

'No, before all that – how did you know about Louise and Simon?'

'I only discovered a few days ago. I found a letter. When I was going through the stuff from the attic – you know, Ricky's letters to me and stuff.'

'What, a letter from Simon bloody Scott?'

'It wasn't signed or anything. But it was like a light shining over the past. It was so obvious.'

'Well,' said Jude, spearing a scallop on her fork, 'I saw them.'

'Oh, God. You mean . . . ?'

'Fucking,' she said harshly. 'I came back from school early. That girl Maisie – do you remember her? She was one of the ones who used to torment me – she discovered this poem in my bag that I'd written. To Ricky, of course. She showed it round the class. It was a very bad poem,' she added drily. 'Anyway, everyone was laughing at me, saying how could a fat dike like me expect a boy to ever look my way? And I'd had enough. I just thought, I can't do this any more, sit and listen to people sneering and jeering at me, day after day. So I skipped the afternoon lessons and walked home. I didn't think Mum would be there; she'd said she would be at the shop till late. I just wanted to be in my bedroom, safe. Her car was there, but still I didn't think . . . it didn't occur to me . . . I just let myself in and went up the stairs and then I heard a noise coming from her room. A wailing kind of noise. I didn't know what it could be – God, I was so naïve. I thought it was the cat playing with a mouse or something; you remember how it used to make those yowling noises at the back of its throat? So I gave the door a little push and looked in and they were at it on the bed, all the sheets and blankets thrown back. I just stood there and gawped for a few seconds. Her mouth open and her white flesh. His skinny bottom, with spots over it. Agh!' She gave a disgusted grimace. 'Sex can look so ludicrously ugly. Then I backed away and ran out of the house. I ran and ran and then I was sick in a ditch.'

'So they didn't see you?'

'No.'

'God,' said Edie. She didn't want to hold the image that Jude had described in her head. 'How shocking for you.'

'I wanted to tell you. I tried to once, but – well, it didn't work. You were on your way out and you were all happy and I – well, I couldn't say it out loud. And I thought I'd confront Mum – God, I hated her so much. I wanted to get her on her own and rub her face in what she'd done.' She swilled back her wine and poured herself some more. 'But somehow I couldn't and then I went and told Vic instead. Just before he killed himself.'

'Oh,' said Edie softly.

'So, there you are.'

'But Jude, he knew already.'

'What do you mean?'

'He knew, I'm sure of it.'

'Why do you say that?'

'Because – well, I just remember him knowing. Remember in retrospect, that is. When I look back to that time, everything I see is Vic knowing. Knowing and unable to do anything about it. When I think of them together – Mummy and him, I mean – I remember Mummy giggling and flirting. She used to put her hand on his arm or round Simon's waist, or whisper things in his ear or take puffs of his cigarette. And the way Vic looked – he knew.'

'You think so?'

'I'm sure,' said Edie. 'Nothing else makes sense. What did he say when you told him?'

'Nothing really. He came to my room to ask me not to shout at Mum. He said something like, your mother's under a lot of stress at the moment and it's up to us to help her.' And I was so filled up with rage at his stupid, stupid blindness that I yelled it at him. He just put his hands up, as if I was throwing things at him, and said, 'No, no,' or, 'Don't, don't,' something like that. Then he stumbled off.'

'You should have told me. You've been carrying it around with you all these years. You should have said.'

'Well, now I have.' She took a cigarette and passed the packet over to Edie. Together they leant towards the candle flame to light them. 'It doesn't make it feel any better though.'

'Not yet,' said Edie. 'But maybe it will change things a bit, over time. To know how we all saw it so differently and took away our own guilty versions. When really, no one and everyone's guilty.'

'Louise is guilty,' said Jude starkly.

'You're looking at her like a judge would. She's your mother, and she just fucked up. The way I've done now. Or you, even. Or everyone does, sometime or other. Life unravels. You only say she's guilty because Daddy killed himself. If he hadn't, then we'd look at it now like an act of pain and folly, not something unforgivable.'

'I never talked to her about it,' said Jude. 'And she never talked to me. She just used to say that Dad had been depressed. We all put a lid on the past and thought we could contain it. Now look at us.'

'It's never too late,' said Edie meaninglessly. She poured herself the last of the wine. 'My head's spinning.'

'So, tomorrow you'll go back and tell Alex?'

'Yes.' Her heart clenched at the thought of it. 'I don't know if it's the right or wrong thing to do, but I have to, because that's what our relationship is like. And the longer I wait, the harder it will be. Think of me. What will you do tomorrow?'

'Just try and get back into a routine. Prepare lessons. Maybe start making inquiries about old people's homes.'

'So you're really going to do it?'

'I said so, didn't I?'

'What about your affair?'

'What about it?'

'Are you going to continue?'

'The question is: is he?'

'Do you – well, love him?'

'Love? No, dear Edie. He's not available for love.'

'Oh.'

'Don't worry about me.'

They sat in silence. Edie mopped up the sauce with the white bread and chewed it slowly.

'I'll miss you,' she said.

'You always were sentimental.'

'No, really. I'll miss you.' Edie heard her voice slur.

She wanted to say something meaningful, about loneliness, or the past, or the future – anything that would express the sense of anguish and yearning that she felt. 'You're very beautiful,' she heard herself say.

'Oh honey, you should go to bed.'

'I feel I love everyone, that's the trouble.'

'Bed.'

'No, let's go outside first. It's a beautiful night.'

So they stood together in the garden arm-in-arm and looked up at the bright moon and the clustered stars.

'I can't recognize any of them,' said Edie. 'Not like Daddy could.'

'That's the Great Bear. And there's the North Star. That's all I know.'

'I read somewhere that there are eleven dimensions. How can that be possible?'

'I don't think either of us is in the right frame of mind to grapple with that concept.'

'And that our universe is just a little bubble in an ocean of universes, so what we see now, the hugeness that makes you feel like a grain of sand, that's nothing at all.'

'I find that comforting.'

'Do you? Why? I find it so scary it makes me feel ill.'

'The fact that it doesn't matter at all, none of this.'

'That's what's scary.'

'I know.'

'Mummy.'

They turned. Kit was standing at the kitchen door.

'Did we wake you?'

'I don't know. There was this dream . . .'

Edie picked him up. 'Was it a bad dream?'

'I don't know. I can't remember.'

'Well, you're all right; it's over. I'm coming up now and you can cuddle up to me in bed, OK? Come on.' She turned to Jude. 'Goodnight.'

'Night.'

'Sweet dreams.'

'Thanks.' Jude hesitated. 'By the way, I'll miss you too.'

Edie lay next to Kit in the bed. He was asleep again, curled up beside her like a kidney bean, his knees drawn up and his head next to hers. His breath was warm on her cheek. Occasionally he shifted, murmured something, just a wisp of sound. Her mouth was dry; she should get up and have several glasses of water, to stave off a headache tomorrow. But she didn't move. She listened to the sound of their breathing. She listened to the faint sigh of the wind outside. A door banged shut, a car drove off, a cat howled once, something screeched out there in the night. It's never completely silent and it's never completely dark. There are always stars that shine and other people who are awake like you, lying in their beds and waiting for the light to come.

33

'Alex?'

'Yes, my love.'

'I want to say something.'

'I'm listening. Do you want a cup of tea? I've put the kettle on.'

'OK. But I need to tell you...' Edie swallowed hard. She looked across the kitchen at Alex, who was methodically stacking plates in the dishwasher. He was wearing the dressing-gown she'd given him for his last birthday, and his ancient down-at-heel slippers that he always refused to throw out. His hair was tousled and his face creased; there were crows'-feet round his eyes. Everything about him was familiar and beloved.

'I'm listening,' he said, closing the dishwasher and switching it on, standing up, smiling across at her.

'Well,' said Edie. Each word felt sharp and dangerous. Daggers and knives and flinty stones ... 'When I was away ...' But her body was water; everything breaking up inside her.

'Come on. Spit it out.' His expression shifted. 'Is it something serious?'

'Yes.' She took a deep breath and looked squarely at him. 'I had sex with Ricky.'

'Edie —'

'Twice.'

How long was there silence? Maybe a second, maybe a minute. Enough time for her to see the way light faded in his face. To see how his hand, lying on the back of the chair, tightened convulsively so the knuckles whitened, and then went slack. How the kettle sent puffs of steam into the kitchen, its lid jumping. How he frowned slightly, as if he was baffled by an irritating mathematical problem.

'I see,' he said at last, in a low voice.

'Alex –'

He lowered himself into a chair. His dressing-gown parted and he pulled it tighter, then he gave a small sigh and rubbed his face all over with his hands. 'Why?'

'I don't know.'

He made a small sound, as if she had punched him in the belly.

'All I know . . .' she stopped hopelessly.

'The kettle's boiling dry.'

She took the kettle off the hob and turned back to face him. 'There's nothing I can say to make it better. But I love you very, very much.'

'Oh,' he said dully.

'At first I thought I wouldn't tell you. I thought I could treat it like some act of madness, as if it wasn't really me who did it. But I found that I couldn't not tell you.'

'I thought we were so happy,' he said.

'We were. We are. Oh, Jesus, I'm so sorry. Alex, I'm so so sorry.' She put out a hand to touch him but he jerked away.

'Don't.'

'No. Sorry.'

'Are you . . . ?' He hesitated, then said, 'In love with him?'

'No! Not one tiny bit! Only with you, my darling, darling Alex. It wasn't that. It was like the past crashing in on me. Oh, but I don't even want to say things like that, as if I'm making excuses. It was like I was doing the worst thing I could possibly do to myself, all of us, and I knew that all the time.'

'Twice,' he said.

'Yes.'

'While I was here looking after the children and worrying about you and missing you.'

'Yes.'

'Jesus.'

'What are we going to do?'

'Do?'

'Yes.'

'I don't know. I can't think.' He stood up, scraping the chair loudly. 'I'll make that tea, shall I?'

'Alex, I –'

'I don't want to talk about it. Later, Edie, not now.'

They lay side by side in their king-sized bed, two pillows each, the alarm clock on his side, the box of tissues and the phone on hers. They didn't touch each other, but kept their legs straight and their arms wrapped around their own bodies. They listened to each other not sleeping, and didn't talk.

Edie went round the local schools. In two of them, there were spaces in Year Four. She chose the smaller school, whose head, a woman in her fifties with wild grey hair, thick glasses and a laugh like a machine-gun, she trusted at once. There were only a few weeks left of the summer term, but she decided Kit shouldn't go back to his old school at all. He spent a week at home, being looked after by Kirsty and spending most days in the garden, reading books with the cats at his feet, pottering by the pond with his fishing net, or building elaborate Lego constructions. It was as if he was a convalescent – and in a way, Edie thought, he was. Whenever she could, she spent time with him. They baked cakes; he painted pictures. She taught him the first moves of chess. His face lost the pinched and anxious look that had marked it before.

On the first day at his new school he got up at six and was sick three times. His eyes were red-rimmed. But he walked to school with his hand in Edie's, and never once said he was feeling too ill to go. The head met them at the entrance, and he squeezed Edie's hand convulsively, then released it and stepped forward through the gates, into the milling crowd.

She rang Jude and Stella almost daily. They arranged for a removal van to collect the furniture and put it into storage. They discussed an offer that had been made on Louise's house. Jude had found a home that she approved of and Ellen would move there in a month's time. They all needed to sign papers and discuss finances. And they decided to scatter Louise's ashes on the river. They would meet up in three weeks' time, and do it all together.

Stella announced that she and Bob were going to counselling; she sounded happier than she had done in ages. 'I suddenly realized,' she said to Edie, 'that I don't have to live like this.' Jude said nothing about her affair, so Edie assumed it was continuing, for the time being.

She put Vic and Louise's wedding photograph beside the rather blurred photograph of herself and Alex, standing outside the registry office on the day they married, Alex in a pale suit and herself in a long red dress. Louise and Vic looked so young. Their photograph had the feel of long ago, and they glowed with the sense of the past.

Once in a while, she would pick up it up and stare at it, as if one day she might come across something that had eluded her. She didn't know what she was looking for. Every day, she went swimming. Sometimes in the early morning, with other professional people; in the changing-room afterwards, Edie watched the women putting on their smart clothes, efficiently applying make-up in front of the mirror. Sometimes at lunchtime, when the other swimmers were usually older and slower. Or even at the end of the day. She always did twenty-five lengths of crawl, her head lifting sideways every fourth stroke to catch a gulp of air, white bubbles rippling off her rhythmic arms, and then fifteen of breast-stroke, breathing in and breathing out, lifting and dipping her head, feeling her arms pointing forward like arrows before pulling back, feeling her legs aching. Up and down, amidst the thrash of other swimmers. In the turquoise water, she stopped thinking, or even feeling. She just swam.

*

For some time, Edie and Alex were very careful with each other, treating each other with courtesy, never snapping at each other, respecting each other's privacy. Every evening before supper, they would sit in the living-room with a glass of wine and tell each other about their day, listening attentively, nodding, making small comments to show their interest. He still rubbed her back, and she still ironed his shirts and cut the stray hairs on his neck. Sometimes they held hands. They didn't kiss, except the kiss on the cheek in front of the children, to say hello, goodbye. Nor make love. In bed, they wore night-clothes for the first time in their marriage, self-conscious about their bodies. Sometimes, Edie saw Alex examining himself in the full-length mirror in their bedroom, pulling in his stomach, turning his head to see himself in profile, and her heart would turn over with pity.

Bit by bit, like easing a cork out of a shaken-up bottle, they talked. When they were driving together, or clearing up the supper things. In the supermarket, loading food into their trolley while the children roamed the aisles in search of treats. Sometimes early in the morning, after the alarm had rung but before they shook the children awake. Once on the phone, he in his car parked outside the school, and she in her office. Sore details, one by one.

One day, they both took a day off work, delivered the children to school, and went for a walk that took them through the park, then along the side of the railway track to Alex's new allotment. They stood by the freshly turned soil, where there were small shoots of peas in rows, courgette plants, a few tiny lettuces that had been half devoured by slugs. They talked then about forgiveness, what it meant. If you forgave someone, was it like a Catholic act, whereby the sinner is washed free of his sins and can begin all over again? Or is the wrong that was done always there, lurking in the undergrowth of one's life, ready to leap out? In other words, said Alex, was he going to remember, or forget; trust or be wary; hold it against her, or discard it?

'I don't know,' said Edie. 'You can't forget, can you?'

'You can make yourself act as if you have,' said Alex. 'What's intolerable is to turn what happened into a weapon that I can always use against you. Every time we have an argument, it can be my trump card, or every time I upset you, I can still claim the moral high ground. Aha! But you were unfaithful. We can't live like that.'

'Maybe you should go and have a fling,' said Edie, smiling ruefully. 'Then we'd be equal again.'

'I've thought about that.'

'Have you?'

'Well, not really, actually. I don't want to.'

'Have you thought about leaving me?'

'I've imagined what it would be like if I did.'

'And?'

'Unimaginable,' he said.

'Alex.'

'Yes.'

'We'll be all right, won't we?'

'I hope so.'

She took his warm, rough hand in hers and held it to her lips. She looked up again and saw there were tears sliding down his face. 'Let's go home,' she said, and she led him back through the park in bloom, back into their ordinary, untidy house, up the stairs and into their bedroom, where she closed the curtains against the afternoon sun.

'We've got forty minutes before the children come home,' she said, and took his tired face in her hands and kissed it. She tried to pull his shirt over his head, but the buttons needed undoing. His shoe-laces were tied in double knots and his socks caught on his heel so she had to tug at them. She fumbled with his belt. 'I'm being clumsy,' she said. 'I must be nervous.'

'Don't be.'

'Alex, I really am . . .'

'Sssh.'

She took off her own clothes, one by one, and he watched her. She felt shy; her skin was covered in goose-bumps, in spite of the warmth of the day.

They slid under the duvet and held each other. They watched each other's faces in the dim tent of bedclothes. When he kissed her, she didn't close her eyes. She didn't want to see anyone's face but his. When he came, she cradled him in her arms and called him by his name.

The three sisters met on a muggy Thursday morning in July. They all parked by the river, where Edie had left her car on the day she had climbed the bridge. Stella had the ashes in a plastic container; they rattled when she walked over to them. Edie saw at once that she'd had her hair highlighted and had lost weight. She was wearing the orange shirt that Louise used to wear, long ago, and a necklace that Edie remembered her mother putting round her neck when she went out in the evenings – leaning forward in the mirror, lips pursed, concentrating on the clasp behind her neck.

'You look fabulous,' she said warmly, and Stella flushed with pleasure.

'Thanks. I've taken myself in hand.'

'And you, Jude. I feel underdressed.'

Jude was in baggy lavender trousers and a silk shirt that came down to her knees. Her hair was artfully wild, her earrings jangled, her lips were scarlet.

'It's going to rain,' said Stella.

'Just as well – then there won't be other people around while we do this.'

'Shall we go, then?'

They walked together along the river bank. The grass and shrubs were bleached. The path was baked, cracked mud.

'Maybe this is exactly the wrong place,' said Stella nervously.

'Maybe,' said Jude. She stalked along in front of them, her clothes billowing behind her.

They came to the bridge and all stopped to look up at it.

'I always forget how high it is,' said Stella.

'Imagine how . . .'

'No. Don't imagine. Come on.'

They passed underneath it and came to a spot where the bank sloped down to the water's edge.

'So what do we do now? Just tip it?'

'Or we could throw handfuls in.'

'I don't think so.'

'It doesn't feel very poetic – especially not in this bloody tupperware.'

'We should have done it from a boat.'

'How about if we all hold it and ease off the lid and just chuck it in?'

'What if the wind blows it in our faces? I've heard of that happening.'

'There isn't any wind.'

'Ought we to say something?'

'You mean, about Louise?'

'Yes.'

'What?'

'I don't know. Like, goodbye to her, I suppose.'

Jude gave a mad shout of laughter. 'Goodbye,' she said.

'Please!'

'We should be serious.'

'Yes.'

'It's just us three now.'

'The front line.'

'Ellen's in front of us.'

'That's not the same.'

'No. I suppose not. OK, just the three of us. Oh shit, I don't want to cry.'

'Lift the lid off then.'

'Now?'

'Yes.'

'It doesn't look how I imagined.'

'That's all that's left of her.'

'No, not all. We're left. Us three.'

'We should scatter her.'

'It suddenly doesn't seem funny any more.'

'There. Over the water.'

'Like that.'

'She's gone.'

'Gone.'

For a few seconds, the ashes lay on the surface of the water, then they disappeared. The muddy waves slapped at their feet. A branch floated past, twisting in the current. The three sisters stood arm-in-arm and watched the water. Then, with one accord, they turned and walked in silence back along the river bank, under the high bridge, going home.

From time to time, Edie still woke in the middle of the night, suddenly, as if something had roused her, and she would lie in bed with the mysterious sense of anticipation that accompanied her sleepless vigils. She would listen to the secret sounds of the night: the murmur of pipes, the whisper of wind, the slow, steady breathing of Alex beside her, and occasionally, at her feet, the faint guttural purr of cats. She would wait for fear to subside, morning to come, shadows to shift. When she was a young girl, she had been scared of sleeping for a while because it had seemed too much like a kind of death. Now she was scared of lying awake, like a lonely swimmer on the surface of the water, when everyone else was sucked down into the dreaming deep.

In the middle of one such night, she thought she heard him calling her name. 'Edie,' he said, 'Edie.' A drawn-out cry, as if he was falling from a great height, and calling to her at the same time. His voice echoed in her head, greeting her or saying goodbye or asking for help or simply shouting, shouting for her to come to him. She hadn't heard it for such a long time. Only in her dreams. She knew it wasn't him, of course, how could it be, and yet the feeling that he was near was so strong that she swung her legs out of bed and stood by the window, listening. Inside, the house slept, each person wrapped in their own warmth. Outside, it was a clear and silent dark. There were white-pricked stars in the sky and a low moon tangled in the trees. She pressed her forehead against the glass and waited, but the voice didn't come again. It would never come again.

Vic parked the car and put the keys under the mirror flap. He got out of the car, did up his suit jacket, and began his slow walk up the bridge. He felt tired, and each step was an effort. The sky seemed to press down on him, cold and grey. Dark clouds in his head. Every so often a scatter of raindrops would sting his cheeks. The road was empty of cars, and beneath him, the river was brown and swollen from the night's rain. He remembered, as if it was another person's life, walking along this bridge with Louise. They had held hands then, stepping in time. Or with Edie, when she was tiny and her brown hair was tied in bouncy pigtails, and she held a melting ice-cream cone in her hand. She had put her chin on the railings and he'd pulled her back sharply to the safety of the pavement and held her tightly against him. But that was another land.

Now he was near to the high middle of the bridge. He stared at the water, the swirl of the cross-current. Then he clambered over the railing. It wasn't too hard, except he was so tired and every part of him seemed heavy as mud. He just wanted to stop thinking, feeling, being, hurting, loving, hoping, losing. Stop.

He was standing now, holding on with one hand, which was cold on the rusty metal. He just needed to let go and fall. He took a breath and held it. Then he let it out again. He looked up for a moment, and the sky filled his eyes. In it he saw a sudden shape of birds in shifting formation, wings beating, bodies like forked arrows. The swallows were flying away, towards the sun, but were they leaving, or were they going home? He closed his eyes. He uncurled his fingers and felt his body tip. He stepped out, into the rushing air, into the healing water.